LOSING AUGUST

ALSO BY W.S. SIMONS

A Second Look

Stone by Stone

COMING SOON

Weeding Out the Lies

LOSING AUGUST

A Novel by
W. S. Simons

Copyright © 2023 by Wendy Simons
All rights reserved.

This is a work of fiction.
Names, characters, places and incidents are drawn from the author's imagination. Any resemblance to actual events, locales or persons, living or dead, is entirely coincidental.

For information about permission to use or reproduce any part of this book in any manner contact
info@wssimonsbooks.com

Cover Design: WS Illustration
Cover photographs:
Alex Melnick/SHUTTERSTOCK
WS Illustration /TWS Photography
Author & Spine photographs:
WS Illustration

ISBN: 979-8-9893594-2-4

This book is dedicated to Mik, Mary, Tim, Francesca and Amy, whose encouragement over the decades has allowed me to keep chasing words.

CHAPTER ONE

As the sun rose on a warm summer morning, Manny Horowitz and Lou Waterman, lunch boxes in hand, shuffled along an abandoned track bed just like they had nearly every summer day since they retired nearly a decade earlier. Stopping at an old shanty, Lou withdrew a clutch of keys from his coveralls and unlocked the padlock. He retrieved two aluminum chairs, both with frayed strapping, and carried them, one under each arm, a few yards away to the edge of a jetty on the Sturgeon River.

Little more than an outcropping, the jetty was contained by two concrete walls, the third having given way long ago, leaving a muddy slope upriver. As young boys, Lou and Manny had been chased up the tracks when timber barges arrived to unload logs to the train. They thrilled at the dangerous dance of men working block and tackle, a giant claw dangling from steel scaffolding, grabbing a log like a stick, swinging it as it tipped precariously, gears grinding, the log finally piled to a flatbed rail car. There was nothing left of tracks or the steel trestle. Like Lou and Manny, the jetty was no longer of use. Manny gathered the fishing poles, both lunchboxes, and followed Lou. The men didn't speak. Lou was a man of few words, and Manny saw no point in conversing with a stone. Most everything they had to say had been said. There was no advantage in rehashing political grievances as they changed little between one administration and another in that no one was ever happy, and somebody was always attempting to wrestle power from someone else. Talking changed nothing, so they didn't talk about Vietnam, though it was waged in their living rooms every evening on the news. Having fought in two world wars, it was apparent there would always be war waged somewhere, families on all sides left in grief. And, as their wives hadn't changed much in their mannerisms or demands over the years, talking about them became little more than a report on an especially good pot roast or a tally of preserves put up. Occasionally, one of the wives had a bit of gossip the men could chew on. Mostly, these old friends remained silent.

    Lou opened his lunchbox, pulling out a cottage cheese carton. Carefully prying off the lid, he slid his fingers into the bloody mass of chicken livers, rummaging until he had a good grip on one. As he baited the first hook, blackish-red ooze dripped onto his coveralls, blending with older stains. Manny lit a cigar after baiting his own hooks. He glanced up and downriver, noticing the current had quickened from the day before. With catfish lines in the water, two poles each, propped in pipes embedded in the soil, Manny and Lou began their morning's endeavor.

Discordant whining carried from upriver as two speedboats approached, screaming full throttle as they passed by. Lou mumbled an obscenity under his breath as their bobbers rocked with the first waves from their wake.

Just upstream, in a honeysuckle thicket along shore, something large heaved back and forth with each successive wave until it broke free of its entanglement and drifted to the mud of the jetty, where it lobbed in quieting waters.

Lou glanced over his shoulder, scowled, and grumbled something indiscernible. Both men rose and went to investigate, finding the body of a man half-submerged face down in a black stir of river muck.

"Huh," Lou grunted. He could have said, "Don't see this every day," the way one or the other of them said at least once a week during their decades picking up the town's trash. But it didn't need saying. It was a fact without contradiction. Neither of them had ever come across a dead body on their route.

"I'll go," Manny said. Being the more limber of the two, he walked back up the track bed to the lumberyard to report it. Lou went to check on his lines. A bobber was dipping.

Chief Schroeder arrived soon after and stood near the body, by then hauled out of the water by two young officers. He dictated details to one of them. "White male. Five-eight, maybe. Probably two-twenty, give or take ten pounds." He told the nother officer to roll the body, calling on the first to assist. With concerted effort, they finally rolled it, the muddy face turning skyward, revealing one eye swollen shut, a split lip, and a gash on his cheek. The chief reluctantly wiped mud from the right shoulder and sighed, shaking his head. "Christ almighty," he grumbled, looking at a lightning bolt tattoo.

Searching for answers, Chief Schroeder roamed the track bed upriver. To his right, the bluff rose up covered in sumac, sassafras, and black locust. To his left, willow trees, sumac, and honeysuckle crowded the riverbank. He found a wrinkled taffy wrapper and followed some duck-footed tracks to a trestle bridge, picking up a cigarette butt as cars droned overhead. He wandered on until he came to a place where the path appeared disturbed with scrapes and slide marks. Glancing up the bluff, he saw more slide marks, broken sumac stalks, and a small space beaten down with impressions of much smaller footprints. A sheriff's boat sped upriver, banking hard by the jetty. When its wake swept shore, it set bushes to rocking. Something bouncing on a branch a couple feet from the edge caught Schroeder's eye. He stepped into the shallows and noticed several willow branches stripped of leaves as he retrieved a single, small, white gym shoe hung up in the honeysuckle. Shaking water from his shoe, he saw bloody taffy wrappers in the weeds. Entertaining his worst fear, that a young girl had also been lost to the river. He instigated a search of the shoreline and prayed they didn't find another body .

    So began the end of summer in Edgewater, Michigan. August 25, 1965.

CHAPTER TWO

    Three months earlier, before summer was yet underway, Garfield Sanders leaned on the westward windowsill of his office perched high on the railroad swing bridge, a massive trestle structure resting on an island of pilings in the Sturgeon River. Lake Michigan spread out before him, its dark, placid waters cutting sharp against the star-filled sky. Warm air slipping off the water felt more like June than May. He perused the shoreline with an uneasy melancholy. Even in darkness, he could see its sandy ribbon in both directions, delineating what could easily have been the end of the earth. The shrouded tree line rose and fell with the undulating dunes, sand almost aglow in moonlight. In front of him, two concrete piers reached out into the lake. Flanking the river channel, a lighthouse perched on the north pier. On the south stood a secondary navigation light.

    After thirty years on the job, Gar was still awestruck by the beauty. This would be his last summer. Mandatory retirement.

    He took his pocket knife in hand, paring away a small slice of basswood, carving what would become the bill of a duck in flight. The wings were nearly formed, feathers delineated by delicate cuts of a well-practiced craftsman.

Downing the last of a tepid mug of coffee, he heard muted voices below. Three, maybe four. Boys. He cussed quietly and waited, certain no man replacing him would pay attention as he did. "You best get the hell off this bridge while you still can," he yelled at the skittish shadows darting behind girders.

The voices drew closer. Gar grabbed his flashlight and leaned out the up-river window, shining the tracks, hollering again. Their laughter carried as they continued over the bridge. A low droning moaned from the south. A coal train. "This isn't a game!" The droning grew louder. The voices were right below him, three boys laughing at the old man in the box. Like a resonant chord from a giant harmonica, the train sounded again, its pitch higher on approach. He heard one of the boys say they should go back. Another called him a coward. The third howled like a wolf.

The beam nearly blinding, the horn became a deafening wail. Gar shouted, "You better run!" Another blast emanated from the first of two locomotives as the train took the bridge; a full load, heavy, long, unstoppable. Vibration strained every rivet. Slowly, it plowed forward, horn blasting. Teenagers caught in the flood of light, eyes wide, ran, feet frantic for cross ties. One fell, his foot slipping, the horn a constant yowl as another boy jumped aside, clinging to a girder, hanging off the edge. The third helped the first, both falling out of the light.

One hundred coal cars rumbled through, one after another, after another, after another. Once past, Gar searched the track, his light illuminating a boy climbing back up, running for the end. Gar gave his siren a short burst and set the gears in motion, the giant rig turning slowly away from land. He heard the boy cussing as he jumped the ever-widening gap, tumbling onto solid ground. Scanning the channel wall, Gar saw two boys swimming against the frigid current toward a ladder. They were lucky this time.

~

Jason Hudson knelt between bushes and pushed on the narrow basement window, confident of his stealth. Sliding through headfirst, he braced himself on the workbench and pulled his legs in. Climbing down, careful to avoid kicking the vice on the end, he went upstairs to the kitchen but stopped cold when someone struck a match in the dark and lit a cigarette.

"It's five in the morning," said his father, shaking out the match. "This is going to stop. Right here. Right now. This stops."

Jason stepped up from the landing. "I'm going to bed," he said, walking through as if nothing his father said meant anything to him.

"Who were you with?"

"Nobody."

"Stop right there. Was it Randy and Wes?"

"So?"

"No more. I see you with them and . . ."

"Yeah, yeah," Jason mumbled.

"I don't need any of your back talk."

"Fine. Can I go to bed now?"

"If you're lucky, you can probably get about an hour in before it's time to get up for school."

Fred was a man who tried to keep a tight grip on things, but no matter how tight the leash he put on Jason, the boy always broke free. At fifteen, his son was reckless. Whether it was just his nature or the result of decisions made on his behalf years earlier was a question that haunted him. Sitting in the dark listening to coffee perk, he wondered how many of his choices concerning Jason were the result of nearly losing their first boy. Eric had been premature and almost didn't make it. Though Fred had been to war, he didn't know real fear until he saw his tiny son struggling to breathe. He wondered if that experience made him too cautious, if it made him weak.

Rose insisted the boys start kindergarten together even though Jason was barely five and Eric almost six. Whether Jason was ready for school or not, she wanted them both out from under foot for half the day, insisting two-year-old Patricia was enough for her to manage. He could have fought harder to keep Jason home, but that would have meant coming to terms with Rose's aversion to motherhood, and he had no idea how to fix that, much less face her head-on about it. So, because Fred was a coward, Jason entered kindergarten too soon.

Though the boys were in different classrooms, Jay Jay was still held to Eric's standard. When he didn't progress as fast and was prone to tantrums in school, there was discussion about having Jay Jay repeat kindergarten. Rose, however, wanted both boys in school all day, not just the half. Fred gave in to her again.

Jay Jay's first-grade teacher said he was ready for second-grade academically, but Fred felt he wasn't emotionally on track. They held him back. There would be fallout. Jason's temper had him in the principal's office at least once a month that next year. He demanded everyone stop calling him Jay Jay. He settled down eventually, but there was always a tension between Jason and everyone else, like a frayed wire about to spark. It was easy to blame Rose, but Fred had allowed it, and in the intervening years, he came to accept that any decision he made could have resulted in the same outcome. What he could not accept was the ever-present guilt he felt for failing as a parent.

Too nerved up to go back to bed, Fred Hudson pulled the chain to the light over the sink and put the coffee on, and noticed the wet footprints on the floor.

~

It was still dark when Ben Finney stood in the driveway stretching his hamstrings. A quiet kid, he was co-captain of the track team as a sophomore, a first at Edgewater High. A week earlier, he'd taken the state in the 800-meter and the mile while placing third in 300-meter hurdles and triple jump. If he kept it up, he'd go to college on a full ride. He adjusted his baseball cap and hit the street with ninety minutes to run ten miles. It was an aggressive goal, but he wasn't happy unless he was pushing himself. He ran down the middle of empty streets lit by streetlights on every corner. The first four blocks through his tree-lined neighborhood was a gentle jog, picking up a bit three blocks west, crossing the south end of Main Street, spilling into the alley behind the IGA. He cut over through a neighborhood of brick ranches, a few with a window or two lit, then through an old section of larger homes before taking the path along the tracks, following them down a long curving grade to lake level, the tracks slicing through woods along Lake Michigan on a straight shot to the river.

Twilight lit his way now, budding trees etching twisted branches on a brightening sky. The last star faded as the rising sun cast its soft glow, lending scattered clouds a spectacular pink aura. It was Ben's favorite few moments of the day when it was easy to believe there was a God. If people stopped piling into church pews and just woke up early to take it all in, they'd be less likely to doubt. Get rid of all the words, all the sermons and choir robes and hoopla, and simply observe. They'd find God on their own. Or not. Running alone let him ponder such things. Living in a house full of younger siblings, there was little space to think. He filled his lungs with sweet air rolling in off the lake, clean, soul-cleansing air.

He came to a small collection of run-down houses along the shore. When he hit the beach, he had yet to break a sweat, but the groin muscle he'd pulled running over loose sand in March was barking at him. It took most of April to heal, and he'd pulled it again on his last event at state finals, the high jump. He'd been tired and lost focus. It was a stupid move. Powering through the pain, he sprinted on the hard, wet sand at lake's edge to the south pier, where he ran to the end. His next-door neighbor called out from a small Boston Whaler heading out to the lake from the channel. Ben waved back. Circling the navigation light stanchion, he slapped it and turned back without stopping, waving at the other end to Gar up on the swing bridge. He ran past five camping trailers sitting end to end on a weed-speckled gravel lot, one a blunt-nosed Airstream, the rest a variety of shapes from boxes on wheels to flat-fronted, round-butted, bullet-looking rigs, most of them twenty years old, hold-overs from the forties. Morning sun, coming on full, cast long lavender shadows in front of them. A collection of odd chairs sat scattered about like mismatched castoffs, not unlike the trailers' inhabitants. The little enclave nestled between railroad tracks and the boardwalk of Sunset Beach, a dilapidated old amusement park.

Ben bolted onto the boardwalk, running past a Ferris wheel, boarded-up dancehall, arcade, funhouse, and game booths, cutting short of the roller coaster through a narrow passageway between two buildings. He crossed the tracks again, running across a gravel lot behind an abandoned warehouse, then along the river to the city marina with its high docks and parking lot still crowded with big boats on racks, cabin cruisers, and forty-foot sailboats waiting on summer. Up to his right, atop a grassy bluff, sat Edgewater's downtown. Following the river around, he ran on an abandoned track bed by the lumberyard and past a dump to where the tracks disappeared, leaving only a wide dirt path. He ran past a small jetty, then under a bridge. Up the bluff was the hospital. Beyond it, a couple blocks away, was his house. Further down the track bed, the path grew narrower, where the smell of the river was as acrid and dense as the overgrown brush until he came to Casper's Cove, a small upriver marina carved out of a marsh. A workingman's marina, it was small and unpretentious. There were no sailboats, no grand Chris-Craft. The river that far up was tricky with ever-changing shallows where anything with a draught greater than three or four feet could get hung up. There were no boats on racks at Casper's. Anyone who docked there stored their boats in backyards or garages, and put in come spring. It had been warm recently, and half a dozen boats sat tied to low splintery docks. Looking at his watch, Ben swore and berated himself, then ran up the hill, feeling the burn. Landing in his neighborhood and home, he went to the basement, stripped down, and climbed into a small shower stall next to the washing machine. Ten minutes later, he grabbed a piece of toast from his mother and took off on his bike, hoping to make it to school before the eight o'clock bell. It had taken ninety minutes to run eight miles. Next week, maybe, he'd finally get to ten in that time.

~

Down at Sunset Beach, a persistent squeaking of metal on metal emanated from the undercarriage of the trailer closest to the river as it slowly listed from one side to the other. It was as unique as the others, a round-cornered box painted yellow up the sides, and white on top, though much of the white had peeled off, revealing naked aluminum. Two doors, one on each end, had round porthole windows, like the dead stare of wide-set eyes. A door swung open, its hinges screeching in resistance. When a woman appeared in the doorway, it seemed her girth would be too much for the narrow opening, yet she maneuvered through, stepping a bare foot down onto the bent step ledge below. It gave some with her weight, but held firm, the whole trailer listing with the effort.

Geneva stepped down and out, closed the door behind her, turned, and looked to the heavens. Something resembling a smile came over her face, though it could just as easily be a wince. She wore an orange and yellow muumuu covered with flowers, sweat-stained at the neck and armpits. Her hair was slicked back into a ponytail, her face haloed by an array of split-ends illuminated by morning sun. A meager clump of bangs hung in flyaway strands over her eyes. Her skin was pale to the point of pallid. Dark sacks under her eyes appeared almost translucent as if the slightest touch might burst them. Though only pushing forty, she could have passed for a woman many years older.

She reached for a pack of cigarettes on a rusty metal table, lit one up, slipped into a pair of ratty canvas shoes with the backs cut off, and sat down, weary. She was already a good hour into her day but soon would be off-task for the rest of it.

~

Out on the lake, Schroeder reeled in one of his three lines, landing a nice pan-sized perch. He tossed it in a cooler and leaned back. He liked fishing alone, nobody demanding his attention and no decisions to make. He could think out there on the water. Or not think.

By the summer of 1965, Andrew Patrick Schroeder had been on the force for twenty years, chief for over ten. He was the youngest police chief Edgewater ever had. Other men who'd been there longer wanted the job, but none of them had what Schroeder did – an innate sense of people, a skill useful in Edgewater, a quiet town. Small. People died by sickness, accident, or altercation gone too far. The only murder of record happened back in the twenties when one of Al Capone's men shot a cop over a busted taillight.

Schroeder looked upriver beyond the piers. The river marked the town's northern border, reaching eastward and curving south. Bathed in morning light, a person might believe the riverfront was still vibrant, not a broken-down pre-Depression relic of a time when big steamers shipped in Chicago tourists and hauled out Michigan fruit. The abandoned warehouse looked as if it waited for men to arrive with trucks and handcarts to begin the day. The amusement park looked inviting, with the Wicked Flyer's wooden scaffold towering above the boardwalk like a dare. For that brief moment, when the sun caught the edges of the Ferris wheel, it appeared to be made of gold, its gondolas dangling jewels.

All that remained of the renowned twenty-acre resort with carnival rides, boat livery, gazebos, restaurants, and tourist cabins, was the boardwalk between the Ferris wheel and the Wicked Flyer, and it existed in a constant state of disrepair, a ghost too stubborn to move on.

Over the objections of the town council, Sunset Beach Amusement Park was preparing to open in a week over Memorial Day. There wasn't a parent in town who trusted the roller coaster anymore, yet people still came from out of town every year, lured by the nostalgia of their youth, only to be disappointed by decay. If this summer was like the rest, after sunset, after families went home, the night crowd would filter in, seedy types and bored teenagers looking for diversion, inviting inevitable scuffles and a few drunk and disorderly calls. No one could tell whether people would still come or not. Schroeder would rather they didn't.

Chief Schroeder was a son of Edgewater, third generation, raised as much by the town as by his family.

His grandfather came down from Canada as a young man and became a Great Lakes steamship captain for the Graham & Morton Line. His position offered prestige in town until the ships stopped running and money came up short. Schroeder saw his town as an intricate puzzle where the past dovetailed into the present. He saw linkages most people missed. He knew the regular drunks from the holiday drunks. He knew the Barley Tap and Mac's over-served on Saturday nights. He knew whose car was in the wrong driveway, and who was running the local card game, and where. He knew Reggie Harrison came back from the war-damaged in ways a person couldn't see and that he sometimes hit his wife. He knew the twice-divorced Marjorie Dodge had been assaulted by her uncle when she was young and was never quite right about men because of it. He had a pretty good idea Aaron Arnold committed suicide but ruled his drowning an accident so his widow and six kids could collect on his insurance. He knew that old Carl Hoxie's scar from an altercation with Capone's men had really come from falling off a ladder, drunk. He knew, above all else, that after twenty years of marriage, his wife, Grace, was still his best friend and his steady reservoir of sanity.

One of his fishing poles dipped and bounced. Schroeder pulled it from its cuff and gave it a little tug. Reeling in, feeling the weaving pull on the line, he thought about his daughter for some reason. That's how it was on the water alone, his mind sifting through random thoughts, tangents leading nowhere, yet often landing on something significant. Tammy was a beautiful, genuine, grounded person about to head off to college in a year. As much as he would miss her, Schroeder knew she was ready. Whether Schroeder was ready to let her go was another issue altogether. The bass he caught was too small. He threw it back.

~

About to wrap up his shift, Gar's radio crackled, and the captain of the Elizabeth announced her imminent arrival. Out the north window, he saw the freighter coming in early with her load of cement. He glanced at the clock, grumbled, and told her captain to wait out the freight train coming across at 7:25. Gar hit the siren, a brief whine, and set the gears in motion to close the bridge. The enormous gears began grinding and moaning as the trestle pivoted from its point mid-river.

A heavyset young man with an awkward duck-footed gate ran toward the river, stopping abruptly at the end of the tracks, waving to the tender's box as if his life depended on being seen. Gar appeared in the window and gave him a casual wave. Augie Maxwell flung up both arms in response before turning his attention to the bridge slowly moving toward him, toward the riverbank, the steel singing with the effort. Augie's heart pounded as he stepped back, watching the giant structure swing ever closer toward him, the tracks slowly moving into alignment, coming to a halt with a reverberating clunk. He smiled and ran away, hollering. "Gotta get back, or Mama's gonna have my butt!"

Out on the lake, the bridge siren was Schroeder's signal to get in to the station. Normally, he'd be at work by a little after seven ahead of the day shift, but he allowed himself an occasional late arrival when perch were running. Stowing his rods, he headed into the channel.

Gar climbed down from his cabin, the iron steps proving more difficult these days. His wife berated him constantly about the dangers, saying all it would take would be one slip, and he'd tumble down to the tracks and crack his head open, or maybe bounce off the pilings into the river. Then where would she be? A pitiful widow who'd have to go looking for a new husband because he knew she didn't like to be alone.

Gar spotted Schroeder's boat approaching the bridge. "Looked like you were doing pretty good out there today, Chief."

Schroeder smiled and throttled down. "You don't miss much, do ya?"

"Nope. Not much. Chased a few rowdy teenagers last night walkin' the tracks."

"Don't suppose you radioed the station. They'd have sent someone to haul them in, ya know."

"Naw. You should have seen 'em scramble when that northbound came at 'em, that big old light comin' straight at 'em. Big one, too. Long one." He smiled with great satisfaction. "That ought to teach 'em."

The day tender approached, a middle-aged man who seemed he wanted to be anywhere but there. Gar told him the Elizabeth was holding steady. The day tender grumbled something indiscernible and climbed the ladder up into the office.

"Next time," Schroeder told Gar, "call us."

"Not many next times left," Gar reminded him. "Retire end of August. I guarantee the next guy won't watch like I do. I guarantee it!"

They waved each other off as Gar walked down the tracks, and Schroeder cruised slowly upriver to his slip at Casper's.

~

Geneva caught a glimpse of Augie running onto the boardwalk. "That taffy better not be ruined, boy!" She shook her head and smiled, snuffed a stub of cigarette in the gravel, and rose from her chair. Taking a second to get her feet under her, she slowly made her way, her body swaying side to side with each step. She skirted the Ferris wheel with its big BUSTED - OUT OF SERVICE sign on the gate and passed by the former ballroom with its boarded-up doors, glassless window frames, and rotted-out floor.

The penny arcade doors were propped open, revealing dozens of ancient freestanding games congregated in the center and lining the walls. Harold Caruthers fidgeted with a Flash Gordon pinball machine, trying to get one more season out of it. A withered man in his late sixties, Harold had spent the better part of his life as a fix-it man. He'd kept Sunset Beach up and running to ever lesser degrees, and it was getting more and more difficult. In the off-season, Harold and the others wintered at an amusement park near Brownsville, Texas, doing the same work. Both places were falling apart, and he needed more than he could do, but management was short on money and incentive. He used to hire locals to run some of the games, but there was no more money in it. Their little crew was all that kept Sunset afloat. Some days, he longed for the past when families thronged to the boardwalk when the paint was bright and the rides safe. Other days, he watched the degenerates who ambled their way along, throwing bottles at faded posters, riding rides that were just as likely to break down as run, and he thought it was time the place was put out of its misery.

"Mornin' Mrs. Maxwell," he hollered to Geneva. She looked over to him and nodded without stopping. "Mornin' Mr. Caruthers." It was a pleasantry they shared, a formality where none existed. Mrs. Maxwell was not, in fact, a missus. Though Augie was her son, she'd never married, and to everyone else, she was Geneva or the taffy lady.

Geneva walked past shuttered game booths that would not open this season. She'd never played a game at the arcade, gone into the funhouse, or ridden a ride.

She looked ahead to her concession stand and saw Augie hard at work pulling taffy. Draping the large mass of banana yellow goo over a hook, he let it fall, slapped the two sides together, gathered it up, wrapped it on the hook again, all the while making grunting sounds with the effort. A sweet bear of a man, Geneva's son was twenty-three going on eight. His belly strained against too-tight pants. His large, round face still carried the innocent, slightly vacant expression of a child, but he was strong and eager, always willing to do the heavy lifting for anyone who asked.

"Good job, Augie," Geneva said. "Good job."

"Good thing you got us up early, Mama. Gonna be hot today. I'm already hot. If you waited one more hour, I'd be too hot to do this. Look. I'm sweatin'!"

"Had nothing to do with the heat, boy. Have an order to fill up in town." Geneva gave the taffy strand a squeeze. "Feels perfect. Let's get it cut."

He gave it one more pull, then collected it, and hauled it inside the stand, and slapped it onto a large marble slab. Geneva followed, the floorboards creaking under their combined weight. She pulled a long, wide knife from a drawer. Augie reached for it, but she laughed him off. "I don't think so," she chided him, and patted the lightning bolt tattoo on his shoulder, something he got for her but got smacked upside the head when he showed her. "Could have at least been a heart if it was for me," she had told him.

Two men ambled their way down the boardwalk. Sam, the younger of them, in his thirties, was tall and lanky. A man of generally high spirits, his smile had more gaps than teeth. The other, Ivan, was pushing fifty, overweight and indifferent to almost everything. Both men wore pinstriped coveralls covered with stains. There wasn't a repair in the place that didn't take the both of them to fix, and this day, they were on their way to Kiddy Korner to repair the Aeroplane ride. Geneva asked Ivan if he was going to get the Ferris wheel running or not.

"Don't see how," he grumbled. "They won't spring for parts."

Harold walked up. "This used to be one fine place."

Sam snorted. "In what century?"

Chesterfield Lee Perry, known as Barker to anyone who bothered with his name, sauntered by in his pointy steel-tipped crocodile boots. A sinewy man with long, greasy hair and one bad eye, he ran the ball toss booth and lived in the storeroom behind it, sleeping on a mildewed cot among boxes of cheap stuffed animals and prizes hardly worth the price of the game. Any hard look at him would set most people back in much the same way they wouldn't want to look a wild dog straight in the eye. There was, however, something just below the surface of the man, like an apparition, a suggestion there had once been handsomeness. "What a fuckin' shit hole."

"Do you ever have anything worth saying, Barker?" Harold sniped.

Geneva muttered under her breath. "Used to." Then she spoke outright. "You used to have lots of fine things to say!" She whipped up her massive arm, flesh swaying, and pointed at his right hand.

Barker fiddled with a large onyx ring, dodging her glare, then rubbed his swollen knuckles. "What's your point?" he snapped, walking away. "What a fuckin' shit hole."

Augie hollered after Barker, saying that he didn't have to be so grumpy all the time. He waited for Barker to turn back around, but he didn't, and the other men headed off, too, toward the kiddy rides. Augie turned to watch his mother heft the big knife into the tough wad of taffy on the slab, leaning on it to cut through. He asked if he could go down to the beach to see if the water was warm or cold.

"What? No! Of course not. You know you can't swim."

"But I won't go in."

"What did you do last time you said that?"

"I went wading."

"That's going in. I said no." She looked at her watch. "Almost time."

"Mr. Gar!"

"You be careful over there! You hear me?"

"Yes, Mama."

Geneva watched her boy hurry down the boardwalk, between game booths, out of sight. She took the big knife, moved it a couple inches up the slab, and leaned on it for another cut.

Augie met Gar out behind the arcade along the tracks. The northbound freight train had already cleared the bend in the distance, slowly making its approach, its horn wailing. Augie unwrapped a piece of taffy and threw it in his mouth the way someone might pop a pill. After he'd chewed it a bit, he crammed another one in. His smile dripped blue ooze.

Gar stood with Augie as the train cleared the station a block away. Augie leaned in too far, and Gar grabbed his arm, pulling him away from the track. Like rolling thunder, the train rumbled by. Augie hollered to Gar, but the train drowned his words. "Have a good night, Mr. Gar?" The freight cars and tankers rolled by, their steel wheels whining and clanking. "It was a hot one, wasn't it, Mr. Gar? Did you get hot up in your little box?" Gar responded with slight nods.

All summer, Wednesday through Sunday, it was the same routine. They watched the morning train together, waving to the engineer who always, no matter who it was, waved back. Then they walked the tracks behind the arcade buildings, skirted the Wicked Flier, and crossed the parking lot to the edge of the neighborhood of old bungalows. Every day, they parted company on the same broken square of sidewalk, and Augie would tell Gar to get a good day's rest. It was a routine that seemed to give both of them a sense of continuity, though Augie would not have recognized it as such. This day was no different, except that a ship was about to come through the channel, and Augie was afraid he'd miss it. Gar assured him it would be a good thirty minutes before she made it in, but Augie left Gar and hurried to make sure he didn't miss it.

On the edge of the river, at the top of the channel wall, Augie held on to a chain-link fence, watching the bridge swing open, watching Elizabeth make her way slowly from the lake, between the piers, inching her way toward the bridge. Tall on both ends, she was long, wide, and low in the middle. Augie was afraid every time a ship came in, it might slam into the bridge and wreck it. He waved frantically at the Elizabeth's captain to warn him, but the captain did not wave back, and the ship slipped through with seemingly inches to spare. Only after she was securely docked did Augie go back to the concession stand and his mother.

CHAPTER THREE

Wednesday after Memorial Day, Hamilton Jr. High spilled its hormonal brood out onto the street for summer break. Jason Hudson stood like a post as pimple-faced kids surged around him. They were not his people. His people, the class he started out with, were up at the high school. He blamed his father for holding him back. That betrayal and humiliation, watching his friends move on without him, fueled an animosity Jason could never quite shake off, embedding in him a sense of never being good enough. Jason became an instigator, predictable only in his unpredictability.

He was a short kid, well-muscled and athletic, with quick reflexes. He'd have ridden his bike to school that last day of school if he hadn't bent the front wheel careening down the ravine the day before. His shaggy light brown hair gleamed as he stepped out of the shadow of a school bus into the sunlight. He saw Randy and called out.

"Well fuck you very much," Randy said.
"What do you mean by that?"
"That little stunt of yours last night?"
"Yeah?"

"Well, guess who's going to military school next year. My dad was waiting for me, pissed as hell."

"No shit. He'll cool off. Want to walk the tracks?"

"Did you hear me? Fuck no. I'm as good as on house arrest. And if my old man sees me with you?" He threw his hands up and walked away. He turned around to say Wes's mom was sending him to live with his father in Detroit. "Have a nice life, shithead."

Jason shrugged. The absence of Randy and Wes from his life meant little. They were fallback people, the ones always up for an exploit.

A few blocks away, his brother Eric sauntered out of high school with Ben Finney and a crowd of other newly minted juniors. Eric was a people pleaser, confident, with an air of quiet self-control. They lingered at the bike rack with a dozen kids, talking about drivers ed and meeting up at North Beach on the weekend.

Over at Orchard Elementary, Jason and Eric's sister Trish stuffed notebooks, papers, pencil boxes, and all the paraphernalia collected throughout the year into a paper sack. She tied together the laces of her scuffed white gym shoes. A nondescript girl, she had quick gray eyes that seemed to take in everything they fell upon with equal scrutiny. Her dark blond hair parted down the middle, exaggerated her high forehead. Her braids hung just below her collarbone. In most ways, Trish was like all kids, worried she wasn't good enough, afraid she didn't fit in, and certain she was the only one who felt that way.

At the bulletin board, Ben's sister Linda, an exceptionally tall girl, reached high for a drawing, taking it and several others down for shorter kids. She was a helpful girl and bookish, a girl who pressured herself to do well. A towhead, her long blond hair looked like the bleached blonds of old movies.

Across the room, Jane Donahue finished packing the last of her eraser collection and her gym shoes into her sack. A round-faced girl, she had long mahogany-colored braids and bangs that hung like a curtain above her brow line. Janey was a follower, quiet. Everyone liked pleasant, submissive Janey.

Mrs. Burns, the school principal, recently made aware she had not run the requisite number of duck and cover drills during the year, initiated the last one. At 11:50, a loud bell blasted three times, and kids all shot to attention. Mrs. Hasselbaum clapped her hands and hollered without any particular urgency, her tone easily construed as a combination of boredom and annoyance. "Tornado drill everyone," she said. "Stand up and file out in an orderly fashion." The kids were quick to correct her. Three bells was a duck and cover drill. "Yes, yes," she said. "Duck and cover. Be quick about it."

Exuberant chatter rose as kids dropped to the floor, crawled under their desks, and pulled their knees up to their chins. Trish tucked her head in tight to her knees, trying to collect her skirt to cover her underpants before grabbing the back of her neck with both hands.

"I see London, I see France..." a boy hollered.

"Eyes down, Stanley," Mrs. Hasselbaum scolded. "No talking." The kids settled down, in position, quietly waiting.

When the all-clear bell rang, Mrs. Burns' chipper voice came over the P.A. "This was only a drill. I hope everyone has a good summer. Don't forget to read a book or two. Be safe." The bell rang one long blast, and kids clamored to their feet, gathered their things, and surged out the door, into the hallway, funneling down the stairwells until four hundred joyously screaming kids poured out onto the playground, to the buses, running to bike racks, spilling into surrounding neighborhoods exhilarated with anticipation of summer vacation.

Once outside, Linda and Janey cut away from Trish and ran off together. Trish called after them. "I'll see you later!" The girls waved and kept running. From that distance, watching Linda with her long legs and graceful gate, Trish thought she could easily be mistaken for a teenager. She envied her.

Trish turned to walk in the opposite direction, toward Maple Lane, sensing an instantaneous shift from communal exaltation to singular isolation. She was beginning to form the opinion that anticipation of a thing was usually greater than the thing itself.

Compact Cape Cod houses lined the streets of Trish's neighborhood, each one nearly identical to the next with postage-stamp yards, crisp curbs, and two maples on every tree lawn. There were ravines at both ends of Maple. Butter Creek ravine, a deep meandering crevasse, reached woodsy fingers all through town. The other ravine, un-named, led to the river skirting town.

Mothers delivered off-limits warning on both ravines like a disclaimer against the inevitable. When

Roger from four doors down broke his arm sledding down Butter Creek the winter before, every mother echoed the same thing as they marched their kids up from the icy woods, plastic saucers and Flexible Flyers dragging behind them. I told you not to play in the ravine.

~

Rose Hudson stood in the kitchen shaking a BubbleUp bottle at the ironing board, the corked sprinkler cap releasing errant drops of water to a pillowcase. She pressed it end to end, folded it, and pressed it again, all the while some woman on the radio yammered on about the upcoming art fair. Behind her, smooth white shirts hung from one cupboard knob, two of Trish's dresses from another. Rose was thirty-five that year, somewhat pudgier than her mother preferred, but pretty. She wore a dress, a comfortable cotton shirtwaist with an apron tied tight. The apron came off only after the dinner dishes were done each evening, a gesture indicating she was off duty.

Trish walked through the back door into air thick with the aroma of brownies. She could almost tell the day by how the house smelled. Floor wax meant it was Monday. Fried onions, preparations for spaghetti sauce, or a casserole meant it was Thursday or Friday. Wednesday was baking day. She dropped her gym shoes to the floor and her sack on the table, nudging a vase with one stem of lilacs, probably cut from one of her grandmother's bushes across town. Quick to grab it before it fell over, Trish moved the vase back to the center of the shiny white Formica. She eyed the brownies on the stove.

"No," Rose said with a little smile. "Still hot." A newscaster on the radio said the soon-to-launch Gemini-4 mission would attempt the first-ever spacewalk, important in the race to get to the moon before the Russians. A commentator touted the idea that an American floating in space generated optimism. Rose rolled her eyes, grumbling it wasn't enough to distract from the National Guard attacking civil rights marchers. "And that ridiculous war in Vietnam. Why are we even there?"

"Where?" Trish asked.

"Never mind. Your laundry's on your bed," Rose said. "Put it away, please. Grandma brought some snap beans over. You can clean some for dinner."

"I'm on vacation."

Rose raised her eyebrows, something Trish chose to ignore.

"Can I go to Linda's tonight?"

"No." It was an autopilot response, the kind that sometimes left the door open to negotiation.

"Why not? There's no school tomorrow."

"Because I said so. And pick up your shoes."

"But Mom . . ."

"Stop whining. It isn't becoming."

"But, Mom . . ."

"No means no."

"Crap." Trish let it slip under her breath, but Rose caught it loud and clear.

"What did you say?"

"Nothing." She picked up her shoes, grabbed her sack, and sulked down the hall to her bedroom.

"Stop pouting," Rose told her as she pulled a dustpan and brush from under the sink to sweep up the bit of dirt Trish tracked in. Rose, like her mother before her, was prone to abrupt dictates. Stand up straight. Smile. Be quiet. Stop pouting. Disappear. Rose never said it outright, disappear, but Trish felt it hiding behind her insincere smiles.

Trish plopped on her bed and turned on her transistor radio. Jackie DeShannon was in the middle of "What the World Needs Now is Love." Rose appeared in the doorway, smiled faintly, grabbed the doorknob, and pulled the door closed. "Keep it down," she said.

It was not uncommon for Rose to close Trish's door. The practice had begun with Eric and Jason when they were babies. Closing the door kept household noise out so they could both take naps or sleep through the night. When Trish came along, the boys were moved upstairs, and she took the front room. Closing the door, by then, was habit, and even as Trish grew, it had become routine to wall her off.

Rose had no idea how her daughter relished the slow sweep of that door closing, followed by the click of the latch. She liked being left alone in her inner sanctum, surrounded by her own things, never having to share. Alone in her room, Trish could forget she had brothers.

She became an only child. Her transistor radio, always tuned to WLS, generated the soundtrack of her life, music sweeping from Chicago over Lake Michigan into her bedroom. Like a meditation, every song took her deeper into the communal consciousness of teenagers everywhere, like a vast soup of dreams where everyone was cool and anything was possible, where she wasn't an awkward ten-year-old forced to wear white anklets.

Trish changed out of her dress and put on a pair of shorts from a tidy stack on her bed. She took the stuffed monkey and giraffe off her bed and tossed them into the closet. She did it every day, and every day, her mother pulled them back out when she made beds in the morning. Girls in Seventeen Magazine didn't have stuffed animals on their beds.

Trish wanted nothing so much as to be a teenager. Pushing eleven wasn't good enough. She wanted to be pushing fifteen, wearing skirts and hose and heels – better yet, flats. She still played with dolls, but they were Barbies and Kens, with intricate stories. There were love triangles, romantic comedies, and tragedies. She spent hours alone in her room, inventing their lives.

She turned up the radio when Little Stevie Wonder came on. Singing along, she leafed through her latest Seventeen with deep longing to be everything she wasn't: Thin, pretty, clever, popular.

CHAPTER FOUR

Rose carried a stack of clothes upstairs, depositing some on each twin bed, wiping a wrinkle out of Jason's bedspread, straightening a pillow on Eric's, caught off guard by the thought of almost losing him at birth. It wasn't often those memories came to the surface, but when they did, they stirred deep disappointments. She'd gone into labor three weeks early, and the birth was difficult. His lungs took in fluid. It was touch and go for the first couple weeks, and she was certain every day would be the day they'd tell her he didn't make it. Fear hardened her expectations in preparation for the worst. And, in this, she buried the love. Her mother supported this approach, telling her daughter, "Don't get too attached." It was cold, an attitude without explanation ingrained into her mother's bones.

When Eric was strong enough, he came home, heightening Rose's fears. If he died at home, it would be because of something she did or didn't do.

Watching Fred revel in every moment he had with his son only served to make her own reticence more painful.

Eric was born in mid-October, and by mid-January, Rose knew she was pregnant again. She went straight to her mother to find someone to commiserate with, but Myrtle couldn't abide such carelessness. "Have you no respect for your body? For the way this will look? Do you have no idea how these things work? I taught you better! I told you when to avoid your husband. What kind of man is Fred to come at you so soon after having a baby? What kind of woman are you? A baby at your breast, and you let him . . . it's disgusting," she shouted. "You should be ashamed of yourself!" Myrtle's rage was irrational even for her.

Walking in the back door with an armload of firewood, Bert heard Myrtle's outburst, his daughter's sobs, and baby Eric crying. He dropped the wood into the rack and stood center room between the two women like a referee. "What the hell is this about?"

Myrtle demanded Rose tell her father, but when she didn't do it fast enough, Myrtle blurted it out. "She's pregnant again!"

Bert looked to Rose with softened eyes. "Irish twins, is it then?"

"Oh, Daddy," she cried, rising to seek his reassuring embrace, but he nodded to the baby.

"I think he needs your attention."

Rose did as she was told, hoisting the baby and bouncing him. He did not quiet. Bert slipped out of his coat and took Eric in his arms, immediately settling him.

"See that?" Myrtle scolded. "You can't even take care of one, and you're having another?"

Where anyone else might have had harsh words for both of them, Bert looked at his wife with an expression entirely counter to the moment. It was one of love and consolation. In his welling eyes, Myrtle found release and understanding. Her rage fell away. Embarrassed for having been so vicious, she left the room, grabbed her coat, and went to the screen porch, where she sat in the big wicker chair, staring out through snow-covered pines to Lake Michigan.

"What was that?" Rose demanded as if her father had taken the wrong side.

"You mean your mother?"

"I mean, you letting her get away with it!"

He turned a stern face to his daughter. "She is your mother, but she's my wife. Don't ever forget that."

"But, Daddy, she . . ."

"You must be exhausted," he said, with the expectation she would take the hint. "I'll get this little guy wrapped up, and you take him home. That's where you belong. Your home. With Fred. Not here."

"But, Daddy. . ."

"Go home to your husband."

Rose crying to Fred later about the argument with her mother is how he learned there was another baby on the way.

~

Raising children wasn't what Rose expected. It had been joyless from the start, and she laid the blame directly at her obstetrician's doorstep. With each of her three deliveries, she'd been given a morphine and scopolamine cocktail, one to minimize the pain, the other to make her forget it. The process somehow managed to break the tether between Rose and her babies. After each delivery, she woke alone in a room with only a vague memory of giving birth. Because of Eric's complications, she was not allowed to hold him for the first few days. He was too frail. He wasn't breathing well. Later, with her other two, a nurse, always smiling, so superior, brought the baby in, placing it in Rose's arms. She found herself searching each of their tiny wrinkled faces for any indication of familial connection. Failing to see it, failing to feel it, she believed they could have brought her any baby and claimed it was hers. Rose said nothing, all the while blaming them for the alienation she felt when her babies did not calm to her touch or nurse well from her breasts. At some point in every day with all three babies, Rose clenched her teeth and fists and powered through the urge to throw something against the wall. The predominant feeling in each day was never love. It was more akin to entrapment.

Had Rose consorted with any of her neighbors, she'd have learned that two doors down, Alice Schulz got so frustrated with her three kids, she once sent them to their rooms, shut the doors, got in her car and drove away. She was ten miles out of town before she turned around. Eloise Cantor piled her five kids in the car one day, the youngest only four, and dropped them at the door of the small local museum, went to a bar, and drank herself into a stupor. Her husband got a call at the chassis plant when somebody recognized her. Down the block and across the street, Tom Price came home to find the twins screaming in their crib and his wife locked in the bathroom inconsolably sobbing. And Sharon Finch used to dose her babies with bourbon to quiet them when she couldn't take it anymore. These things were not spoken of. The mothers of Maple Lane kept their little insanities to themselves, thereby appearing to love their children wholeheartedly and unconditionally. Because of this, Rose believed there was something inherently wrong with her.

As the years passed, she came to see her children, chiefly and above all else, as an ever-present responsibility. As toddlers, they spit up, smeared their food, and spilled everything. Then, they began to speak and refuse. They turned into independent humans with words and ideas foreign to her,. They were strangers constantly morphing into new versions of themselves. She found it impossible to keep up with them or take pride in their accomplishments. Each day, week, month, as her children took her more and more for granted, she grew further apart from them, fearful they might sense she felt little but obligation toward them. The guilt of these feelings only served to enhance her sense of inadequacy. As her touch had not quieted them as infants, she withdrew from direct contact as they grew. She cooked for them. Cleaned. Kept their clothes clean and pressed. She hounded them to do homework and intervened before they tore each other to shreds. She had always heard that a mother's love is instinctual and automatic, but Rose didn't much like her children. How could she expect to love them? She put up and shut up, her subtle self-loathing hidden behind eyes that couldn't smile with her mouth.

~

    The tinny sound of the Beach Boys drifted from upstairs as Fred, still dressed in his white shirt and slacks from the office, finished the last page of his newspaper, folded it carefully, and headed to the kitchen. "Eric," he called upstairs. "Turn it off and come down to dinner."

    At forty-one, Fred was a reserved sort of man who rarely smiled. He was an accountant for a small company that did finish work for area tool and die shops. His office was too cramped, his challenges too few, and every day he fought against boredom. Yet, he stayed on out of his sense of loyalty and security. The owner had lent him the $500 down payment on their house and was good about bonuses and insurance for the kids. His paycheck covered the mortgage, utilities, and groceries with little left over for unexpected expenses or vacations. Rose was the one who made it work, skillfully managing every penny.

    Rose brought a bowl of peas to the table, reaching around Fred as if he were a piece of furniture. She straightened the stack of Wonder Bread on a plate, poured milk for everyone, and called the kids to the table a second time as she sat down.

Eric showed up first, walking in without making eye contact with either of his parents. He sat down and drank all his milk. Without a word, Rose refilled his glass.

Out in the hall, Jason pushed Trish out of the way with a laugh and sauntered into the kitchen. Trish pushed past him and sat down before him, jostling the table, drawing a glare from Rose.

This was the Hudson household, a constant war of wills.

Fred filled his plate. "When do your games start?" he asked the boys, neither of them answering.

"Answer your father," Rose said with a grin and cocked head.

"Huh?" Eric said.

"You boys play tomorrow?" Fred asked with a little more vigor.

"No," Eric told him. "Friday. 4:30."

"Jason, are you going to pitch?"

Jason mumbled with a mouthful of mashed potatoes. "Probably."

"Eric, you catching?"

"Yeah."

Fred said he might miss a couple innings but he'd make it to the game.

Rose started in on the agitation of the day with a singsong lilt to her voice. "There is a hamper in the hall upstairs." She took a sip of milk, smiled wide, and shook her head as if telling a joke. "For the life of me, I don't know why you can't put your dirty clothes in it. Why I should have to pick your clothes up off the floor every day is beyond me." As she prattled on, she didn't notice Fred watching her with an expression that might have spoken volumes, or nothing at all. He sighed, retuning his gaze to his plate, and loaded up his fork with a chunk of leftover meatloaf.

Silence returned to the table until Trish looked at the boys, sat up a little straighter, and announced she wasn't going to any more of their baseball games. She wanted to stay home. Baseball was boring.

"Don't be ridiculous," Rose said.

Fred ignored them both.

Trish accepted defeat, proud to have at least spoken up.

Evenings in the Hudson household were spent sprawled around the living room watching a barrage of TV shows hawking family values. They were a fiction Trish never wanted to emulate. The characters had no privacy or secrets. They always smiled and their problems only took twenty minutes to find tidy little solutions. Grandmas were always sweet. Parents never argued. Brothers didn't beat up on sisters. The Indians always died, and the sheriff always got his man. She didn't know much yet, but she knew real life was messier than that.

CHAPTER FIVE

Down at the amusement park, deep in the night, Harold Caruthers sat alone in the darkness by his old Airstream. He leaned back in one of the fan-back metal chairs, legs spread wide, his head resting back with his face to the stars, hands on his belly, holding an ice pack on his knuckles. A breeze set the line of frayed triangular banners overhead to flapping, and he liked that. Nobody else heard that particular sound, not in their cozy backyards, not up on the main street through town. It was his sound. Personal. Geneva stepped out of her trailer and sat down. She asked if the pain was getting to him again, but he didn't answer.

The banners settled as the breeze died. The two sat in stillness. Geneva rustled a pack of cigarettes, struck a match, and lit one up, the red glow sweeping with the drop of her arm.

"I was watchin' you over there this mornin'," Harold said quietly. ". . . how you're always so patient with your boy, and it got me to thinkin' about old Ralph and how he used to love that boy of yours." Geneva did not respond. "That was a good man. And, I have to say it, you were good to him."

Geneva laughed a little. "Ugly as sin," she said and took a deep drag, blowing it out in a long, steady stream. "I mean, my God, he was the ugliest man I ever saw."

"Was he? I guess men don't notice that kind of thing about other men."

"What, so you can see ugly on a woman but not a man?"

Harold grunted, and they returned to silence. Neither of them should have been awake, but there they sat. The breeze rose again, stirring the banners, then changed its mind and settled.

"I suppose it's more that Ralph was more than what people saw," Harold said. "I suppose if he'd been mean, he'd have been ugly, but he was kind. Decent. That's all I saw."

Geneva didn't argue. She snuffed out the last half of the cigarette and groaned as she stood up. "Good night, Mr. Caruthers. I hope the pain lets up."

"Good night, Mrs. Maxwell."

The undercarriage of her trailer creaked as she stepped inside. She hesitated when Harold spoke again.

"The man had no chin, though, did he? No chin at all. And those teeth."

"Good night, Harold."

From inside, Augie could be heard asking if Harold was all right. Geneva assured him he was and told him to go back to sleep. Augie called out. "Good night, Harold."

"Sleep good there, Augie. Dream somethin' beautiful."

~

Geneva Maxwell was the best mother she could have been under the circumstances. By the time she was a teenager, she was good at two things: One got her pregnant, and the other ingratiated her to Ralph Lester.

In another lifetime, before she became the bloated, bitter version of herself, Geneva's family owned a candy store on Coney Island. She grew up in the shop, learning the recipes and waiting on customers. She and her sister were pretty back then, bright, delightful girls. But Geneva had a wild nature. When her father found out she was pregnant and then discovered she couldn't be certain who the father might be, he kicked her out. She was only sixteen the spring she took up residence in an abandoned building, waiting for her parents to take her back. They didn't. She was alone when she went into labor. Someone heard her scream and called the police. The baby arrived as they did. He wasn't breathing until one of the cops smacked him on the back a few times.

Geneva's parents were charged with child neglect. The family business closed. The newborn survived but with "expectations of retardation" and was declared a ward of the state. Geneva stole her baby boy from the nursery and hopped a bus. Mother Nature, as if to abet the escape, covered their tracks with a great storm.

Later dubbed the Long Island Express, the hurricane left people with more important problems than tracking down two strays.

Geneva arrived in Myrtle Beach, South Carolina, with the dazed little creature she named August. The tourist season was in full swing when she walked into Ralph Lester's saltwater taffy shop looking for work. She said she'd work in trade for room and board. He took them in.

In his mid-fifties, Ralph had never married. Perhaps he hadn't found a woman able to look past his appearance. One side of his face was moderately proportional, the other askew. One eye opened too wide, the other hardly at all. His nose had a prizefighter's crook from being repeatedly punched as a kid. His jaw was too small, his teeth too big, and his eyebrows marched from one side of his face to the other. He lived above his taffy shop in a tiny apartment barely big enough for him. But he made room for the girl and her infant.

Geneva would have done anything he asked, but he never laid a hand on her. He was grateful for the company and took on the role of surrogate father figure to her. They managed to keep Augie alive, but he had problems. He didn't nurse well and was slow to take to the bottle. Once he got the hang of it, he could never get enough. He cried a lot, never slept through the night, and pushed Geneva's patience to the limit. None of it seemed to rile Ralph.

When asked about Geneva's presence, Ralph said she was his niece, shunned by her parents up north for having the baby. Close enough to the truth no one doubted him. When school started, no one questioned her absence. Ralph said she was eighteen. So certain was she that no one would come looking for them, she didn't even change her name. She was born Geneva Maxwell and would remain so.

Geneva expanded their inventory with candy she made from her family's recipes. Selling it at nearby stores helped get them through the winter when the park closed. Ralph grew attached to his new family. The next season, Geneva's efforts brought more business.

Augie didn't walk until he was nearly two and didn't string more than a few words together until he was going on five. When he turned six, Ralph thought the boy should be in school, but they turned him away. "Too slow," they said. "We're not equipped for retarded children."

It took another couple of years for Ralph to get up the nerve, but with nothing to tie them down, he bought a camper and a truck, packed up his taffy machine, and the little family hit the road, looking to meet up with a small traveling carnival he knew about. He'd always wanted to tour the country, and Geneva somehow gave him the wings to do it. "We've nothing to lose," he told her. Ralph sublet his apartment and store, and they hooked up with the Stone Carnival, traversing the countryside.

Stone brought Chesterfield Lee Perry into their lives, and in him, Augie found a friend. There was no separating the two.

~

Born in Emporia, Kansas, Chesterfield Lee Perry was an only child of parents who drank too much, yelled too loud, and hit too hard. When he was a baby, his mother gave him whiskey to make him sleep. By the time he was five, he drank it on his own for the same reason.

When he was eighteen, the Stone traveling carnival came to Emporia. They showed up the same day he was released from county jail, having served thirty days for conning some old lady out of her fur stole. He was strikingly handsome then, with stunning blue eyes, thick black hair, and an infectious smile.

He started a dice game behind a filling station on the fringes of the midway, luring those otherwise headed to the carnival. His hawking drew the attention of Mr. Stone, the operator of the show. Stone stood off to the side, watching the boy work the crowd, amazed at his instinct to say just the right words to get each man to throw his money down, not just once but repeatedly. He watched the boy flash his smile and wave his arms, grin and cajole, and laugh out loud, ramping the small crowd into a frenzy, dimes and quarters leaping from pockets to his hands. He watched women flush in the wake of a wink.

Though Stone had his rousters break it up, he invited Chester to work for him. Over the course of one season under Stone's tutelage, Chester discovered his true calling as a barker. He was rotated game to game. Any booth he worked pulled the highest gross of the night.

Stone started calling him Barker, and it stuck. Chester found a life with Stone, a future.

Geneva, Ralph, and Augie had been with the operation a year by then, and Augie was having a tough time acclimating to constant change, moving from town to town every few days. But the moment he saw Chester, Augie came to life. He latched onto him, following him everywhere.

It was easy to see Augie wasn't quite right. He was a chubby child, clumsy, and his smile was too eager, yet Chester talked to Augie like he was no different from anyone else. Augie loved him.

Anyone making the mistake of calling Augie retarded backed off when they saw the threat in Barker's steel blue eyes, a fierceness no one chose to challenge. Each night, Augie occupied whatever booth Barker was running, handing out prizes of cap guns, yoyos, cheap stuffed animals, and occasionally a knock-off Swiss Army Knife. Barker gave Augie purpose. Anywhere Barker was felt like home, no matter where they set up.

Geneva was still pretty then, yet immune to Barker's charms. No man was ever going to get the better of her again. Being several years older than Barker, Geneva thought of him like a little brother.

Mr. Stone's appreciation was as mammoth as his greed. At the end of every year, he singled out the highest earner in the company and gave them a cash bonus. One year, he went a step further. Barker was the top earner four years running. In honor of his fifth year on top, Mr. Stone gave him a solid gold onyx ring with a diamond chip in the middle. It stood for respect. It proved his worth. It was the only gift Barker had ever been given, and he wore it proudly.

There were other people in the company, rosters, ticket takers, and concessionaires, who never had the opportunity to bring in the big bucks. To them, seeing that huge ring on Barker's finger was a daily reminder of the inequities of the system. The kid was cocky. Ignorant. He was becoming more important than those who'd been with Stone from the beginning.

One night outside Omaha, Mr. Stone stood face to face with Barker, flanked by four beefy rousters. Stone accused him of shorting the take. Barker's denials fell flat. Stone turned his back and walked away. Barker yelled after him. "I'd never do that! You know me! I'd never steal from you!" The first gut punch doubled him over. Stone kept walking as the beautiful young man he loved took the beating of his life.

Morning found Barker abandoned in an empty field amid the rubbish. He would never regain the sight in one eye or hearing in one ear, and the pounding to his head left him damaged in other ways. He would never again be charming, or witty, or pretty. And, they'd taken his ring.

Augie didn't understand why Barker disappeared without saying anything. He cried for days. He shouted at people gathered at game booths. He threw taffy at people. He was a teenager by then and big. Stone told Ralph to rein him in or else.

One day, he ran off and couldn't be found. Stone left Ralph and Geneva behind. It took two days for a sheriff to bring Augie back. He was scraped up and hungry. He wouldn't talk to anyone.

Ralph heard about a park in Texas that needed a new concessionaire, so they headed west. Ralph and Geneva set up shop, leasing a booth from an outfit with other parks scattered around the country. That's where they came across Harold, Sam, and Ivan.

Augie was slow to warm up to anyone. All the progress he made with Barker vanished. He didn't smile. He shuffled. He spent his days sitting in the camper eating. He refused to hand out taffy at the stand. It took the whole of the winter for Augie to settle down, settle in, and come out of his shell.

Then, in the spring, Ralph sat down to dinner, grabbed his chest, keeled over, and died. It was too sudden to feel real. Augie didn't understand and he folded inward yet again.

Geneva thought going back to the Carolina shore would be good. They'd have a place to call home. She'd run the store. Harold tried to talk her out of it, telling her to follow them up north for the summer. But she was set on striking out on her own, making her way, running her own store, finding a stable home. She packed up and left, driving to the east coast stopping along the way at campgrounds as if they were on vacation. Augie hated it.

When the landlord in Myrtle Beach wouldn't let her take over Ralph's lease, they found themselves homeless. The current tenants felt sorry for her and gave her some money for Ralph's equipment in the shop, but hardly what it was worth. Geneva headed north to Lake

Michigan to meet up with Harold, Ivan, and Sam at Sunset Beach. Seeing them was nothing short of a miracle for Augie. He ran to them and hugged each one tight, telling Ivan he smelled bad. When the bridge siren whined and began to open, Augie ran to watch. Seeing a man in a little window in the middle of it, he waved. Gar waved back, and Augie made a new friend.

    Geneva took over the food concession, relieving the old man who said he was getting too old to run both it and his café up in town. She bought his refrigerator, hotdog roaster, and popcorn machine with the cash from the Myrtle Beach equipment. It wasn't long before she began filling saltwater taffy orders for the local Five & Dime and a grocery store. The expanded menu was more work than Geneva was used to, but with the old man's help, she learned how to manage the inventory of fresh buns, hotdogs, condiments, and paper products. It turned into her most successful summer yet. In the fall, she packed it all up, and the troop headed back to Texas. Over the next couple of years, with the routine in place, Augie found his footing again.

    One afternoon on the boardwalk in Texas, Augie jumped off his stool in the concession stand and went running after a man, hollering for him to stop. "Barker! Barker! It's me! It's Augie! Stop walking, Barker! Stop! You're not dead! I thought you were dead!" He finally caught up with the man and nearly knocked him to the ground, trying to hug him. Barker spun around and punched him. It wasn't out of anger. It was reflex. Augie cried, looked at Barker's face, and cowered, stumbling away. Barker saw Geneva up ahead with her arms open wide to take in her boy. Augie was almost seventeen by then and was as confused as ever, especially by old friends who turned mean.

Even from a distance, Geneva could hardly believe Barker's appearance. "They told me they left you for dead," she said. The man standing in front of her was only a shadow of who he once was. The old Barker was gone. This one had a hardened gaze with a foggy eye, its pupil misshapen. "Can you see out of it?" she asked, but he didn't answer. She was talking to his bad ear.

Geneva fed him and made a bunk for him in her booth. Later that night, she came to him with something in her hand. "One of the rousters, the big stupid one with the ponytail? He got drunk one night and started bragging about how he set you up. Stone had him disappeared. I found this in his stuff and kept it." She handed him the onyx ring. "I thought maybe one day I'd give it to Augie. We thought you were dead." He took one look at the ring and threw it in the corner, cussed at her, and told her to get the hell out. He gladly took her next gift, a bottle of whiskey. The next day, the ring was on his finger.

She convinced Harold to take on Barker, giving him a job on the boardwalk. But he wasn't good at games anymore. He didn't lure people so much as taunt them. When spring came, they all headed north to Sunset Beach in Edgewater. Barker wasn't the same man who let Augie sit in his booth and hand out prizes, yet no matter how nasty Barker talked or how mean he looked, Augie still loved him. He still saw the wonderful man he used to be. Augie saw only good in everyone.

As tenuous as it was, this little troop of misfits managed to get by, people inextricably stuck together like weed seeds clinging to the same old sock.

CHAPTER SIX

The third Saturday in June was the annual Edgewater Art Fair on the bluff. Early that morning, Trish stood in the hallway watching her mother apply makeup. A methodical process, Rose gave the flat, stained pad a couple of swipes across her pressed powder compact and looked in the mirror as she carefully spread a nearly invisible layer over her entire face, starting with her nose and chin, then circling her face and cheeks. Wetting a small brush, she dabbed it into a little black tray of mascara and brushed it onto her lashes. She took a golden tube of lipstick out of the medicine cabinet, twisting it open to a bright red nub. Her bottom lip got a quick swipe, but her top lip was traced with great care. Then came the subtle lip press to a single square of toilet paper folded in half, then final inspection in the mirror, giving the corners of her mouth a little swipe.

"Go get in the car," Rose said. "We're late." Rose tightened the belt of her shirtwaist dress and slipped into a pair of blue flats. "Go on," she insisted.

They parked four blocks from downtown, walking the old stately neighborhood to the bluff where the art fair was setting up. It was a chaotic mess of people trying to put up awnings and partitions around stacks of paintings and pottery. They finally found a balding middle-aged man with a clipboard. Merv Demorrow, in charge of volunteers, told Rose to go to the fountain at the other end and find Mrs. Haley, in charge of the ice cream social. Then he gave her a safety pin with a green ribbon tied to it, signifying she was a volunteer. As Rose headed away, she told Trish to stay out of everyone's way.

When Trish turned around, she collided with Augie and fell flat to the grass. His box of saltwater taffy scattered everywhere.

"Hey, you idiot!" Merv hollered to Augie. "Watch it!"

Augie couldn't catch his breath and started shaking both hands like propellers. "I'm so sorry! I'm so sorry!" He reached for Trish's hand and yanked her to her feet so hard she almost went flying in the other direction. Merv grabbed Augie by the arm and told him to leave her alone.

"I'm so sorry!" Augie said again, his eyes glued to the ground. Trish glared at Mr. Demorrow, insisting she was fine and didn't need his help. Merv stepped off, grumbling.

"It was my fault," Trish said. "Are you OK?" She could see there was something not quite right about Augie.

"I dropped my taffy," he whined. "She's gonna gut me if I don't deliver it." He looked at Trish's shorts and pointed to fresh grass stains. "You're in trouble now!"

"Oh, I'm always getting stains on my clothes." Trish laughed, and like a mirror, Augie laughed, too.

"We can pick it up," she said with a smile. "I'll help you."

With a goal clearly defined, he got down on his knees and started gathering the wax paper-wrapped nuggets. "My name is Augie," he said.

"That's weird," she said, dropping several taffies into his box. People kept walking by, dodging their bodies, stepping on taffy.

"I was born in August," he said. "When were you born?"

"In June."

"Is that your name?"

"No. It's Trish."

"But it could be June. June could be a girl's name."

"Yes, it could."

Somebody picked up a piece of taffy and walked off with it, prompting Augie to yell, "Thief!"

Trish noticed a black streak sticking out from under his T-shirt sleeve. "What's that?"

He stood up, hiked up the sleeve, and leaned his shoulder into her so she could see it better. "My mama thinks lightning is pretty, so I put lightning on my arm for her. It's a tattoo."

"Did she like it?"

"She whipped my butt."

Trish laughed, and then he laughed. When the box was as full as it was going to get, Augie crammed two pieces of taffy into his mouth. He talked through the wad, walking backward with the box. "If I don't deliver this, I'll be in big trouble."

~

Merv watched Augie scuffle off until his attention was drawn to the edge of the bluff, where a small clutch of people stood together, looking down. The bluff was the front porch of town, a pristine tree-lined grassy park with a forty-foot vantage point from which to view Lake Michigan and Sunset Beach.

"You can't be serious," one woman groaned.

"No, no, no," said a man nearby. Someone pointed to the source of their contempt.

Merv looked down and saw a bright green bus in the Sunset parking lot. "Not again," he said, watching a stream of Negro families and teenagers file onto the boardwalk. "Every year, the same damn shit."

"Are you kidding," asked a woman with a clipboard. "There's more now than ever!"

"This is bullshit," said a sharply dressed woman in her seventies.

A man in a suit said they'd better not come up into town.

~

Down below, the Battle Creek Baptist Church community bus let out its last passenger, a pretty young woman wearing a yellow cotton dress. Helen ambled across the parking lot, her gaze taken by the snapping crisp line between water and sky. She took a deep breath of the fresh, clean air and hurried to catch up with her friends.

Happy screams and giggles came from within Kiddy Korner's colorful picket fence. Small children refused to be organized into ride lines, and Helen was recruited to help. Suddenly, a whistle pierced the air, and the little roller coaster, empty this first time, pulled away from the platform, rising to its ten-foot peak and charging down and around and up and down. Then Andy the Aeroplane's chubby planes began spinning, slowly at first, then faster, and the little kiddie carousel began spinning. Children flocked to the safety fences around each ride. One by one, the rides stopped, filled up, and started up again. All this chaos was orchestrated by Ivan alone, rotating between the three rides, taking nickles, setting one ride, then another, funneling kids on and off. The music box tune from the kiddy area was nearly overpowered by the calliope music from the big carousel down the boardwalk.

Looking way beyond the kiddie fence, Helen watched her friends disappear into the funhouse.

Geneva sat on her stool in her concession stand, sweat swimming in the creases of her neck. She gave a cold stare to two Colored teenagers trying to decide if they wanted to buy taffy, popcorn, or a hot dog. The girl flirted and pretended to beg the boy for candy, but the boy saw Geneva's disgust. Grasping the girl's arm, he pulled her away.

An arriving White family held tight to their children as they traversed the boardwalk, staying clear of the kiddie rides.

With little enthusiasm, Barker called out to a clutch of teenagers to draw them to the ball toss. Some looked but turned away. Others didn't even look, just kept on moving. White parents with three young boys walked up. The father handed over three dimes, and the boys each took the first of three throws, all failing to knock over any milk jugs. Two Colored families stepped up with young boys equally anxious to win something. The White mother drew her young daughter close and backed up. The White father pulled his sons away, smacking one of them on the head for his backtalk. One of the Colored dads gave Barker a dollar. It bought him a bucket of balls. The White family headed to the parking lot, the three children complaining all the way.

Behind it all, the big carousel spun, its off-key calliope ringing out with its orchestra of automated instruments, its tinny glockenspiel and raspy snare drum.

Down at the funhouse, a mechanical clown bounced in its glass box, its hideous laughter blaring from the speaker. Harold sold tickets to all the Coloreds seeking entrance, but turned away Whites. It was the surest way to avoid any confrontations inside. And, as Coloreds outnumbered Whites that day, it was just good business. He directed the Whites to the arcade, keeping an eye on things as best he could. Sam was left to rotate between the carrousel and roller coaster.

Helen had not witnessed any of these interactions, and no one on the bus talked about it on the way home. They talked about a rug burn from the spinning floor in the funhouse, about the wicked flyer's first steep fall, and how funhouse mirrors changed their perception of reality.

~

The next Tuesday, Mayor Abbot Carver sat at a long table with eight of the town's ten council members. The missing members had made feeble excuses as to their absence, fully aware of what was about to happen. Impatient attendees fidgeted and muttered, waiting out forty-five minutes of agenda items. Finally, Mayor Carver took a deep breath and opened the floor to new business. Merv Demorrow stepped forward, the first in a long line of people waiting to speak their minds.

"Sunset Beach!" Merv shouted. "Shut it down! Doze it to the ground!" The crowd cheered. "Look, maybe I'm the only one with the nerve to come right out and say it. Sunset Beach is bussing in Coloreds. And we, the merchants," he said, waving his arms to include the entire audience, "We don't want them up in our town, coming into our stores and pawing our merchandise!"

"And using the bathroom in my restaurant," somebody hollered. "Without ordering any food!"

A man in the back, with a voice resonant enough to be heard without yelling, countered. "What the hell? You wouldn't have served them if they tried!"

"We don't want a Selma riot here," somebody else hollered. It drew groans and jeers from some and shouts of agreement from others.

"Look," Merv whined, "I'm no bigot, but they're not Edgewater people."

"Come on, Merv," said the mayor, "Just what the hell does that mean?"

A woman told Merv to look up the definition of bigot. The crowd laughed.

Mrs. Hanford stood up. A fourth-generation Edgewater native, she was a stately woman known for her committee work for the hospital and her church. "You might as well break out the fire hoses, Abbot, if you let this continue. Before you know it, we won't look any more civilized than Birmingham was a couple years ago! You think it can't happen, but it can! And I, for one, will not stand for it!" The crowd exploded in opposing voices.

"And it's people like you who cause it," someone shouted.

Mayor Carver banged his gavel without effect.

Schroeder gave the mayor a look from the corner that pretty much said he'd better get control of the meeting. Then Schroeder ripped the room with a piercing whistle. Everyone quieted. "I think the mayor has something to say," the chief said in a normal tone of voice.

"I do," Abbot said. "I've been keeping abreast of the situation on the boardwalk. They've done nothing to break the law. Let me say that again. They've done nothing illegal. People have long come from far and wide to Sunset Beach. So long as I am mayor, this will be a welcoming town. Welcome to all law-abiding citizens."

Father Merchant rose to his feet, shouting. "I'm a man of God and hold all his people in my heart, but that place is a den of sin, a magnet for troubled teens, and a danger to families everywhere who dare ride those broken-down rides! I say condemn it or do whatever you have to. Just shut it down!"

The room broke out in chaos. The mayor looked for Schroeder, who was already out the door.

CHAPTER SEVEN

The end of June finally arrived, and Trish received a new bike for her eleventh birthday. A 5-speed. She awoke the next morning with a sense of independence, presuming the bike came with privileges and freedom to leave the four-block radius of her neighborhood. She would no longer have to be driven to sleepovers with Linda and Janey. It was a moment both Rose and Trish looked forward to, though for different reasons.

Rose sat on the ottoman, running a comb down the middle of Trish's head, dividing the hair into two sections, then each one into three sections. She tugged one tight, folded it over another, tugged tighter, and continued until she wrapped a small rubber band around the end of the braid. The back screen door slammed shut. Jason was out and off as usual, his cereal bowl and half-eaten toast left on the table.

"Where you going?" Rose hollered to him through the side window.

"Don't know."

"Be back by dinner," Rose shouted as she started in on Trish's other braid. "Eric! Get down here. Your father wants you to mow this morning." Trish said he already left, and Rose took her frustration out on the braid, yanking with more vigor. Trish took the abuse, relishing the moment when the last rubber band snapped. She charged outside, got her bike from the garage, and hollered to the house, "See ya later." Yet, as she peddled past the back door, Rose appeared.

"Where do you think you're going?" she asked, her tone calm, expectant.

"Don't know."

"Get back in here. If you want to go to Linda's tonight you need to clean your room."

"Did the boys clean their room?" The look from her mother suggested Trish was half a step over the line. She parked her bike and tramped through the kitchen.

Rose headed upstairs, a new reprimand with every step, her voice growing ever more edgy. "What do you mean just taking off like that? Without telling me where you're going. You want your father to take that bike away?" Trish slammed her bedroom door. "Don't you slam that door, young lady!"

After dinner that night, Fred stood on his front porch. The warm evening air was thick with the smell of fresh-cut grass from a few doors down. Eric and Jason tossed a football. He could hear a faint clatter from the kitchen as Rose cleaned up dishes. All was right with his world.

He watched Trish stuff a paper sack full of clothes into her bike basket. She looked so eager. "Call your mother when you get there," he said. She rolled her eyes. "Would you rather stay home?"

"No, sorry," she said. "I'll call."

Dealing with the boys was difficult enough, but Patricia? From the moment she learned to walk, then ride a bike, he was certain that a car driven by a teenager or a distracted mom would swerve and slam her to bits. Every time his kids left the house, when any of them left his sight, he choked. He loved them so hard, sometimes he could barely breathe.

He feared Trish's trusting nature made her an easy target. He was certain some asshole would take advantage of her and knock her up. He'd been there. He knew. Granted, he'd planned to ask Rose to marry him anyway, but he thought they'd wait until she got through college. It was no sacrifice when she told him she was pregnant. He took it in stride, and they were making a go of it. The routine, however, the responsibility, and incomprehensible monotony of it all sometimes wore him down, and it was all he could do not to explode.

In what few solitary moments he had, when Fred pondered useless philosophies, he came to consider himself a pragmatic fatalist. When he was ten, his little brother died from an infected cut on his leg. A year later, his father went out to mow the alfalfa and died in the field of a heart attack at forty. A few weeks after that, Fred came home from school to discover he and his mother were moving away. The bank took the farm. Life had shown no regard for plans, so he stopped making them. The best he could do was try to be prepared for any eventuality. He decided life without expectation kept disappointment at bay, an attitude that limited his aspirations as well as options.

In another life, one where Fred allowed himself the slightest expectation, he might have become a writer. He'd have written about his brother so no one would ever forget him, about how they spent long, languid hours daydreaming in the hayloft or sitting in the century-old elm between the field and pasture. He'd have written about moving in with his aunt and uncle, who argued every night, and about the house his mother rented at the beach. He'd have written a novel about a careless young man who took his mother for granted, who came home from college to find she was sick and had been for a long time, but he was having too much fun to notice until it was too late. He'd have written about Lake Michigan and dunes and storms. But in this life, he had to settle. Having just enough was always going to have to suffice.

~

Trish careened out of the driveway to the school grounds, peddling hard past the church, the Tastee-Freez, and the skating rink, now just a big grass field. It was her first shot at independence, an adventure replete with supplies and rations – pajamas, clean underwear, and a full package of Oreos she took from the cupboard. It would just be Trish and Linda for the night, two-thirds of a whole. Janey was off visiting cousins.

All the way there, she thought about Linda's brother Ben. He stirred something she didn't yet understand, a twinge, a yearning. There was a four-year difference in their ages, at least until November, when he'd turn sixteen. They would never be in high school at the same time, so there would be no invitations to homecoming or prom. But she had Linda. So long as they were best friends, Ben would always be within reach. Hope and expectation let her believe he would eventually really see her. Like all the stories she concocted for her Barbie and Ken, she laid out her life with him. He would come home from college and suddenly see her as a woman, sixteen, her legs longer, leaner, her ankles more defined, her waist narrow, her breasts full and round. He would call her from college. They'd talk for hours. He would come home every weekend to see her, kiss her gently, hold her, and promise to always be there for her. In the meantime, all she had were her fantasies. She had to be patient. She had to be careful. The first glimpse of him always made her flush, something she hoped to hell no one noticed, especially her brothers. Jason, Eric, and Ben were as tight as she was with Linda and Jane.

Cruising into the neighborhood where Linda and Jane lived, Trish shot fast by the pastel houses to the yellow one with white shutters. She flew into the drive and slammed on her brakes to make a dramatic entrance to impress Ben if he was in the backyard, but her only greeting was a bark from Hoover, their ancient black lab.

She parked her bike against the side of the garage and heard Linda from the window upstairs telling her to come up. Walking in without knocking, Trish paused on the landing, looking for a light in the basement, listening. Mrs. Finney pulled two beers from the fridge and told Trish to be quiet upstairs. She'd just put the boys down.

The Finney house was packed with kids. Three boys, three girls, three bedrooms, toys everywhere, inside and out. The youngest boys were two and four. Then there were two more girls younger than Linda, all three sharing a room, twin beds lining the walls, toys and dolls cluttering the floor. Ben slept in the basement.

From the hall at the foot of the stairs Trish caught a glimpse of the living room where Mr. Finney in shorts and a T-shirt slouched in a big chair, arms folded behind his head, hairy legs stretching long and straight in front of him, his bare feet crossed at the ankles. Mrs. Finney brought him a beer and sat on the arm of his chair where his hand came around to collect her, embracing her outer thigh. Trish had never seen such affection. Her father never went barefoot. Her mother never sat that close to him.

The little girls, already in pajamas, were curled up on the couch. Ben was on the floor on his back, arms behind his head, barefoot in jeans, his faded ones, and a white T-shirt. He did not appear to notice Trish.

She went up to Linda's bedroom, then shot back downstairs and called home to report in. Back upstairs, she shut the door, and for an hour, the two girls sat on a bed, combing through magazines, drinking pop, and eating cookies and potato chips. They painted their nails bright orange and put on pale pink lipstick so dense it covered the natural blush of their lips. It's what the models wore.

When it was time for the little girls to go to bed, Linda and Trish went down to the living room. The screen filled with Tina Turner's gyrating hips as she belted out a song on a "Shindig" rerun. Linda's dad got up and changed the channel. Almost simultaneously, Ben left the room. The girls followed.

Ben had carved out a space for himself in a corner of the basement. A flowered sheet nailed to the floor joists served to wall it off from the laundry area. A tall dresser stood in front of a quilt hung to serve as a wall on the other side. He had a table and chair in one corner and a reading lamp by his bed. It was a tidy space where the dense aroma of Tide competed with mildew.

Linda and Trish parked themselves together in a beanbag chair as Ben turned on a little portable TV with rabbit ears, and they watched the rest of "Shindig" on the fuzzy screen. Ben sprawled on his bed, a twin mattress on a metal frame.

Trish watched every move he made. He folded one arm behind his head against two pillows. He crossed his feet and then uncrossed them. One foot occasionally kept time with the music. He laughed at a joke. He did not acknowledge Trish's presence but did not seem to object either. She was in his inner sanctum, reveling in the closeness until one word, his first word, was spoken when the show was over. "Out."

Linda and Trish removed themselves to the backyard picnic table until Linda's mom called them in a little after eleven. Inside, Mr. Finney disappeared into the downstairs bedroom. Linda's mom followed, telling the girls to be quiet and go to bed.

Upstairs, in the dark silence, the girls sat on a bed, fully dressed, and waited. When Mr. Finney's snoring resonated through the house, Linda and Trish crept downstairs, aware of every floorboard creak and crack. Walking through the kitchen, they stepped over the sleeping dog. At the back door, they listened for any sign of life from the basement before pulling the door open and pushing the screen door out. It squealed ever so slightly as they stepped out into the warm, still darkness undetected.

It was not the first time they'd taken a night foray. It had become almost a ritual, and as a rule, Janey would climb out her bedroom window to join them. The farthest they'd gone to that point was three blocks away to the play park.

They bolted to a hedgerow four doors down, then to a fat bush at the next house, and to another at the corner house. They skirted streetlights and scooted between garages, stopping and listening before moving on. Arriving at the play park, they each, independently of the other, continued walking. Without a word, they moved on to where alleys, like secret passages, cut through neighborhoods. Trish did not look at Linda as if doing so might affect their momentum. Only when they got to the bridge over the tracks did they stop, their glance to each other merely a matter of confirmation to continue on.

Over the bridge and down, they landed in the neighborhood of shabby bungalows at the beach. "Don't let the sand rabbits get you!" Linda teased.

"What?"

"Nothin'."

"Take it back." Trish stopped and glared at Linda.

"Take what back?" Like most slang picked up from adults, Linda had no idea the connation her wise crack carried. It was tantamount to calling the inhabitants White trash, another term neither of them understood.

"My dad grew up here. In that house there."

"OK, OK. You don't have to be so touchy."

They continued on in silence to the shore, where water lapped sand. Trish took off her sandals and waded in to her knees. It was warm until a river of coolness wrapped around her legs like a serpent drawing her in, and she jumped back to the beach.

The girls stood transfixed by glittering lights down at Sunset Beach. Colors blinked on the stationary Ferris wheel. Bright white dots defined the roller coaster scaffolding where a streak of red dashed up and around, down and out of sight. While Sunset Beach was a broken-down relic in the daytime, at night, laced in sparkling lights, it seemed a magical paradise.

Like explorers stumbling onto a hidden city, Linda and Trish ventured forth over the sand, drawn forward by calliope music. They hid in the low dune. Behind them only darkness, dune grass, then open beach to the water. As they drew closer, flaws became more evident, shadows menacing. Rounding the old dancehall with its busted out and boarded up windows, they stepped onto the splintery boardwalk into a tunnel of light formed by strands of bulbs strung from buildings across to poles and down.

A clutch of teenagers huddled by the roller coaster ticket booth, sullen and quiet, smoking cigarettes, drinking beer from longneck bottles. Ivan did his best to ignore them as he hit the buzzer and pulled the lever, sending the string of five cars ratcheting up the incline with only four passengers onboard. A couple of the boys looked Trish and Linda up and down. Trish sneered at them. They laughed at the would-be tough girl.

The girls stuck close to the poles as they stepped deeper into the lights. Two couples ambled past, the women in skin-tight tops exposing pushed-up mounds of breast. Trish watched as one allowed her boyfriend's hand to roam her body like a lion on the hunt. The men walked with a kind of strut, one flicking a lit cigarette. Their hard smiles and raucous laughter seemed to carry a threat. Linda grabbed Trish's arm and pointed to a dark recess between buildings where all Trish could see was a pair of high heels wrapped around a pair of undulating jeans, unaware of what it signified.

Barker called out from his ball toss booth, his enthusiasm dampened by the general disinterest of the sparse crowd. "Try your luck. Only ten cents. Win a watch. Ten cents. Walk this way." He looked straight at

Trish, taunting. "Just one thin dime gets you three big balls."

She couldn't help but stare. His black hair was slicked back, his T-shirt rolled up over a pack of cigarettes on his shoulder. His eyes were set so close together and so deep into his head, he reminded her of Abraham Lincoln, except one of them didn't look right.

~

Out in the parking lot, a young black woman applied fresh lipstick in the back seat of a Ford Fairlane. "Is this the right place?" she asked. "There's hardly anybody here?"

Her friend Helen was already out of the car, straightening her skirt, her long dark legs punctuated by white flats. "I told you, Shirley," she said. "I was just here with our church group. It was fun. It's safe."

Charles, nineteen and black as a coffee bean, sat in the driver's seat surveying the boardwalk. Deon grumbled from the back seat. "I don't know about this."

Helen leaned in through the passenger window with a teasing smile. "Are you coming?" When she started walking away, Shirley pushed the seat forward and maneuvered out, hollering for her to wait up.

"Shit," Deon said as he climbed out, his muscular frame unfolding as he stood up.

Charles called out for the girls to wait. They turned, giggled, and waved him off. He got out and stretched, his body looking inordinately huge next to the small two-door.

"You sure about this? Looks pretty damn white from here," Deon asked.

"This isn't Georgia. It's Michigan."

The girls hit the boardwalk first, laughing and talking, totally engrossed in their conversation, glancing back to see if the boys were following them.

"Helen!" Charles called from the parking lot. "Come back here! Helen!"

She ignored him.

"I don't like it," Deon said. "What the hell, man? What are we doing here?"

"Helen wanted to," Charles said. He squared his shoulders. "We belong here as much as anyone."

They started walking, both of them nervous, trying hard not to show it.

~

A slow freight train rumbled from the north about to make the long, slow climb up the grade southward. Its whistle blew on approach to the bridge, and again, as it passed behind the arcade and game booths, and again, crossing the road at the station.

Linda and Trish came up to the concession stand where Geneva sat, huge and sweaty, her bulging grey bags sagging under her eyes. The counter seemed a mini-amusement park with leathery hot dogs skewered on long prongs, turning on a spit behind grimy glass, and the mesmerizing taffy machine grinding away as two rotating arms caught a pink ribbon of thick goo just before it fell, lifted it, and stretched it, always in motion. Above it all hung the pungent aroma of popcorn, hotdogs, and body odor.

"Bag of taffy, twenty-five cents," Geneva muttered. A cigarette stuck to her bottom lip bounced, and a small length of ash fell, resting on the bosom of her muumuu. Linda pulled a quarter from her pocket. Geneva took it. "Better get your butts home," she said. "No place for you down here."

Just then, Augie stood up behind her with a wax paper bag of taffies and hollered out, "June!"

"No, Augie," Geneva muttered. "It's July, sweet boy. It's July."

Trish recognized him, but Linda grabbed the bag and yanked her away before she could say anything. Trish gave Augie a little wave as they walked away.

Lured by hideous laughter blasting from a speaker, the girls stopped near the funhouse to watch a mechanical clown gyrate in its big glass box. Its rusted gears clicked as a metal shaft rotated in and out of view through a hole in the diamond-print fabric. Several grumpy teenagers spilled through the doors, yelling at Sam in the ticket booth.

"What a waste!"

"Yeah," another hollered. "We demand our money back!"

Sam flipped them his middle finger.

~

Helen and her friends approached Barker's ball toss, Charles and Deon arguing over who had the better aim. The White kids from in front of the roller coaster closed in. Helen and Shirley suggested maybe it was a mistake coming there. "Please, Deon," Shirley said. "I want to leave."

"Please, Deon," mimicked a White boy from the safety of his crew.

Charles, standing head and shoulders above them all, turned to them. "We don't want any trouble here," he said.

Deon gave Barker a dollar, but Barker refused to take it.

"This one's pretty," said one of the White boys, pointing to Shirley's face, then lowering his gaze to her chest and below.

"Lay off," Deon demanded.

"Lay off, he says," chided one of the boys.

Barker told them all to move off but one of the boys stepped toward Helen, reaching for her, and Charles blocked the approach with his body. The boy, dwarfed by Charles, made an attempt to shove him and Charles pushed back, knocking him into his friends who bolted forward. Barker climbed out of his booth to break it up, yelling at all of them to get the hell off the boardwalk.

Trish and Linda heard the commotion. Sticking close to the light poles, they watched a handful of people gather across from the concession stand, shouting.

Barker pulled the White boys off Charles, who was blocking their swings but not fighting back. A loud buzzer sounded as the Wicked Flyer began its ratcheting climb for a run. Two boys pushed Barker into Deon, who pushed back, igniting Barker's rage, and he swung at Deon, but Charles stepped in to take the punch.

The growing crowd began to shout. "Fight! Fight! Send them the hell back where they belong!"

Barker's punches appeared to make little impact, and Charles said repeatedly he didn't want to hurt anybody. Chants swelled and receded seemingly in unison with the coaster's rumbling rise and fall.

Trish and Linda edged toward the concession stand, catching a glimpse of Barker's arm swinging in a grand gesture, hitting, missing, hitting with a quiet flesh-to-flesh thud not at all what it sounded like on TV.

Sam watched from the coaster, casually picking his teeth.

Barker rarely landed a solid hit, but with one punch, his ring ripped Charles's shirt and cut into flesh. Charles let go with one swing, clipping Barker across the jaw on his blind side, knocking him to the ground.

Two young police officers, making their regular rounds, pushed their way through the pack. Ted and Frank were well accustomed to breaking up fights at the boardwalk. Ted grabbed Barker. Frank reached for Charles but withdrew, intimidated by the boy's size. Charles put up his hands in surrender and stepped back.

As if to signal the end of the fight, the coaster buzzer pierced the air, and the lead car slowly hit the bumper. Though the calliope music had stopped as well, the clown laugh persisted in the background, lending an eerie sense of dread to the night.

~

"We have got to get the hell out of her right now!" Trish whispered in a panic.

Augie heard them and made eye contact with Trish. "June!" He waved the girls to the back of the booth and shook his finger at them. "You get out of here!" he shouted. "It isn't safe down here. These people are really, really mean."

Frank and Ted walked Charles and Barker, both handcuffed, to their squad car. Chief Schroeder drove up. Linda and Trish saw him and stayed plastered to the back wall.

When Augie motioned it was safe, Trish and Linda bolted into the dune grass out of sight. They ran across the beach to shore and dove over the breakwater like a bunker on a battlefield. Catching their breath for only a moment, they took off again, up between houses, over the bridge, into the alley. Trish's whole body vibrated with a strange concoction of fear and elation. They shouldn't have been there. Something horrible could have happened, but it didn't.

As their pace slowed and they caught their breath, brief giggles bubbled up and escaped, followed by a spattering of "I can't believe we did that" and "I thought for sure Chief Schroeder would see us." By the time they made it to Linda's neighborhood, the girls walked silently. They did not dart from bush to bush or dodge streetlights. They sauntered down the middle of the street. They owned the night.

The screen door made its faint squeal as Linda pulled it. Stepping through to the landing, the light in the basement came on. Ben stood at the bottom of the stairs. He asked where they'd been. Trish tossed him a saltwater taffy. He caught it, looked at it, and his face twisted into an angry glare. She heard him muttering stupid little shits as he turned off the light.

Stepping over the dog, they made their way up to bed.

~

Back at the boardwalk, the group who'd watched the fight had quieted, but did not disband, their attention split between the cops in the parking lot and the three Negroes in the shadows. Schroeder stood in front of the concession stand pointing to Shirley and Helen.

"You two," he said, "and your boyfriend back there. Stay put."

Deon crossed his arms and leaned on a wall, his eyes on Charles out in the parking lot.

"Well," Schroeder asked Geneva, "Who started it?"

"Well," she said, mocking him, "Can't say as I know. Maybe Barker didn't like the look of those kids."

"Why might that be?"

"Gee, officer. Can't imagine. Maybe because they're kind don't belong here."

He cocked his head and stared at her.

It was moments like that, of hatred spoken freely, that Schroeder feared most. He turned and yelled at the collection of degenerates. "Alright! Go home! Now!" They backed off only so far, waiting for whatever might happen next. "I said go! This place is closed for the night."

Geneva hollered he couldn't do that, and Schroeder hollered back. "I just did!"

The crowd sauntered off the boardwalk, Deon and the girls among them.

"Not you three," Schroeder said, rolling his shoulders and popping his neck. He walked over to the two girls. "Where do you two live?" he asked abruptly. "Got any I.D.?" They didn't answer. He asked with more authority. "I asked, where do you live?"

"Battle Creek," Shirley said.

"Battle Creek. That's a long drive from here. You have names?" he asked. "And how old are you? The truth."

"Shirley. She's Helen. We're eighteen."

"I said the truth."

"It is the truth." Helen pulled her wallet from her purse.

The hideous clown laugh seemed to get louder, and Schroeder threw an annoyed glance down the boardwalk. "This is a Michigan State student ID," he said.

"Yes, sir," Helen said, her voice almost too soft to hear.

"Helen and I are from Battle Creek," Shirley said. "She got into Michigan State. That's a Big Ten school." Her words were meant to impress. "They came down from East Lansing," she said, pointing to Deon, then Charles.

Schroeder glanced over to Deon, who advanced with a swagger that belied his fear.

Schroeder looked at the three, dressed better than everyone else in clean, pressed clothes. "What exactly are you doing here?" he asked.

"Just killing time," Deon said casually. "Having a little fun." Then, his demeanor changed and he looked the chief straight in the eyes. "We're doing the same thing everybody else is."

Schroeder sighed. "I really don't want any trouble here."

"You saying we aren't welcome here?" Deon challenged.

Schroeder looked to the bystanders still loitering in the parking lot. "I'd say that's pretty obvious, wouldn't you? Come on. I'll walk you to your car."

"We don't have to go anywhere." Deon squared his shoulders. "You can't make us leave." The two girls drew closer to each other, their eyes wide.

"Oh, I can play it your way," Schroeder said, "and this can get real ugly, real fast, but I'd rather we not make any more of this than it is." He glanced out to the parking lot where Ted held Barker on one side of the squad car while Frank and Charles stood on the other side. "I don't want any more trouble here tonight. Let me see your license."

Deon pulled out his Georgia license and Michigan State ID and handed them both over. "You know who that is?" Deon asked, pointing to Charles. "That's Charles Morgan, the starting halfback for Michigan State."

Schroeder let out a long, hard sigh.

"I want to go home," Helen said quietly.

Deon stepped closer to the chief, whispering so the girls wouldn't hear. "Look, man. We didn't come here trying to make a point or take a stand. We were just trying to make two pretty girls happy. Ya know?" He looked at the girls and back to Schroeder. "This isn't right." He said, defeated. Then, defiant, he said it again. "This isn't right."

"I know," Schroeder said in a tone suggesting he agreed. In one sense, he admired their nerve. But to have said anything to encourage them would have been a mistake. He had to get them out of there. "Let's go."

He escorted the three to the parking lot and collected Charles. The girls climbed into the backseat of the Ford. "You, too," Schroeder said to Deon.

Schroeder looked up at Charles and half chuckled. "Damn, you're big." Charles cocked his head and looked away. "You alright?" Schroeder asked with a tone of true concern, pointing to blood on his shirt. The boy didn't answer. "I'm sorry about this," he said. "Your friend said it. This isn't right."

Charles looked down at Schroeder. "So fix it."

Of all the comebacks the boy could have used, that one stung the most.

"Deon and I are from Georgia," Charles said quietly. "It was supposed to be different up here." When Schroeder had no response, Charles slowly got into the car. He sat there, hands on the wheel, working something over, and finally spoke, the words pushing out through clenched teeth. "Are you filing a report? On me?"

"No," Schroeder said. "No reports." He saw a single tear slide down the boy's cheek.

Charles turned the key and drove away.

Ted hollered out from the squad car. "What do I do with this one?"

Schroeder waved him off, and Barker walked back to the boardwalk. "Christ almighty," Schroeder said. "I wish this place would just burn to the ground. And somebody pull the plug on that damn clown!"

CHAPTER EIGHT

Andrew Schroeder had been called Schroeder since he was a little kid. Only Grandmother Fiona ever called him by his given name. His grandfather had been a steamship captain on the Great Lakes, his father a barber, his uncle a banker, and Aunt Eunice worked in a dress shop. The Great Depression eventually put them all out of work and under the same roof with the Captain and Fiona. The Main Street house was big, but not big enough. Aunt Eunice had to give up her room for a smaller one so Uncle Ryan, his wife, and toddler could be together. Schroeder's mother, Angela, fought the move but, in the end, yielded, as they were dead, broke, and out of options. Schroeder was just a kid, and from seven to fifteen, he had a front-row seat to every sort of family dysfunction possible.

His grandfather was a gregarious man loved by everyone who knew him except his wife, having something to do with his overnights in Chicago four times a week when the steamers still ran. Grandmother Fiona ruled the household with pursed lips and sharp tongue. She treated them all like impudent children, especially the adults. Things were to be done her way on her timetable.

The house sat on a large lot back then, over half a block in size, with a view to the lake. Most of it was grass, which the captain turned over into a vegetable garden when the boats stopped running and money was tight. Spring through autumn, he was in the garden. It was orderly, productive. He built a chicken coup, something the neighbors complained about until he gave them fresh eggs every week. Ratchet, the Captain's old German shepherd, guarded the hen house, seemingly pleased to finally have a task after a lifetime of leisure. He had a particular bark for intruders, different from conversing with neighborhood dogs. Whenever he let out with a volley of aggravated barks at night, a rifle shot from an upstairs window guaranteed the thief would hightail it and not return, giving the neighbors something to talk about the next day. Though the captain was generous with his bounty, Fiona always took first pickings, filling the cellar with jams, canned beans and tomatoes, dried peas and beans, carrots, potatoes, parsnips, winter squash and anything else he grew. In the depth of winter, there was something comforting about a full larder. Food for the soul as much as the body.

Fiona resented having her butler's pantry turned into a makeshift barbershop, yet it allowed Schroeder's father to contribute to the household.

Uncle Ryan had been a banker, a talent of little use. When he lost his job along with his big beautiful house, he also lost any semblance of self-respect. Fiona arranged his apprenticeship with a local undertaker, a profession more resistant to failure. Ryan hated the work and the long hours without pay but he had little choice in the matter. So long as he was learning a trade, his mother continued to provide free room and board for his family.

Ryan's wife Marie, accustomed to a comfortable life, indulged in a spending spree as if their lives hadn't financially imploded. She drifted down the staircase one evening, the flowing skirt of a baby blue chiffon dress sweeping the newel post. Fiona took one look and charged up past her, returning moments later with two new dresses draped across her arm and three Madame Elaine's garment bags. "You take that off before you ruin it with perspiration," she shouted. "Now! It's going back. All of them! First thing tomorrow!"

There were tears and yelling. When Marie ran upstairs, the delicate fabric caught on a tiny nick on one of the banister spindles and ripped. Marie froze where she stood. The Captain, silent to that point, said he thought Marie looked very pretty and said he'd pay for the dress.

The next day, Marie suffered the humiliation of returning the two dresses, as well as a scarf and a hat Fiona found hidden in a dresser. Fiona told the clerk to stop extending credit to anyone in her household, even the captain. She then marched into every store in town with the same directive.

Schroeder was nine when he heard Uncle Ryan and Aunt Marie arguing in their room. His mother ushered him down the hall. When he heard it again days later, Grandmother Fiona told him to mind his own business. The third time he heard arguing, something crashed. He charged in to find Aunt Marie on the floor next to an overturned table. Uncle Ryan stood over her with his hand raised high, about to strike. Schroeder took one step into the room and stood there without a word, his mere presence enough to extinguish Ryan's rage. Schroeder watched the man collapse to the floor next to his wife, both of them in tears. Schroeder's grandmother and mother appeared at the doorway. He would never forget their faces as they silently went to Marie, righted the table, and helped both of them to their feet.

At dinner that night, the table was a bounty of boiled potatoes, green beans, wax beans swimming in buttery milk, biscuits, and a stewed chicken, an old hen who'd stopped laying. Everyone ate in silence. Glances passed between Fiona and Ryan, between Ryan and Marie, between Schroeder's parents. Aunt Eunice, as was typical, paid no attention to any of them. With food still on his plate, the Captain rose from his chair and stood there for what seemed like forever. Forks clinked to rest on china plates. Heads hung down, waiting, until eyes eventually lifted to his. He looked at each of them, one by one, saying nothing. He walked over behind Ryan and Marie, resting a hand on their shoulders, the weight of the gesture delivering a powerful expression of what Schroeder interpreted as love and forgiveness but could just as easily have been a threat. Without a word, the Captain headed out for his evening walk. As his hand grabbed the doorknob, Fiona made a grunting sound, like an authoritative last word, and he stopped. He did not have to turn back around for her to feel his silent reprimand, and she straightened. Ryan never raised his voice to his wife again. And Fiona showed young Schroeder nothing but respect going forward.

~

Whenever life at the captain's house got too tense, Schroeder would go a block over to Grace's house. They'd been best friends since kindergarten. Circumstances at her house hadn't changed much, as if the Depression didn't exist. Her father was vice president in charge of engineering at Hamilton Manufacturing. Though they'd cut back production, they hadn't stopped entirely. He found laughter in Grace's house in direct opposition to his own.

Over the years, he saw a pattern emerge within his family, a dynamic of cause and effect. He began to see every harsh word and action at home to be the result of deprivation, fear, or inequity. His dad and uncle were ashamed of not being able to support their families. His mother and aunts were forced into submission by Fiona, unable to speak their minds for fear of retribution. Fiona's bitterness stemmed from her belief that her husband was a philanderer, though she had no proof. And Aunt Eunice, who by all accounts had been a wild child since birth, certainly could trace some of her issues back to a distant mother and often absent father. There was not enough trust, love, or employment in the household to foster any self-esteem, much less joy. As a teenager, Schroeder would discuss these things with Al Hightower, owner of the Barley Tap, a corner dive by the docks. Though good observations, Al told him, they weren't necessarily truths, and there was something in the manner in which he said it that led Schroeder to think Al knew more than he was saying.

Much of what Schroeder knew about human nature he'd learned in Al's bar. Aunt Eunice was a party girl with a habit of getting herself into precarious situations from which she had to be extricated. The police brought her home one night with a bloody nose and black eye. Fiona took Eunice by the ear and dragged her upstairs, scolding all the way. After that, any night Eunice wasn't home by nine o'clock, Schroeder was sent to retrieve her. Each evening, he'd watch the clock, hoping Eunice wouldn't show. He was ten years old the first time they sent him. Prohibition had just been repealed. He would invariably find Eunice in the Barley Tap.

From the very first time he found her, she set him straight. "You tell anyone in that house what I do, and I'll rip your ears off, you hear me?" He swore his silence.

Whenever Schroeder showed up asking after her, Al would pull a stool behind the bar for him, plop him down, and give him an Orange Crush. Schroeder discovered the world from that perch. The big bald man at the far end of the bar sometimes yipped and hollered, happy, his arms stirring thin air. Other nights, he'd be head down and silent. Schroeder asked about him once, but Al told him there was no knowing what goes on in another man's head.

"Whatever I told you wouldn't be the truth," Al said. "Wouldn't be his truth. Only he knows that." Twenty years later at Al's funeral, Schroeder spoke of Al as a philosopher and a good listener. "He gave sound advice. Most importantly, he knew when to keep his mouth shut and pour, and when to cut it off."

Eunice was never ready to go home with her nephew. Most times, she kept drinking and laughed at the boy. She sometimes shouted at him, depending on how the night had gone or how drunk she was. The walk home through the neighborhood could be boisterous. Sometimes, he'd notice a sliver of light in a window, someone peering out between curtains.

One particularly hot night stuck in Schroeder's memory the way the first of any enlightenment registers. It was sweltering in the bar, air still and thick with nicotine, sweat, and perfume, floorboards sticky underfoot. Al waved him in as he always did, pulled out the stool, and opened a pop for him, like opening a beer. There was no sign of Aunt Eunice. "Your aunt just stepped out for a bit," he said. "She'll be back."

The waitress slapped her small tray in front of Schroeder and wiped her forehead and neck with a towel from her apron. Her dark hair was tied back. Wet, clingy strands dangled in her face. Her eyes were heavy with eyeliner and purple shadow. Schroeder could see the remnants of bright red lipstick on her mouth as she grinned wide at the sight of him. Her red-tipped fingers reached for his cheek, but he ducked before the pinch.

It was a quiet night. Too hot to be rowdy. Two tables down the middle harbored couples. Two couples filled a booth on the wall. An old married couple sitting at the bar, bored, drinking whiskey together, stared at the big mirror behind the bar, hoping to find who they used to be, disappointed to see who they'd become. Schroeder was still too young to interpret it all but would store it, every detail, and in later years come to better understand what he'd been witness to.

Schroeder's eyes fell to the booth in the corner. Two bodies, fused, faces hidden, roiled in the dark. One high-heeled foot slipped out, then was snatched back.

Smoke clouds hung suspended, seeping into Schroeder's shirt, his hair, his memory. He lifted his pop bottle to his mouth in unison with, and in the same manner as a man down the bar lifted his beer, with an awkward two-finger and thumb embrace. Syrupy carbonation filled Schroeder's mouth. He swallowed, lowering the bottle only when the man lowered his beer.

Finally, Eunice appeared through the back door tucking something into her bra, straightening her dress, wiping the corners of her mouth. Her eyes glanced across the room to Schroeder. He couldn't read her expression, whether one of fear or something altogether different. She disappeared behind the ladies' room door. A man walked in, straightening his belt.

As if by instinct alone, or taking a cue from Al, who pretended not to notice, Schroeder said nothing as he watched Eunice walk back through the bar, past him, and out the front door, where he followed behind her the silent five blocks home.

No curtains shifted to peer, no dog barked, not even a car passed by. Schroeder's young mind could not fully imagine what transpired out back of the bar that night, but he knew it was a humiliation, some sort of disgrace, and for reasons he couldn't have explained, he felt more sorry for Eunice than for anyone ever.

At his grandparents' house, Fiona sat waiting on the porch, arms crossed, her face taut with contempt. Schroeder watched Eunice ascend the steps and walk past her mother, eyes forward, no comment made. He, too, walked up and in, careful to avoid eye contact, to avoid anything that might require him to speak, being unsure of what he'd seen, yet having a strong sense that it was no one's business. Fiona saw the shift. He would no longer be sent to fetch his aunt.

He was fifteen when the captain and Fiona passed away within weeks of each other. Siblings anxious to be on their own sold the Main Street house. At Ryan's suggestion, they hung on to the land to section off later when people were flush enough to begin building again. Schroeder's dad took over a barbershop and rented a little house. Uncle Ryan leased the mortuary and lived above it. Eunice bought into a dress shop.

Later, when the land was divided into seven lots and sold, Ryan and Marie returned to their old lifestyle, buying a large house on the bluff with a mortgage. Schroeder's parents bought a modest house for cash and took a mortgage out on the barbershop building, leasing out two apartments upstairs and a small gift shop below. Eunice purchased an old house that had been turned into apartments, moving into the smallest of four units.

Twenty years later, Schroeder's parents, Aunt Marie and Uncle Ryan, were gone. Ryan Jr. ran the mortuary. Aunt Eunice was an inebriate and a recluse, holed up in her recently condemned home.

CHAPTER NINE

June of 1965 had been one of the hottest on record. When the rains finally came in July, it was a relief. On a drizzly Monday morning, Schroeder stood in the doorway of the kitchen watching Grace sip coffee in her cotton robe, bathed in the humidity from the open window. "Let's go back to bed," he said with a little grin.

Grace turned and smiled. "I love you, too, now go to work."

"Tell the girl I love her," he said, glancing at the ceiling. He sauntered out to the car and climbed in. Grace spoke from the window. "It's beading up nicely." He'd waxed it over the weekend, and the drizzle was pooling and running in fat rivulets down off the hood. Pulling out the drive, he looked at his house and thought how lucky he was. His life made sense. There was love. There was health. They were happy.

He drove down the block, thinking about when the whole area was old man Patterson's orchard, how he used to get paid fifteen cents a bushel to pick apples and peaches when he was a kid. He was a good picker, careful, and Patterson was particular about who he let touch his trees. More times than not, Schroeder took payment in fruit, taking a bushel home for Fiona and his mother to can. Now Patterson was long dead, and his orchard was a tree-lined neighborhood of two-story houses filled with families. Schroeder could name almost everybody who lived within a three-square-block radius, all the kids and even some of the dogs. In a couple of weeks, the moms would pull together the annual potluck block party, and he'd meet any new arrivals. Everything is right with the world, he thought.

He stopped at the corner just as Ben jogged across the street, shaggy brown hair sticking out from under his pale blue ball cap. Right on time, Schroeder thought. Ben waved. Schroeder watched in his rearview mirror as the boy slowed his pace to a walk and disappeared into the house next door to his.

~

On the first Saturday in July, the parents of Maple Lane all went to the annual Elks Club dance downtown. Even the Finches down the street, who never went anywhere, went to the dance. It was as if they all communally disavowed family life, turning their backs and driving away as fast as possible, leaving their offspring parked in front of their respective televisions to be lulled into compliant passivity.

Rose and Fred were getting a late start. Trish pleaded to stay at Grandma's house. Rose patted her lipstick, surveying her makeup in the bathroom mirror. "They're busy tonight."

"But I don't want to stay here with the boys."

Fred walked by Rose, pointing to his watch. He didn't even look at Trish when he told her to stop whining.

Trish went into her room and slammed the door, thinking it might be enough to make them stay home, but there came no recrimination from the hallway. Looking out her window, she saw them drive away.

Trish came out to the living room, where the boys watched TV.

When she sat on the couch in the corner opposite Jason, he stretched out until his feet came within an inch of her in a silent declaration of territory. There was a discordant vibration within Jason, almost as if dust could dance on his skin. The energy ramped up like a turbine, churning faster and faster until the excess had to be discharged one way or another. If Trish was nearby, she usually took the brunt of it. It could start with a look, then a demand. "Get out of my way! That's mine! Get out of my face! I'm sick of looking at you! What are you looking at? You think you're so smart? You're not! You're an idiot!" What he lacked in creativity, he made up for in other ways. The slightest touch of his finger to her shoulder could impart a warning. His cold stare backed it up. The more she resisted his taunts, the more amped up he got. Only when she lost control, screaming, crying, and pushing back, was his energy released. Sometimes, things got thrown, like the ice cube that hit him smack in the eye and got them both grounded for a week. He didn't know why he did the things he did. He only knew he had no reason to not do them.

When his toe touched her leg, Trish got up, went to her room, and closed the door.

Downtown at the dance, Fred and Rose drank and danced mindlessly, laughed with friends, and generally let loose of anything resembling responsibility. Back at home, Trish's bedroom door crashed open. Eric spilled in, crumbling to the floor, moaning, clutching his stomach, covered in blood. Trish screamed as he crawled to her bedside. "Jason's gone mad!" he groaned. "He stabbed me! Get out while you can!" Trish looked up to see Jason standing perfectly still in the doorway, glaring at her, with the bloody bar-b-que fork raised high over his head, pointed at her.

"You're next," he sneered.

Trish hit the floor, scrambling to get under the bed, but she didn't fit, and Jason and Eric both broke out laughing.

"Ketchup, stupid," Eric told her. "It's ketchup," he said again, crouched on his knees, looking at her cowered against the bed. Jason yanked Eric to his feet and out of the room, laughing hysterically.

Eric stepped back in to find Trish standing still and straight in the middle of the room, her eyes narrow, her expression tight, unyielding.

"I hate you," she said.

~

Mid-week, Rose called her mother to ask if they'd take Patricia with them to the cabin for a few days. She had no idea what transpired between her kids over the weekend, but whatever it was, the tension between Trish and the boys was worse than usual. It was their silence that grated on her the most. It was the kind that, if broken, would shatter.

CHAPTER TEN

Trish was waiting on the back stoop with her overnight bag in hand when the Lincoln pulled in. Gramps got out wearing his threadbare Levi's and a cotton shirt frayed at the collar.

"Escaping, are we?" he said to her, opening the trunk.

He stuck her bag next to two sacks of groceries and three canvas totes of fresh sheets, towels, and clothes. Trish climbed in the back seat. Myrtle glanced at her from the front with an expression more curious than pleasant.

Riding through town, Trish watched stores and businesses pass by. It wasn't until they cleared the last bridge that she felt a sense of relief settle in. Bert and Myrtle's moods began to shift as well, a loosening of the shoulders, relaxing of the brow. Pulling into Keeter's farm stand for blueberries and corn, they sat for a moment, letting the rhythm slow, their breath deepen. By the time they pulled off the main road onto the two-track into the woods, pretention flew away with the dust kicked up by the tires.

The lake was only fifteen miles out of town, but felt like another country.

Until that spring, Bert and Myrtle had lived executive lives. His mild heart attack in May, the second in a year, forced Bert into retirement from Hamilton Manufacturing. It was a difficult adjustment for them both. Bert was used to being important. When he took the reins of the company his father started, he turned it into one of the leading manufacturers of washers and dryers in the country. As the chief employer in Edgewater, Bert still felt responsible for the livelihoods of hundreds of families.

Myrtle was used to being the consummate entertainer, capable of throwing together a gourmet meal for as many as eight when Bert would call mid-afternoon with out-of-town businessmen to entertain. Her house was tastefully decorated and always spotless. Those days were behind them, yet they still lived up to expectations of presentation. They had dinner parties and kept up with social events at the country club. Myrtle had her committees and bridge club. Bert was a bit at a loss to fill his days but managed to maintain a level of respect within community organizations.

In town, they were always on. At the cabin, they switched off.

Passing an array of cottages on a large lake, Trish heard the familiar drone of a ski boat. Turning onto what seemed a mere path through pines, oaks, and walnut trees, they eventually came to a row of modest bungalows. She waved at an old man fiddling with a boat motor on a stand behind a cottage three doors down from Bert and Myrtle's place. He waved back, and Bert stopped, asking about the man's wife.

"She'll be back by the weekend," he said. "Hard to leave that grandbaby, but those kids need their privacy."

Bert motored slowly to the end of the row to their little cabin. Its plank siding was shiny with dark honey-colored spar varnish, little bits of it fraying at joints. Moss grew thick on the roof as the sun never reached the shingles once the trees leafed out.

There was something comforting about pulling up to the cabin, a sensation of absolute calm. Trish felt it. It was the only reason she was allowed out there on her own. If her parents and the boys had been along, there would be no such feeling. They brought chaos wherever they went. Bert and Myrtle were not fans of chaos.

Bert turned off the engine and grinned at Myrtle.

"Don't worry about it," she said. "I've got it." Though only in his early sixties, he was under doctor's order not to strain himself. There was to be no hauling of heavy duffels and such. He ambled down to the water.

The lake itself was quiet, a fisherman's lake. Nothing beyond a trolling motor allowed. He took the canvas cover off his wooden skiff and folded it neatly on the dock. With an eye to the cabin to see if Myrtle was watching, he rolled the canoe over in the grass to check for critters, finding nothing but a couple spiders. He looked out to a swimmer's raft anchored forty feet off shore, a wooden platform secured to four steel drums. If you couldn't swim to it, you couldn't use it. That was the rule. For much of the summer, it floated empty. Today, a pair of ducks commandeered it.

    Myrtle and Trish took a load of groceries in. Unlocking the door with a satisfying click, Myrtle pushed hard to get it open. Summer humidity made it stick when left for a few days. Stepping inside, Myrtle dropped her purse to a drawer and took a pale yellow blouse from a peg next to her plaid flannel shirt, two yellow rain slickers, an old canvas jacket, and her fishing hat, the kind with a small wavy brim all around. She took off her earrings and put them in a dish with the key, then kicked off her polished town shoes and walked barefoot into the bedroom to change out of her shirtwaist dress. When Trish came back with another load, she smiled to see her grandmother in baggy shorts and the yellow blouse, her hair in a scarf tied at the back. There was no concern for appearances in the woods. No lipstick. No hairspray. Myrtle slid into a pair of old canvas shoes with a small hole at a little toe. Stained and worn, they never left the lake.

    Trish liked her grandmother better at the lake. Myrtle didn't boss or criticize or gripe. It was the only place Myrtle seemed happy. Yet, always in plain view were the earrings in the dish at the door, a reminder of another life full of obligations and pretense.

    The cabin was cozy with two bedrooms, each barely big enough for a double bed and a dresser. The knotty pine walls made it dark inside. One wall in the main room held fishing poles on a rack. A small chest of drawers under them housed reels and fishing gear.

The attic, only tall enough to stand in the center, was a bare-bones bunkroom for the kids with beds framed into knee walls. Not that Fred, Rose, and the kids went there often. The quarters were cramped. Fred didn't like spending his weekends stuck in the woods with his in-laws, and the boys would rather be with friends in town. Trish was the only one in her family who enjoyed it out there.

Myrtle unpacked groceries to the scrap of counter next to the stove in the corner kitchen and filled the small refrigerator. She wiped a dead bug out of the iron-stained porcelain sink and put fresh towels in the bathroom.

She gave the furniture a quick dusting, lifting Bert's pipe off the mantel and putting it back. Though it was a small fireplace, it was surrounded by a massive stone wall with a window on one side and a door on the other. It's not the door they used to come and go. It swelled stuck as soon as Michigan humidity set in.

The cabin was Bert's domain, not Myrtle's, a distinction she accepted without resistance. She could do what she wanted with the house in town, but out in the woods, she deferred to Bert on everything. They had a radio for weather reports and baseball games. There was no television.

Families with kids tended to populate other lakes in the area, bigger lakes where ski boats keep them occupied. The sound of laughing children rarely filtered through these woods, not by intent or decree, but more an inclination toward quiet, as if dappled shade precluded rambunctious behavior.

Bert wandered over to talk with a neighbor through the woods, a conversation that carried no weight or stirred agitation. They talked about fishing, weather, grandkids, and baseball while Myrtle, inside, dug through a box of paperbacks, selecting one with its cover half torn off. She filled a gallon-sized mason jar with water, dropped in three tea bags, and tightened the lid. With the book under her arm, she grabbed a folding beach chair and the jug and made her way to the sunny end of the dock. As the sun tea brewed, she disappeared into a lusty story of tightly bound bodices and well-endowed men.

Trish sorted through a collection of "Hardy Boys", "Nancy Drew" mysteries, and "Boxcar Children" books. She'd read most of them already but was always content to revisit them. She pulled out her favorite Boxcar book and settled in at the picnic table on the screened porch.

As this quiet day unfolded, Myrtle made sandwiches for lunch. Bert raked a bit of tree debris from the foundation. Myrtle took a walk. Trish went swimming, walking through shore weeds to get to deeper water. Bert grilled steaks for dinner, after which the three headed out to fish.

Trish loved the smell of gasoline as Gramps started up the little Mercury and the way it puttered them across to one of the deep holes on the other side of the lake. There was no talking on the water aside from Gramps suggesting a bobber adjustment for Trish, or a different lure for Myrtle. Muted on-shore conversations carried across the water, as did the occasional smack of a screen door somewhere. With only a handful of cabins, most of the lake was rimmed with trees and bushes right down to water's edge. Bert filled and lit his pipe. Sitting in that boat, flanked by her grandparents, Patricia Hudson was content, something she never felt anywhere else.

Myrtle's pole dipped and she jerked it a bit, embedding the hook. Bert grinned. As her pole bent in the fight, she laughed, and Bert lowered the net into the water, collecting her catch, a nice pan-size bass. The air suddenly cooled, and they motored slowly back to the dock through a mist.

Not yet dark, Bert lit a fire. He and Trish played rummy, Trish beating him handily. Myrtle worked on a small needlepoint Christmas ornament. There was little in the way of conversation.

As night fell, Bert refilled his pipe, and he and Trish headed out for their evening stroll down the road behind cabins with windows aglow. A TV show could be heard coming from one, a radio from another, the clatter of dishes from another. The silence between them was filled with a chorus of crickets, cicadas, and tree peepers. Other summers, they walked to the main road and back. This visit, they didn't even go so far as the last cottage.

Upon their return, they went to bed, Bert crawling in with Myrtle and Trish settling into the front bedroom. Through her window, coyote yips carried from across the lake somewhere. She heard a giggle from the next room.

Myrtle Hamilton never giggled in town.

~

As a young woman, Myrtle adopted what she presumed were the affectations of wealth and privilege: Perfect posture, insincere eye contact, quiet hands, and an expression void of any genuine emotion. Everything she learned, from how to dress to how to speak, came from the movies. She was careful not to pronounce theatre with the accent in the middle. She softened her voice. She spoke only when necessary and then briefly, without expressing anything but inconsequential opinions. When Bert met her, she was nineteen, a waitress in an Indianapolis hotel coffee shop. In town on the first of several business trips, he struck up a conversation with her. He was taken with her poise, her delicate frame and posture, and believed she was far too beautiful to be waiting tables. She always seemed interested in what he had to say, but rarely shared anything personal about herself. He found her to be very pleasant company and asked her to dinner. She refused. On his second and third trip in a month, he asked again. Again, she refused. He asked again on his fourth trip. She accepted that night and every night for the next two weeks.

He'd been in town to assess and acquire a small washing machine manufacturer. It was their three patents he wanted more than the facility, but the owner was adamant about his men keeping their jobs. In the end, Hamilton won out, and the shop was cleared of equipment, all sent up north. Only three of the twenty employees were asked to relocate. He didn't like dismantling a perfectly good enterprise, but it had to be done. The only upside to the time it took to make the deal was spending time with Myrtle. His task having been accomplished, it was time to go home. Never seeing her again was not an option. Bert asked her to marry him. She refused.

"I am not who I pretend to be," Myrtle said, tears welling. At Bert's insistence, and fully expecting him to walk away, she confessed she came from dirt-poor transient day laborers. She left them when she was fifteen and never looked back. Bert showed nothing but compassion and praise for what she'd made of herself. In a story contrived to quell the curious, Bert told his mother and father Myrtle's parents were lost to the Spanish Flu. Their ruse carefully constructed and maintained, no one suspected Myrtle carried the shame of poverty in her bones.

She told Bert she'd give him one child. Just one. When he pressed her, she told him she'd already helped raise her siblings. He pressed harder, only to learn Myrtle had assisted in three of her mother's births and watched her nearly bleed to death once. He pressed no further. She never told him about the soiled diapers she washed by hand from the time she was seven, or the grimy little fingers reaching for her, tugging her skirt, pulling her hair, one in her arms, two at her feet, others running, yowling, begging for food and attention because her mother was too sick or too busy with the rest of her brood.

Once Rose was born, there would be a three-day window each month when Myrtle let her husband near.

Bert abided by her cautions. Only he understood why every misstep by either her daughter or her daughter's daughter, any act that did not reflect decorum and respect, disturbed her so deeply. Nothing could be allowed to lead anyone to speculate.

Myrtle made sure Rose grew up with every advantage. If her shoes were scuffed beyond what a fresh polishing could remedy, they were given away and replaced with shiny new ones. Rips and stains were reasons to discard a garment. Mother made sure her daughter's hair was always stylish, her manners impeccable, her posture straight. "Stop giggling. Don't touch your face. Be quiet. Stop fidgeting. Don't stare. Smile. Stop crying. Don't pout. I said behave!" The dictates were quick and emphatic.

When Rose fell in love with Fred, a man so beneath her station, Myrtle's resentment was too much to contain. Rose's ill-timed pregnancy put Myrtle to task, attempting to hide the proverbial shotgun behind magnificent sprays of roses and camellias.

Four years later, when Rose delivered her third child, a girl, Myrtle set out to give her granddaughter all the advantages Rose had thrown away. But Trish was resistant to crinoline and lace. She was not a docile child. As Patricia entered kindergarten, Myrtle was already making arrangements to enroll her in boarding school as soon as she turned twelve, believing six years under the tutelage of refined educators would surely groom her for a life of status and wealth. Fred said no. He wasn't about to let strangers raise his daughter.

Late July brought canning season. Among the ladies who lunched, homemade jams and conserves were a source of bragging rights, presented at bridge parties in cut glass bowls, dollops scooped with ornate silver spoons. Rose had ten pounds of sour cherries waiting to be pitted.

Rose finished Trish's first braid. When she asked for a rubber band, Trish gave her a blue one. She complained that the braid was too tight, but Rose snapped the rubber band in place and started on the other side. Trish held up the second rubber band, a red one.

"Where's the other blue one?" Rose was impatient.

"I don't know. It doesn't matter."

"It does matter. I'll put this one on, but you need to go find a blue one or another red." Rose snapped on the rubber band and headed to the kitchen. "Now go wash your hands."

"I don't want to pit cherries."

"Go wash your hands. Your grandmother will be here any minute."

The Lincoln delivered Myrtle and just as quickly left. Myrtle's first comment upon seeing Trish at the door: "Rose, dear, Patricia's braid bands don't match."

As a huge canning pot steamed on a back burner, Trish sat at the table in front of a giant bowl of cherries, halfheartedly punching out pits, one at a time, juice running down her arms. Her mother and grandmother entered into verbal combat over boiling pots of burping ruby sludge. Rose cranked up the heat on the canner. Myrtle waved her spoon to make some point, dripping sticky cherry juice to the floor. She looked down at the linoleum, and something about the striations on the tiles made her think of blue cheese and thus began the argument.

"When your mother was your age," Myrtle told Trish, "she loved blue cheese."

"I have never liked blue cheese," Rose countered, taking the dishcloth to the spatter on the floor.

"Of course you do," Myrtle said with absolute certainty.

Trish watched the exchange like a tennis match.

The lid on the big canner started dancing.

"You're thinking of Betty," Rose said.

Myrtle came right back. "Betty? Your cousin Betty? No. I took you into the city the summer you'd just turned twelve, and you ordered extra blue cheese in the Walnut Room. The waiter brought a special bowl of it for you." She stirred the cherries with a long-handled wooden spoon.

"I was at camp that year," Rose said. "You took me to Marshall Field's at Christmas."

Myrtle whipped out the spoon and pointed it at Rose, sending a bit of hot jam flying past her. Another drop fell to the stove. "We skipped the trip to Chicago that Christmas. I had the flu."

Without missing a beat, Rose picked up the dishcloth again and wiped the stove. "That was the next year," she said, "and we all had the flu. You took Betty that summer and me at Christmas. You said it was easier with just one of us."

"I said no such thing. You and Betty always got along."

"Got along? Where were you? Betty griped about everything."

"Well, yes, she was a griper."

Landing on a point of agreement was not acknowledged so much as tolerated. Both went back to stirring their respective pots of roiling cherries.

The tension between Rose and her mother was like an unconscious chipping away at a fortress. Rose knew nothing about her mother except she'd been born in Ohio somewhere. Sometimes, it was Toledo, other times Defiance. As if Myrtle had been born an adult, she never spoke of her childhood, nothing about her life before Bert. Rose asked once, as a child, about having another set of grandparents somewhere, but Myrtle said they were all dead and told her never to ask again. In that refusal, Myrtle extinguished any likelihood Rose would ever truly know her mother.

Trish started in on another bowl of cherries when the back screen door opened, and Gramps stepped in.

"I'm taking the girl," he announced. "There's a storm coming."

Trish jumped up, wiped her hands on a towel, and dropped it to the floor on her way out. Rose and Myrtle both shouted reprimands.

Trish soon stood beside her grandfather at Lake Michigan, her toes buried in wet sand. The air was still, yet waves washed in one after another, generated by a storm making its way across the oceanic lake, each one arriving with a pounding thud as it crested and broke in front of them. The northern horizon was bright and clear, but southwest, the sky looked dark as midnight. Blue sky directly above gave no hint of warning.

She looked to the trees for any sign of arrival. Not a leaf twitched or fluttered. There was only stillness, as if every living thing held its breath. As the dark wall approached, lightning illuminated a massive thunderhead. Distant thunder grumbled, still too far away to feel. Soon, it seemed they were straddling the border between day and night.

"I give it a minute," Trish said. Then came the smell of rain, and Bert grinned.

"Nope," he said, pointing straight out to spray rising from the water. "It's here!" The temperature suddenly dropped and a cold hard wall of wind hit them full on. "To the car!" Bert hollered, reaching for Trish's hand, and together they ran across the sand as the first bolt of lightning cracked the air around them, the thunder breaking immediately with concussive force. Trish screamed in giddy terror, jumping into the car. Gramps pushed her door closed, and the rain came down in sheets. He dashed to his side and slid in, sopping wet.

"Your grandmother's not going to like this," he said, trying to catch his breath. He shook his thick white hair, sending water splattering everywhere. Wind and rain buffeted the car as lightning struck all around, followed immediately by raucous bellowing thunder. In minutes, calm prevailed, and the time between lighting and thunder grew longer. The heart of the storm was already inland, leaving behind a steady, uneventful rain.

At the same time, up the shore, disgruntled beach people thronged a covered area on the boardwalk to dodge the downpour. Barker tried to lure them into the ball toss, but they weren't interested. They were never interested. He sat on a stool, smoking a cigarette, drinking cheap whiskey from a pint flask.

CHAPTER ELEVEN

Schroeder stood in front of a building shedding its shingles like a mangy animal. What had once been a solid two-story house with four apartments now had a condemned notice nailed to the front door. The musty smell of neglect greeted him in the entryway of Aunt Eunice's apartment house. He was there to convince her to leave. The front hall, piled high with unopened mail, old magazines, and stacks of newspapers dating back years, afforded barely a path to and up the steps.

Schroeder knocked on her door. Her raspy voice came from deep in the apartment. "I know what you want. I'm not leavin'!"

Schroeder knocked again and swatted a fly away from his face. "It wouldn't take much to knock this door in but you could just open it."

"Why should I?"

"Grace cooked you dinner."

This dance never changed. He'd coax her to open up, she'd resist and eventually give in.

With the money from the captain's house, Aunt Eunice could have been set for life. But she'd lost her dress shop after a series of altercations with her clients' husbands and too many drunken tirades unbecoming a businesswoman. The only thing she had left was the uninhabitable apartment house she lived in. Inattention over the years had left it a dump, but as she was quick to point out, it was her dump.

"Go away!" she hollered, and something crashed against the door. A cat screeched from inside.

Schroeder had tried to help her. He'd hired women to clean for her, but she either wouldn't let them in, or if she did, she'd scare them off with her vulgarity and filth. Eventually, anyone he asked just laughed in his face.

"Aunt Eunice," Schroeder said quietly to the door. "I'm not leaving. Grace made you a meatloaf. She thought you might like something that didn't come out of a can for a change."

"She's a sweet girl."

"Yes, she is."

He heard some shuffling toward the door, a clicking of the latch, then shuffling away. He opened the door, but only halfway, as that's as far as it would go. He always tried to prepare himself for the smell but it got him every time. Moldy food, cat pee, dust, and the smell of a woman whose bathtub wouldn't hold water anymore.

Schroeder stood in a narrow aisle amid boxes of trash and piles of papers and clothes and beer bottles. Whatever came into the one-room apartment stayed in. The grocery boxes were receptacles for moldy, half-empty cans. Empty whiskey bottles barricaded a dresser. The sink was filled with dirty plastic utensils, used paper cups, and beer bottles.

"I see you've cleaned since I was here last," he said.

"No need to be a smart ass," she muttered.

Eunice stood in front of her chair, turned her back to it, and fell into it, almost tipping it over in the process. It was a wingback Schroeder remembered from the Main Street house, though now only recognizable through memory, its fabric frayed, stuffing protruding. She lit a cigarette and tossed the still-lit match into an overflowing ashtray on the table next to her. It didn't make it, landing instead on the table, its tiny, dying flame adding another black mark to the hundreds already there.

Though she was not yet sixty, Eunice had the craggy features of someone in her eighties, her face long and thin with little bulging jowls. Her eyelids drooped, top and bottom, revealing less of her irises on top and more of the red-laced eyeball below. Three white whiskers protruded from her chin.

She took a rattling draw from the cigarette, inhaling deeply the way anyone else might take a breath of fresh air off the lake. The smoke she expelled hung in the air before dissipating, adding its nicotine to the layers already staining the walls.

Schroeder attempted to clear a small space on the counter, giving up when he hit a bowl of moldy leftover something he couldn't recognize.

"Don't you dare clean for me," Eunice groaned.

"No chance of that," he said. He unpacked the sack and handed her the plate of food Grace had prepared. She took it and motioned for him to sit in a straight-back chair that had once graced Fiona's Main Street dining table. He moved a box of beer bottles and empty cigarette packs to the floor and sat down. From somewhere near his feet, he heard a guttural growl. A cat batted the back of his shoe.

"You've been evicted," Schroeder said. "Nothing I can do about it."

"Who's doing the evicting? I own the damn place. And where in the hell am I supposed to go?" she said with her mouth full. "Get me a beer."

Schroeder opened the refrigerator expecting the worst but found, instead, nothing but beer. No old food. No moldy cheese. Just bottles of cheap beer. He took two, opened them, and gave her one.

"Drink your own damn beer," she said. "Look at yourself. Still believe people can change, don't ya?"

He took a slow draw from the bottle.

"Still think you have all the answers," she goaded him.

"Nope," he chuckled. "Not so much." He took a swallow. "I found a place that will take you. Remember the farm by Keeter's Corner? It's an old folks home now. They'll take you in."

"Bull shit. Nobody's taking me in because I'm not leaving."

"You want me to carry you out? Because I will if I have to."

"No, you won't. You say that thinking maybe I'll go along with this insurrection. Well, I won't. People aren't always who you want them to be. And give them the chance, they'll always disappoint."

"When did I ever disappoint you?" Schroeder asked. "Didn't I always keep your secrets? Whenever I brought you home from Hightower's bar, I never said a word about what I saw, or what you did."

"Didn't have to. She knew."

"Who?"

"Your grandmother, the grand dam of the house. Miss Fiona herself. She knew. Cause it takes one to know one!"

It was a story she'd told many times, but only to Andrew, and only when she needed to strike out, needed to salve a wound that never healed. The general consensus held that Fiona and the captain slept in separate bedrooms because of his presumed indiscretions in Chicago. Eunice, however, said it was Fiona who did the screwing around. "I was the living proof of it," she shouted. "She'd have left him if my real father hadn't turned her away. So. There she was, stuck with two sons and me, her red-headed bastard, living under the captain's roof." Whether any of it was true or not, it was the reality she'd chosen to live with.

"Three days," Schroeder told her. "I'm coming back in three days. Pack a bag. Or a box." He looked around. "Better yet, let's leave it all here."

Aunt Eunice looked at him with an I-dare-you-to-try grin. He tossed his empty beer bottle into a corner, and left her in her squalor. Pulling the door closed behind him, he heard her hollering. "That's a good boy!"

Three days came and went without the successful extraction of Aunt Eunice. Throughout July, Schroeder made several more failed attempts.

CHAPTER TWELVE

It was already eighty degrees by eight in the morning. Geneva's trailer listed as she stepped out to face the day. She lit a cigarette and ambled to the picnic table where Augie sat with Harold.

"Do you want me to pull today, Mama?" Augie asked as she approached.

"No pulling today. Too hot. We'll let the machine do the work."

She scuffed toward the boardwalk and disappeared around the arcade. Augie got up to follow but caught a glimpse of Barker walking around the warehouse along the channel, heading toward town. He called out, but Barker didn't turn. He called out again, even louder, and set off to follow him. Harold told him not to go too far, then went to work on an old pinball machine.

Running at first, then slowing down, Augie's pace didn't catch him up to Barker, but he could still see him, walking along the channel wall below town. He followed him around to where the box factory rose up four stories.

At the municipal marina, Barker plopped down on a bench near a man standing at a table cleaning his catch. Gulls screamed overhead as entrails flew into the water.

Augie watched the big white birds swoop and dive, grabbing dangly bits in their long yellow beaks. From where he stood, he could see the man take a long, thin knife and slip it through a fish, head to tail, like it was soft butter, lifting a long pink slab of flesh and setting it aside. Entranced, Augie almost lost sight of Barker until a hefty marina worker ordered him to move on.

~

Across town, Trish's morning was starting out like every other: breakfast followed by boredom. She sat at the kitchen table, bobbing a lone Cheerio up and down in the milk, staring at the kitchen cupboards. They'd always been daffodil-yellow with grass-green doors, but Trish hadn't really noticed how ugly they were until that morning, which led her to wonder if bad taste was hereditary.

~

Augie followed Barker into a lumberyard, losing sight of him behind tall stacks of 2X4s. Lost in a maze, turning around one pile after another, he walked a narrow alleyway between 4X4s, trying to find his way out when he heard a loud man yelling at him. When Augie hesitated, the man started to run after him, and Augie ran to the end of the row, and darted around a corner, panting, frightened. He looked back and saw the man had stopped chasing him but was shouting at him again to hightail it out of there. Augie saw trees at the end of the row and ran toward them. Clear of the lumber, he caught a glimpse of Barker disappearing down a train track. Augie called out and ran after him.

Barker didn't hear him as he ambled along, rubbing his stubbly beard. A strand of greasy hair bounced on his face as he jerked his head side to side, muttering random obscenities.

~

Trish got up from the table and put her bowl in the sink. Taped to the fridge was a painting she'd done two years earlier. It was an embarrassment. Picking at the yellowing tape to take it down, she noticed her father's Lucky Strikes in the carton-shaped basket on top of the fridge.

She looked up to the ceiling and listened. The snap of the floorboards on the far side of the room meant her mother was probably making Jason's bed. With confident hands, Trish reached for the open pack of cigarettes, pulled it carefully out, and took one. Creaking overhead stopped. Panic set in. She grabbed a couple more and shook the rest to the opening. Her jittery fingers fumbled, and the pack fell to the floor. Footsteps thumped directly above her, toward the stairs. Trish snatched up the pack. The thumping descended the stairs. She stuffed the pack up into the basket, stuck the cigarettes in her shirt pocket, and tore out the back screen door. She was giving her bike a running start when she hollered in to her mother. "Going to Linda's."

Rose called out. "Be back by dinner. That means 5:00!"

Energized by larceny, Trish peeled off Maple St., checking her pocket for the cigarettes. Still there.

~

As Trish rode figure eights on the playground, pondering a plan, Barker stumbled through an industrial dump littered with cast-off car batteries, rusted machine parts, and barrels of unknown contents with lesser-known origins. He took a swig from a flat brown flask and then pushed it back into his pants pocket. He lit a cigarette and took a long, deep drag, blowing the smoke out his nose and mouth into a cloud that washed over his head and hung in his wake. The flattened cigarette stuck out between his swollen fingers like an extra appendage. When he sat on a crate to rest, Augie caught up with him and sat next to him, trying to catch his breath. Barker said nothing and took another long drag. Sitting there together, they became part and parcel of the debris.

~

When an idea materialized, Trish took off peddling under a lush canopy of oaks lining the street to Linda's house.

Linda's mom was hanging sheets in the backyard, oblivious to Trish's arrival. The dog let out a few barks of annoyance when one of the girls, a tow-head just like Linda, screamed bloody murder, chasing her little brother around the swings as he flailed a Raggedy Andy in the air, threatening decapitation. As she darted in and out of the shade, her hair caught the sun like a bright blinking light. The dog took shelter under the picnic table.

Trish walked in the back door without knocking to find Ben sitting on the kitchen counter surrounded by half-empty cereal bowls and juice glasses. Still sweaty from his morning run, he finished the last of the milk from a bottle. She smiled at him, hoping for any sign he noticed her, but he barely raised his eyes.

Gathering Linda and then Jane, the threesome was soon wending their way on bikes via a deviously circuitous route toward the hospital, behind which was supposedly a trail leading down the bluff to the old train tracks at the river. Linda had heard the boys talk about it. There, they would each smoke their first cigarette.

~

Down at the dump, Barker told Augie to go home and leave him alone, but Augie refused. "Suit yourself," Barker grumbled. He rose and walked down to where the tracks stopped, leaving only a dirt path where ties and rails had been removed.

"Where'd the tracks go?" Augie asked, but Barker just grumbled. Up ahead stood a small ramshackle shanty that Augie confused for a house. "Who lives in that? Must be really small people." Barker ignored him.

Manny and Lou sat in their aluminum chairs, catfish lines in the water. Augie went over and asked if they were catching anything.

"Nope," Manny said. Lou paid no attention to anything but his bobber bouncing with the flow of the river.

Barker asked if they had any cigarettes. There came no response.

Augie sat down on the cement edge of the jetty, dangling his feet above the surface of the river until Barker headed off down the track bed again.

~

The girls cruised through the neighborhood, weaving in unison like a synchronized bicycle team. A woman watering flowerpots called out from her porch. "Enjoying your summer girls?" They smiled and waved.

"Yes, Mrs. Jackson," they said in unison.

Another block over, an old man sprayed something from a hand pump onto weeds inhabiting the cracks in his driveway. "Hey there, Patricia," he called out. "Tell your grandfather he still owes me a trout dinner."

"I will, Mr. Carley," Trish answered back.

When the girls made it into the hospital parking lot, they jumped the half curb onto the grass and ditched their bikes under an overgrown forsythia hedge. Trish, Linda, and Jane sat under its protective umbrella, catching their breath. Below them, the river flowed, slow, wide, and brown, one shore connected to the other by a two-lane trestle bridge.

With a glance of determination to each other and a singular focus to find the track bed, they found the path down. One after another, bare legs tried hard to avoid thorny branches by maneuvering the steep trail. At the bottom, they were surprised to see there were no tracks anymore, only a wide path between the dense sumac on the bluff and the shrubs at the river's edge. Jane questioned if it was the right place. Trish said it had to be. Jane kept looking up and down the pathway to the river only a few yards away and up the bluff. Her hesitancy was quickly corrected by Linda. "Stop it. We're doing this."

Trish checked the cigarette stash and found one had broken. She threw it down and pulled another from her pocket. Linda said they needed to get further away from the bluff trail. In agreement, the trio began walking.

Freedom seduced the girls, drawing them down the path. Cicadas whirred above, their blanket of sound a welcome or warning. The path became an ever-narrowing tunnel with overgrown bushes reaching from each side, a high canopy of hardwood and sassafras filling any gaps above. The hill to their right grew steeper, thick with underbrush. To their left, the river lapped just feet from the path.

"This is a good spot," Linda said with authority. She held up her matchbook. Trish put the cigarette to her lips. Linda lit a match. It went out. Jane cupped her hands around Trish's face, and Linda lit another match. It went out. The next match survived to ignite the tobacco before petering out. Trish gave a little suck to get the cigarette going, wincing at the bitter taste. When they all thought it looked to be well lit, Trish took a draw of smoke, pulling it into her lungs and started coughing. Linda said she was doing it all wrong and took it away, taking a shallow drag with the same hacking results. Jane followed suit, coughing and grimacing. With her eyes still tearing, Trish took it back and tried it again. Linda picked bits of tobacco off her tongue. Around it went one more time until they'd had enough and tossed it to the ground and stepped on it. They walked off slowly, each of them queasy, trying not to throw up.

"Where's the island the boys are always talking about," Linda asked.

"What island," Janey asked.

"There," Trish shouted. Through a break in the thicket, they saw what could have been construed as an island though it was only a spit of land separated from shore by eight or ten feet of water. "Look," Janey said.

"Chairs." Two rickety straight-back chairs, one standing, one lying down, skirted what looked like a fire pit, ashes and burnt bits piled in the middle.

Six white gym shoes and wadded-up socks lay scattered on the shoreline as the girls stepped into the murky waters. Securing a precarious balance on the slick clay underfoot, they probed with long sticks, gingerly stepping forward whenever the sticks found hard ground. Jane stepped into a muck pocket, screamed, and jumped back onto the bank. Linda blasted her for being such a girl.

Confident of an easy crossing, Trish and Linda simultaneously poked and stepped, then slipped into the river up to their armpits, splashing and screaming.

Jane yelled to save the last cigarette. Stumbling to shore, laughing with equal measures of revulsion and thrill, Linda and Trish finally stood upright on solid ground, shaking water from their hands and trying to wipe the oily black river muck from their clothes. The effort only smeared it in deeper. As the thick, acrid stench rose from their clothes, fear rose with it, the only fear they could comprehend at this point in their naive little lives: If caught, they'd be grounded and never trusted again. Freedom itself was at stake. Linda took off her shorts and dunked them in the river. Though some of the muck disbursed, the stench remained.

As Linda saw it, the only option was to go to Jane's. Both her parents worked, and her grandmother was glued to her game shows and soap operas all day. If they made it to Jane's without being seen, Jane could distract her grandmother while the other two snuck into the basement to launder their shorts and shirts. But Mrs. Jackson might still be outside, take one look at them, get one sniff, and surely report their transgression. Adults were like that. Always watching, always reporting.

What came next seemed logical for the few minutes it took to put it in motion. Trish and Linda stripped down to their underpants. Trish told Jane to run back up the track bed with all their clothes and wash them.

"You have to," Linda insisted.

Jane feared she might not find the path up, that her grandmother would question her, that she didn't know how to run the washer, that it was too much responsibility.

"Just go!" Trish shouted.

Standing at the water's edge in their underpants, Linda and Trish watched Janey run off. They stepped in the warm shallows under a dense canopy of willow fronds, rinsing their legs, feeling exposed and vulnerable, eyes darting about like nervous birds. Trish felt the chill of a breeze on her bare chest and stepped away from the shadows into the sunshine.

"Jesus! A boat!" Linda snapped, grabbing Trish by the arm, pulling her to cover. The speedboat zipped along the far side of the river and under the bridge. They put on their socks and shoes and settled into a thicket partway up the bluff, above the track bed, and waited.

~

As two prepubescent girls hid in the brush in their panties and Keds, Barker tried to give Augie the slip at the jetty. When Augie realized Barker was gone, not knowing where he was or how to get back to the boardwalk alone, he ran back onto the track bed, calling out, cramming a saltwater taffy into his mouth. He caught up with Barker under the trestle bridge, finding him peeing into the river. Augie laughed at him and decided to do the same, but his stream wasn't as strong, and he wet his pant leg.

"Can I wear your ring, Barker? C'mon. Can I?"

"No." Barker zipped up.

"It's so pretty," Augie said, fumbling with his own pants.

"Leave me the hell alone!" Barker sat down in the dirt against the bridge abutment and closed his eyes. Augie sat down next to him and reached out to touch the ring, but Barker moved his hand and crossed his arms, hiding it.

Augie sat still, his shirt soaked with sweat, sweat beading and running from his brow. Cars passed overhead. The droning whine, interrupted by rhythmic thuds on the seams, lulled him to sleep.

~

In the hiding bush, nervous giggles subsided, leaving Trish and Linda to sit quietly. "We should just go up," Linda said. "Hide with our bikes. There's no one to see us."

"No," Trish said. "She'll be back soon. We should stick to the plan."

"Why?"

She delivered the one word that bounced back at every why ever asked. "Because."

Linda sighed, slapped at a mosquito, stood up, and brushed away a twig from her underpants. "What do we do if the boys show up? They're always down here. What if they find us?" She rolled her shoulders and sat back down.

"What are they gonna do, tell on us?" Trish said. "They're not supposed to be here any more than we are."

"But, still, what would we do? We're naked!"

"Nothing. We just hide and wait."

Silence wedged its way between them.

Six blocks away, Jane pulled wet clothes from the washer to the dryer as her grandmother dozed in front of the TV.

Linda slapped at another mosquito.

Trish flicked away a beetle in the dirt.

"She's taking too long," Linda said. "I'm leaving."

~

Under the bridge, Augie woke up when he heard Barker shuffle away. He jumped to his feet and followed.

A little way up the path, Barker reached down and retrieved a broken cigarette from the path. He struck a match and lit up. Augie threw a stone into a bush, startling a grouse that flew up and whistled in alarm.

~

Linda stood. Her patience was gone, and she took a step down the hill. A grouse whistled. Trish looked down the track bed and saw two men. She grabbed Linda's arm and yanked her back down. Like scared rabbits, they watched, hearts beating fast. Barker and Augie stopped below them, not ten feet away. When Trish realized who they were, she squeezed Linda's hand.

~

Up in the neighborhood, Ben, Eric, and Jason saw Jane pedaling hard toward the hospital. Ben wondered aloud where she was going alone in such a hurry.

"Don't know, don't care," Jason said.

"I don't get it," Ben said.

"I don't like it," Eric agreed. They followed her to the bush, saw the other bikes, and headed down the bluff after her.

~

Barker took one last hit from his flask and threw the empty bottle to the island. It shattered against a rock. What followed was silence except for the river rippling against a bobbing branch. It was probably nerves that made Linda let out a little fart, and good etiquette that made her let go with an automatic Excuse me.

Barker turned, searching the hillside, and saw Linda's light blond hair glowing like a beacon in the sunlight. Both girls launched straight up the bluff. The sight of skin, Linda's long naked legs, in combination with high-pitched yelps, triggered a primal response in Barker, his mind flashing to the last naked legs he'd seen, the bleach blond spreading to take him in in exchange for a pint of whiskey.

His brain did not translate what he saw, confusing fleeing children with naked women. He charged up the bluff on base instinct alone.

Linda made it quickly up the bluff, her long legs climbing, arms reaching, grabbing one sumac stalk after another. Trish tried to get a foothold but slipped back down.

Barker grabbed her foot. She kicked free, her shoe flying off her foot, soaring over the track bed, out of sight.

"Leave her alone!" Augie hollered, but Barker grabbed hold of Trish's leg. She kicked him in the chin, pissing him off, and he surged upward, no longer motivated by lust so much as anger.

"Augie, help me!" Trish cried out. "Help me!"

"June?" Augie lunged at Barker, trying to pull him down, but Barker backhanded him hard with his ring hand, sending Augie tumbling to the ground with a gash on his cheekbone.

Linda screamed from the sumac as Barker clamped onto Trish's legs and flipped her, nearly wrenching her hip out of its socket. Face to face with him, she saw close up his one dead eye, smelled his sour whiskey and cigarette breath, and began pounding his face with her fists.

From down the track bed, the boys heard the screaming and Ben saw Barker grab somebody, skinny arms flailing, then both of them disappearing down behind the undergrowth. Ben took off on a dead run, way ahead of Eric and Jason, passing Janey, who stood still, gripping the clothes to her chest, too frightened to move.

Barker, fully on top of Trish now, grabbed her fists and held them down, lifting his head up to see better with his good eye.

Ben saw Barker's head and shoulders rise up from the ground. His terrified mind filled in the gap of what he could and couldn't see, and he grabbed a dead branch on the fly charging forward, carried by a rage stronger than he understood.

Barker hovered over Trish for only a moment, his body half on top of her, shocked to see she was just a kid. There was, in that instant, a recognition between them, and he let go of her. But Ben came at him from his blind side, delivering a piercing crunch across his shoulder, and Barker fell away.

Trish recoiled without knowing what just happened. A T-shirt landed on her face, and she yanked it on. She heard Eric yell at her to get the hell out of there.

She climbed partway up to Linda and looked back down, watching Eric run up and smash Barker with a branch. Pieces of it splintered and flew away. Barker scrambled to his feet, but Ben, shirtless, shoved him down again. Jason knocked Augie down and kicked him.

"Stop it!" Trish yelled to Jason. "Jason, I'm begging you! Stop it!" But he kept kicking Augie.

"Barker! Barker, help me!" Augie shouted.

Up in the sumac, Linda stopped screaming and cried.

Down the path, Jane stood frozen, pee running down her leg.

"I didn't do anything," Augie cried, but Jason kept kicking.

"Jay Jay! Leave him alone!" Eric yelled.

Jason looked up, shouting, "Don't call me Jay Jay, you fuckhead!"

Augie stumbled to his feet and ran. Jason followed, chasing him around a bend just out of sight. He shoved Augie from behind, lurching him forward, and Augie scrambled into dense bushes at river's edge. He yelped, and there was lots of splashing, sending waves rocking the shore. Jason stopped, listening to Augie's frantic splashing and cries, coughing, splashing, and twigs breaking. Then came the silence and stillness.

Eric hollered again. "Let him go! Get back here!"

Jason peered into the thick brush and saw an arm lying in the mud at the edge of the water. The rest of Augie appeared to be submerged. There was no movement. Jason could barely breathe. Time seemed to stop as he wrestled between panic and disbelief, waiting for another sound, anything to indicate life, but the water only settled to stillness. Fear flooded his brain until something snapped and he took off running back down the track bed to the fight, tripping when he got there, sliding in the dirt, clipping Barker in the mouth sending a splatter of blood to Eric's shirt. Jason did not stop. He kept running.

Eric and Ben ducked wild punches from Barker and landed a few of their own. Ben shoved him down, and in some hormonal rage, the boys kicked the hell out of him. Trish called out to stop, but they wouldn't or couldn't. She finally ran down to them and grabbed hold of Eric's arm. "Stop it! Stop it!" she yelled, and Eric shoved her hard, sending her to the ground.

"That's enough!" he shouted, suddenly aware it had gone too far. Like a sudden downpour of rain, it stopped as fast as it started, except for a couple more errant kicks, and it was over. Barker managed to stand up and hobble away.

"Get the hell out of here, you asshole!" Ben yelled.

Jane walked over with the clothes. Linda wouldn't come down.

"It's OK," Ben called up to her. "You can come down now. C'mon. C'mon down."

"Turn around," Linda hollered down. "Both of you!"

Eric and Ben turned away. Linda came down and quickly dressed. Trish pulled Ben's shirt off and put her own on. When she handed it back, Ben glared at her, tears welling in his eyes. "What the hell were you thinking?" he shouted.

Linda started crying again.

"All of you," Eric said. "What the hell?" He looked down at Trish's feet. "Where's your other shoe?" he asked.

"I don't know."

"Goddamn it!" he shouted and made them all start looking for it, but it wasn't to be found.

Together, they walked back down the track bed. For all there was to say, no one spoke a word.

Eric hung in the back, instinctively protective, senses hyper-attuned to their surroundings. His heart had stopped racing. Now it pounded, hard and irregular. One word reverberated in his brain: lucky, lucky, lucky. Then came all the what-ifs. What if they hadn't followed Jane? What if one of them had really been hurt bad? What if the guy had had a knife? Or a gun? He pushed his mind into containment mode, trying to organize scattered thoughts enough to figure out what to do next. Keep it quiet. No need to tell anyone. No real harm done. If they played it right, they could pull it off.

When they got to the trail up the bluff, Jason was waiting. Eric said he'd take the girls up to their bikes and told Ben and Jason to wait.

"Who made you king of me?" Jason scoffed.

"Shut up," Ben said.

Eric commanded everybody shut up.

"Yes sir, Mr. I-have-all-the-answers-thank-you-very-much," Jason sniped.

"Shut up!" Eric hollered. He knew Jason was the wild card. His unpredictability made him dangerous. When Jason noticed Trish's missing shoe, and was told they hadn't found it, he started back to look for it. Eric stopped him.

"It's gotta be in the river," Ben said. "We looked everywhere. It's not there."

"Fuck you all," Jason said and took off running toward the bridge, past the jetty, and up behind the box factory. Manny and Lou had long since gone home.

Eric felt the weight of the day's events bearing down on him. He had to be the strong one, the right one, the one to save them all from themselves.

Up at the bikes he told the girls not to say anything to anybody. Whether his words made any sense or not, the girls needed to hear them. They needed someone to tell them what to do and Eric made it sound like he knew what was best. He was confident. He was older. He was angry with them. "Don't even talk about it. Somebody might hear you. You understand?" They muttered that they got it and he watched them ride across the parking lot before going back down to Ben.

Ben waited below, shaking out hands that kept making fists. His mind hit a wall and every thought he had crashed into it. Nothing made sense. The adrenalin rush left him depleted, yet the image of Trish, her nakedness writhing under that man, stirred an aggression he could barely contain. No one else had seen what he'd seen, real or imagined, and in that moment, he'd felt invincible. Standing alone, waiting for Eric, he felt anything but.

CHAPTER THIRTEEN

Mrs. Finney pulled a bed sheet off the line and began folding it, the corners wafting over the grass momentarily before she caught it all up. She saw the three girls return and called to tell Linda she'd missed lunch, to make some PBJs if they wanted to. Beyond that, she paid no attention to them.

The girls ran upstairs to shower. Linda went first. As she dried her hair with a towel, Trish took her turn. Jane sat on the counter nervously, chewing on a braid.

Linda said something smelled like pee.

"That's me. It's dry now."

Trish laughed from behind the curtain. "You peed your pants?"

Janey, not prone to harsh responses, barked back. "What of it?"

Rinsing shampoo from her hair, Trish interrupted their argument. "What am I going to tell my mom about my shoe? She's gunna kill me."

Janey's mouth hung open. "Are you serious? You could have been killed today, and you're worried about a shoe?"

"Don't be so dramatic," Linda said.

Trish worked up a good lather, scrubbing her arms and legs, but the dirt wouldn't wash away no matter how she rubbed until she realized it wasn't dirt. She was bruised where Barker grabbed her. She began to cry. It had all happened so fast. If the boys had been even a minute later, those men would have walked away. She was certain because of his face, the way it looked when he really saw her. He seemed so surprised, suddenly so sad. He was letting go when he got knocked off her. He was letting go, and that was what she hung on to. It wasn't going to get worse. It was going to get better, but the boys came along, and poor Augie took such a beating. The shower washed away her tears.

When the faucet squeaked off, Linda gave her the wet towel, and Trish dropped it. "A dry one?"

"My mom will get suspicious."

"There are seven people living in this house," Trish argued. "She won't notice." Linda gave her a dry one.

"Tell your mom you took your shoes off over here," Janey said. "And couldn't find one."

"That'll work," Trish and Linda said in unison.

Downstairs, Ben perched on the edge of the couch and stared blankly at a game show on TV. His leg bounced wildly. Timmy, fresh off a nap, pestered him to go outside and play catch. Sherry sat on the floor playing Candy Land, talking in high, fake voices, pretending to be three other players.

"Come on, Ben. Pleeeez?" Timmy whined and started tugging on his shirt. Ben heard the girls coming downstairs, yanked his arm free, and jumped up, bumping Timmy aside. Timmy started to cry. Ben stumbled over the game board, scattering the game pieces, and Sherry started to cry. Trish saw him from the hallway and smiled at him, but he shot her a dead-serious glare and charged out the front door.

Over at the empty Little League field, Eric leaned on the dugout wall watching Jason sit motionless on the bench. "You OK?" he asked.

Jason looked up at him, belligerent. "Fine. Why wouldn't I be?"

"You don't look fine."

"Yeah, well, what do I look like?"

"Shit. You look like shit."

Jason pointed to a spot of blood on Eric's shirt. "At least I'm not covered in blood."

Eric looked at the dried reddish stain, and his stomach churned. He would have to change when he got home, then hide the shirt and throw it away in somebody's trash the next day, or go down in the ravine and burn it, anything to get rid of it.

"I'll see you at dinner," Eric said and walked off. He turned back to say all they'd done was kick the shit out of a couple low-life scumbags, that's all. End of story.

Jason lingered in the dugout, trying to convince himself the guy had gotten out of the river, that he was safe, but something nagged at him, and he couldn't get the image of Augie's face out of his mind. He could see it, not the way he saw it when he was kicking him, but for what it was, just a big, scared kid. He picked up a stone and threw it hard, but it ricocheted off the wall and hit him in the eye. "Goddamn it!"

~

Trish left Linda's, compelled to make things right. If she found her shoe, there would be no proof any of them were there, and things would go back to normal. Purpose overtook reason as she rode to the hospital, ditched her bike in the forsythia, and headed down the trail.

Ben had more at stake. He had to find the shoe. His only hope of getting into college was a track scholarship. He couldn't afford an assault charge. He went to look downriver, making his way up from the lumber. Trish startled the hell out of him when she stepped out from a bush. "God damn it," he shouted. "Haven't you caused enough trouble for one day?"

Trish stumbled. He held out his hand, but when she started to get up on her own, it went into his pocket. "You shouldn't be here," he said, calmer. "I've looked everywhere."

She started to push her way back into the thicket.

"Trish! Nothing more to do here. Go home." When she refused, he looked at her with a smile meant to coax her along the way he'd coax his baby brother or their dog. He followed her up the bank to her bike. Lifting it for her, he asked if she was really OK, thinking maybe she was too afraid to tell anyone if things had gone too far. It wasn't concern for her so much as how it would play if it got out. All of it, every stinking minute of that day, held a distinct possibility of crashing his future. Her expression of innocence seemed to support her insistence that nothing terrible happened. "Don't worry about all this," Ben told her. "It will be fine. You were really lucky today."

Trish peddled home, enraptured by the idea Ben was looking out for her. She felt a connection in his outstretched hand when she stumbled, even though it retracted just as she was about to take it. She saw something in his eyes, a sweetness in the way they caught hers then glanced away as if embarrassed. She saw compassion in his smile. In the momentary touch of their hands when he held the bike for her, she felt connection. She felt hope.

~

After setting the table for dinner, Rose yanked Trish's hair into sections to braid. Trish yelped. Fred watched from the hallway, wincing for Trish, but said nothing. Rose looked over her shoulder at the stove and told him to turn the corn off. Fred obliged. Rose attacked the second braid. She was stretching the rubber band to put it on when Trish yanked away, and it shot across the room. Trish undid the other braid.

"I give up," Rose snapped. "I don't know what you had to take them out for in the first place."

Trish went to the table and sat down. Fred carried a plate of cubed steak over and sat down. Eric wandered in from the hall, avoiding eye contact with everyone, and sat down.

"Why did you change your shirt," Rose asked as she brought the corn over and took her place. He didn't answer, and she didn't ask again. Fred hollered to the ceiling for Jason.

"He's not home yet," Rose said.

"What do you mean?" Fred asked. "Where is he? Eric, where's your brother?"

Eric did not respond.

Trish looked at Eric, but he wouldn't look back.

Rose straightened her silverware. Everyone's plates were full when Jason finally walked through the back door and pulled his chair out to sit.

"Hands," Rose said, pointing to the hallway. He walked over to the kitchen sink. "Bathroom," Rose instructed. He ignored her, washing his hands with dish soap. "Not the dish towel," Rose said without turning to see. Jason shook off his hands, wiped them on his pants, and sat down.

Trish asked for the bread. It was by Jason, but he didn't budge. Rose told him to pass the bread to his sister. He didn't hear. He was still at the river, in the fight, at the bushes.

"Jason," Fred barked. Jason looked up. "The bread. Pass it to your sister."

Jason hoisted the plate toward Trish, almost dropping it before she took it.

"Straighten up, mister," Fred said.

Eric shook a ketchup bottle, but nothing came out.

"Trish," Rose scolded. "You need to be more careful with your things. Money doesn't grow on trees, young lady."

"What's this?" Fred asked, looking to Trish.

Eric smacked the bottom of the ketchup bottle over and over until Fred took it.

"Trish lost a shoe today," Rose continued. "How does a person lose a shoe? That's what I'd like to know."

With one good smack, the ketchup broke free onto Eric's plate, sending a red splatter to his shirt. "Damn it!" Eric shouted, shoving away from the table. He couldn't wipe the ketchup off his shirt fast enough.

Rose sat slack-jawed, holding a fork full of corn, some of which fell back to her plate.

Fred took a breath to speak, stopped, and heaved a heavy sigh. He took a gulp of milk as if it were a stiff drink. Jason crammed a huge piece of boiled potato into his mouth. Trish stared at her plate. Rose put her fork down and straightened her spoon. Dinner resumed in silence.

Afterward, Jason got up and started out the back door. Rose told him to finish his milk. He turned, took the three steps back up from the landing, gulped the last of his milk, and left. Eric followed in his wake. Rose was starting the dishes when Trish headed to the door. "Where do you think you're going, young lady?" She said it quietly, the way someone does when the expectation is obvious. "Come back and clear the table." Trish clenched her jaw, took some dishes to the counter, and headed for the hallway.

"Get back here and grab a towel."

"Why do I have to dry all the time? Make Jason do it for once."

"What's gotten into you three tonight," Rose groused, putting a clean plate in the rack. She held out the dishtowel. Trish took the towel, grabbed the plate, and started to cry as she wiped it. Annoyed, Rose asked what she had to cry about in a tone that suggested she had nothing to cry about. The plate hit the floor and broke.

"Oh, for crying out loud!" Rose hollered. "Go on. I'll take care of it." Trish disappeared into her room behind a closed door for the rest of the evening.

Later that night, as Rose and Fred sat in the living room laughing at Johnny Carson, Jason sat on a swing in the backyard reliving how he chased and kicked that stupid fat man over and over, and only then remembering it was entirely one-sided. The man never hit back. Not once.

A wind kicked up, the strange kind that doesn't bring a storm, just blows for no reason. It sounded like rough surf as it whipped the tree tops into a frenzy, yet the space below, the air around Jason was unnaturally calm aside from all the questions swirling in his brain. Why did he do it? Why did he leave him there? He didn't bother trying to believe it had anything to do with defending his sister. It didn't. Whoever that man was or what he had or hadn't done was irrelevant. Like the wind mindlessly assaulted the trees, he had attacked Augie. Some darker nature allowed it, and whether he would ever be able to control his dark urges or not frightened him. What if that was who he really was? Even thinking these thoughts brought the urge to go into the house, to Trish's room, and shake her by the shoulders until she shattered. He blamed her in advance for every future vile eruption, for whoever he would become. It would all trace back to this day, that fight, her stupidity, and the man lying in the bushes at the river, probably dead. Every fiber of Jason's being needed to go back down there to see for sure. It was the not knowing, wrapped in guilt, that tormented him.

Upstairs, Eric sat on the edge of his bed, holding his head in his hands. He was having a hard time wrapping his mind around the day's events. The right and wrong of it all wouldn't line up. He knew he should tell someone but couldn't bring himself to do it in the face of repercussions. In his belief they'd saved the girls, he rationalized justification. Trish was safe. They were all safe. In the greater scheme of things, he felt good about what they'd done. He was proud to the small degree he would allow, and content in thinking how much worse it could have been had they not intervened. He fell asleep listening to the wind plow through the trees.

Downstairs, Trish sat on the floor in the dark, yanking the head off a Barbie doll. What if she had never met Linda? How long would the tenuous nature of life have remained hidden behind obedience? If she had not been emboldened by their night forays, would she have ever stolen the cigarettes, gone to the river, stripped naked in the woods? Would she have ever discovered her curiosity or explored possibility? Or would she have a life built on the limited expectations of those around her who craved only safety and security? Such questions were only beginning to brew in the primordial sludge that would one day evolve into awareness. Yet this night, enraged and exhausted, Trish felt like she was disintegrating, bits of her sliding through the screen, carried away by the wind, wondering how she would pull herself together again, with parts of her scattered.

Trish crawled into bed. The wind howled, sending errant twigs scraping across the screen to taunt her as if the night knew what she'd done and would not let her rest. Everything that happened was her fault. If she hadn't stolen the cigarettes or hidden at the river naked, he wouldn't have attacked her. The boys would never have gotten into the fight. It was her fault. All of it. Exhausted, she finally slept, waking with a start, having felt an imaginary weight on top of her, hands pinning her arms to the bed.

Across the hall, Trish's parents enjoyed the blissful sleep of ignorance.

CHAPTER FOURTEEN

From his perch in his office on the swing bridge, Gar watched the lights go out at Sunset Beach. One by one, entire sections went dark. First, the boardwalk, then the roller coaster, the Ferris wheel, and the parking lot. Only the string of lights by the trailers remained lit, swaying in the wind, illuminating a solitary figure sitting in a chair by her trailer. Gar saw Geneva stir only once that night, about two in the morning when she disappeared onto the boardwalk. He heard raised voices, though not what was said and Geneva returned to her chair. She was still there in the morning when Gar walked off the bridge at shift change. When Augie was not there to wave at him, Gar began to suspect something was wrong.

"Where's our boy this morning?" he called over to Geneva.

"Oh, up in town I suspect," she said. "Hasn't done that in a while, but he gets turned around sometimes. Hides out until morning. Should be home soon."

He walked over and handed her the rabbit he'd carved overnight. "Thought Augie would like this one," he said. "Standing on its hind legs."

"It'll go nicely with his collection," Geneva said. "He does love all those critters you carve."

"I'm going to miss him waving at me every morning. Nobody else I know is ever that happy to see me. Not even my wife."

Any other morning, she might have laughed, but not this day. "When do you retire?" she asked. "Labor Day?"

"The Thursday before. Wouldn't go if they weren't making me."

"Well, he's going to miss you, too."

"We'll see each other, no worries," Gar said walking away.

~

Across town, Schroeder arrived at Aunt Eunice's apartment, this time with two officers in case they needed to carry her out. He knocked but heard nothing. He called out for her the way he always did. Hearing no response, he put his shoulder to the door. The hinges gave way, pulling from the rotted doorframe. He pushed it in expecting it to fall, but it simply tilted in, then slid a bit, and came to rest on a pile of debris behind it. The smell hit him first, more putrid than normal.

He stepped in and glanced to the bed on the far side of the room, the springs so shot the mattress hung low in the middle. Making his way through and around the trash, he saw a bony hand protruding over the edge of the mattress, a cigarette butt wedged between nicotine-stained fingers. Half the spent ash still clung to the filter, the remainder rested in two tidy clumps on the bare mattress. Aunt Eunice's skin was as grey as the ash, and just as cold.

Sandy, one of his officers, walked in. "What in the hell is that stink?" he asked, then saw the hand. "Sorry, Chief." As he stepped closer to the bed, a low growl emanated from under it and he jumped back, fell over a box and landed in a pile of empty cans. "Jesus!"

Schroeder pushed a box under the bed and a bone-skinny cat shot out from under it and disappeared out the door, free at last.

Sandy stood up, shocked at the mounds of boxes, papers, trash, empty bottles, filthy clothes and debris. Somewhere under a pile of beer bottles was probably a sink, but he wasn't sure. "It's gonna take a dozen truckloads to empty all the trash out of this place," he said.

"Well, my dear," Schroeder said to his dead aunt. "You got your way."

From below, a car horn blew and the other officer hollered up.

"On the radio, Chief. Just heard. They're looking for you. Something about a dead body." Schroeder stuck his head out the window, the screen hanging from the frame like laundry.

"A dead body?"

"That's what dispatch says," the officer hollered up. "Somebody called it in. You need help with your aunt, sir?"

"Yeah. Get dispatch to call Ryan Jr. over at the funeral home. We've got a pick up for him here."

Schroeder gave Aunt Eunice one last glance. Her face, sunken in life, looked skeletal in death. Waiting on emotion that did not arrive, he accepted his indifference and left.

~

Down at the jetty, Manny Horowitz held Officer Ted captive in conversation. "City sanitation. Forty years," Manny told him. "Never saw anything like this and we used to see it all. Invisible men. That's what we were. Drove all through town, picked up everybody's refuse, every house once a week, and nobody gave us any notice. Even yours, Teddy. How's your dad, anyway? Ever get over his love of the drink?" A few feet away, Frank stood on the riverbank next to the body they'd just pulled out of the river.

A second squad car drove down the narrow track bed. Chief Schroeder got out. He passed by Ted. "Mornin', Manny. What we got here, Ted?"

Ted took a breath to answer but Manny pointed to the body without skipping a word. "He's another invisible man," Manny said nodding to Schroeder. "Has been since he was a little shit. Everywhere that one, why I can tell you…" Ted looked at Schroeder for relief but instead was motioned to stay put.

Schroeder sauntered over to the riverbank side of the jetty. "Mornin' Mr. Waterman." Perched in his lawn chair, two poles in the water, Lou lifted two fingers in recognition.

Frank stood over the body fidgeting with a Polaroid camera, extending the bellows, adjusting the lens, looking through the viewfinder. He stood back a bit farther, cocked the shutter, and finally took the picture. He pulled a white tab from the housing exposing the larger white tab of the photo packet and pulled, checking his watch.

Schroeder knelt next to the body.

"Ted and I pulled the body up on shore, so it wouldn't go anywhere."

Schroeder looked up with mild annoyance. "And where was the body going to go exactly?"

"The current here is sorta, well, and it was rocking, and…"

Schroeder raised his hand. "Yeah. Don't worry about it. Help me here."

Frank held up the photo packet, negating any possibility of assistance. Schroeder called out to Ted and asked Frank if holding the photograph was all he could manage. "Can you take some notes for me, maybe?"

Tucking the photo packet carefully in his shirt pocket, Frank pulled a notepad from his back pocket and began writing as Schroeder spoke.

"White male. Five eight, maybe. Probably two-twenty, give or take ten pounds."

Frank looked at his watch, dropped the notepad and fumbled with the photo packet trying to peel it apart, holding the black negative backing in one hand, the black and white image in the other. Ted walked up as Frank gingerly peeled a chemical laden edging from the print.

Schroeder watched with evaporating patience.

Frank confirmed it was a good picture. "You can roll him now."

"You're sure." Schroeder's sarcasm took a moment to set in. It took both Frank and Ted to roll the body to its back, a wide-eyed death stare sliding over the men. Ted stumbled and fell on his ass.

"Never seen a dead man before, have you? Either of you," Schroeder said. Frank took another picture, this time of the bruised and muddy face, one eye swollen shut, a split lip and a gash on his cheek. Wiping the mud from a lightning bolt tattoo on one shoulder, Schroeder shook his head. "Christ almighty," he grumbled. "It's Augie Maxwell."

"Who?" Frank asked.

"Sunset Beach. The taffy lady's boy."

"Sure as shit," Ted said, pointing to Augie's shoulder. "That tattoo. That's his lightning bolt. It's her boy all right."

Manny walked over. "Looks pretty fresh," he said. "Saw a lot of floaters in the great war. Some fresh, some not. He's fresh."

Schroeder studied the wound on Augie's cheek. He told Ted and Frank to stay with the body and take a statement from Mr. Waterman.

"Oh, you won't get any answers from him," Manny said. "Silent as a post."

"Try."

"I've seen this boy," Manny told the chief. "Yesterday morning. We were fishing."

"What time?" They walked together back to the track bed.

"Don't wear a watch anymore. Don't have need of a watch. But if I think about it," Manny said, visibly calculating. "I got home at 11:42 yesterday. I know because I found my bride on the floor writhing in pain and called an ambulance for her."

"What? Is she alright?"

"Had to have surgery."

Lou called out from his chair. "Appendicitis. She'll be fine."

"So, he does speak," Schroeder said.

"Occasionally."

"Did you know him?" Schroeder asked, pointing to Augie.

"Nope. Knew the other one though."

"The other one?"

"Yeah, a carnie. A mooch."

"Do you know his name?"

"Nope. But the kid called him a dog, I think."

"A dog."

Manny squeezed his eyes shut as if his brain hurt.

"It's OK, Manny. Just a couple more questions. How'd they look?"

"What do you mean? How'd they look?"

"Did they look like they'd been in a fight? Were they arguing?"

Manny studied Schroeder's face. "Looked hung over is all. Not that one," he said pointing to Augie. "The other one."

"So, no arguing, then?"

"Nope."

Schroeder stepped to the middle of the path, looking both ways. "Which way did they come from?"

Manny pointed with a wave of his arm. "Came from the dump. Went down there."

Schroeder asked how it was Manny wasn't at the hospital with his wife.

Manny grinned. "She knows better than to interfere with my fishin'."

Schroeder put his hand out to Manny. "Thank you, sir."

Manny grabbed it with a tight grip, giving it a firm shake. "No problem. I'll keep an eye on your boys over there," he said with a grin.

"You do that. And I hope your wife comes home soon."

A loud *Ha* came from Lou's vicinity.

Schroeder waved Frank over. "Give me one of those pictures," he said. "I need one of his face."

Frank came over carefully holding a black and white photo by its edge. It was shiny, still damp, and a little out of focus. "Give it a couple more minutes," he said. "It will get better. Just don't touch it." Schroeder sauntered away, waving the photo in the air, then stuffing it into his shirt pocket. Frank watched, shaking his head.

Schroeder walked the track bed, finding the first of Augie's taffy wrappers. "What the hell were you doing down here?" he muttered. He followed Augie's duck-footed tracks to the trestle bridge, picked up a cigarette butt and noticed two smooth spots in the dirt against the abutment, looking like someone sat there for some time. Just past the hospital he found the scrapes and slide marks of the fight. Some of the slide marks looked like stripes in the dirt. He saw the broken branches up the bluff, and more slide marks. The foliage closer to the path was beaten down. Following the slide marks up the hill he found a worn spot behind a bush. "What the hell?" he muttered. The impressions of smallish footprints sent a wave of dread through him.

When the county sheriff's boat sped up river he turned and saw something dangling from a honeysuckle branch. Stepping into the river, he retrieved Trish's gym shoe and noticed willow branches stripped clean. Back on shore, he found the bloody taffy wrappers and his mind split wide open. If Augie was in a fight, he could deal with it. But kids? Was someone else in trouble somewhere? Was he going to discover another body, maybe a young girl? Diligence made him consider every possibility. Good sense told him to keep those possibilities to himself. He ran back to the squad car.

Within the hour he had county sheriff deputies patrolling the river and all his own officers scouring the shoreline all the way to the lake. "Just covering our bases," he told them all, careful not to ignite rampant speculation by revealing his own fears. "The drowning victim seems to have been in an altercation before he died. Let's make sure we don't have anybody else floating around out there."

With the search in full swing, Schroeder went to find Geneva.

~

Barker sat at the picnic table with Ivan, Harold, and Sam. He cracked open a can of beer. In half an hour the boardwalk was supposed to open. None of them were in any particular hurry to prepare since no one ever came before noon. Ivan glanced over to the trailers where Geneva sat in the same chair she'd spent the night in. They were all waiting for Augie to show up. He'd only ever been out all night a few times before, when he was younger. Until that morning, he had always made his way home by breakfast.

Harold was the first one to see Chief Schroeder step onto the other end of the boardwalk. Ivan and Sam turned to see. Barker didn't budge, except to put the cold can to his swollen jaw. Schroeder's pace was slow and deliberate as he approached.

Without a word, he pulled the Polaroid from his pocket and handed it to Harold. Harold looked at it, hung his head, and handed it back. When he looked to the trailers, Schroeder followed his eye line to Geneva, and walked over to her.

Harold sat silent until Geneva's wailing began. "It's Augie," he finally said. "It was a picture of Augie. The boy's dead." Ivan and Sam gasped.

Barker cocked his head. "What did you say?"

"It's Augie," Harold said. His next words pushed out of his mouth like an accusation. "Looks like he got beat to death."

Harold got up and started walking to Geneva.

Barker's grip on the can tightened until it buckled, foam spilling out.

Geneva's hysterics carried to the men. "I knew it," she cried, "I knew it as soon as he didn't show up for last night's supper there was something terrible happened. All night I've been waitin' for him to show up. Oh my poor Augie!"

Schroeder sat with her but the woman would not be calmed, and when Harold came to her side Geneva rose up, faltered, fell to her knees, then keeled over completely, almost taking Harold down with her. Sam and Ivan jumped up. Barker did not.

"Somebody call an ambulance!" Schroeder hollered. Geneva lay in the gravel, a large gasping hulk of a woman. Sam ran off to Harold's office in the arcade to the only phone they had.

As they waited on the ambulance, Ivan, Harold, and Sam stood around Geneva like guards. Barker hung back at the table.

Ivan asked to see the picture, wincing at the image. "Who'd do that to him?"

Sam looked at it. "Aw hell, he'd never hurt nobody. Nothing more than a overgrown kid."

"No telling what he got into," Ivan said. "Stupid as a post, that boy. How'd he die exactly?"

Schroeder didn't want to speculate. "I never knew him to be prone to get into fights," Schroeder said.

"Augie?" Sam laughed. "Ha! For as big as he was he wouldn't hurt a fly."

Harold was silent, his glance fixed on Barker.

When Schroeder asked about the last time they'd seen him, the other two looked over to Barker, too. "Augie went off with him yesterday. Never came home," Sam said.

"It's not like he didn't know his way around," Ivan said. "His mama used to send him on errands. It's happened before. He's gone up to town with me and wandered off. Always came back."

"Yes. I've driven him home a time or two. Lots of people have," Schroeder said.

Harold sighed and lit a cigarette. "Yeah, he used to not come home sometimes, but it's been a long time. He'd get confused and lost up in town. Usually somebody would point him in the right direction. Been a long time though."

"Years," Sam said.

The discordant whine of the ambulance approached. Schroeder flagged it down and left the driver and the carnies to figure out how to hoist Geneva into it.

Barker started away from the picnic table when Schroeder called out to him.

Barker stood in front of the chief, holding his ribs with scraped knuckles. His face was bruised, his lip cut. When he went to step away, he limped.

"Quite the fight?" Schroeder asked.

"Behind Mak's Tavern last night. What of it?" Barker grumbled.

"Any witnesses?"

"One of your boys broke it up. Go ask him."

"I'll do that. So, where'd you leave Augie yesterday?"

Barker didn't answer.

"I have two witnesses who saw two men matching your description and the deceased down at the jetty yesterday morning."

"I ain't got time for this," Barker said. "I gotta get this shit hole open."

Schroeder stood his ground, crowding Barker. "You know anything about how Augie came to get so beat up?"

Barker cocked his head to get a better look out of his good eye. "You come here, tell us our Augie is dead and then you ask me questions like I got anything to do with it. Takes a lot of nerve." He crossed his arms. "A lot of nerve."

Schroeder slowly shook his head and smiled. "I don't believe I suggested anything like that. Just wondered if you knew anything about it, where he went yesterday, who he might have seen. Just a simple question is all."

Barker ruminated for a moment, his gaze falling to the open swing bridge, its full length aligned with the river. A sailboat lobbed its way past it, sails still tied tight. "He followed me a while. I took a nap. I woke up. He was gone. What he did after he wandered off I can't say."

"You didn't see Augie get in any altercations?"

"A what?"

"A fight?"

"I'd never let anybody hurt that boy. Geneva would have my hide."

"Where were you the rest of the day?"

"Yesterday?"

Schroeder cracked his neck. "Yes. Yesterday."

"Well, I sort of went on a bender if you know what I mean. Never did make it back here till after my fight downtown."

"Where'd you get the booze?"

"What booze?"

Schroeder glared at him.

"Oh, yeah. I stopped in at Casper's. Bought me a flask of whiskey. Found myself a comfy log out back and had me a fine day. A fine day."

"Aside from losing track of Augie."

Barker grumbled some obscenities and wandered off.

"Don't leave town, Mr. Perry."

"Where the fuck would I go if I did?"

~

Slips in Casper's Cove were inhabited mostly by skiffs and runabouts. The only cabin cruisers were old and in various stages of refurbishing, a perpetual money pit. A couple Boston Whalers spent their summers there, one of them being Schroeder's. Two charter boats occupied the deeper slips closest to the river, quick in, quick out. Being a Wednesday, most of the slips were full and it was quiet.

A white-haired man sat in the back of an old Chris-Craft surrounded by cans of varnish and solvents, parts from an engine, boxes of brushes, tools and fishing gear. Schroeder sauntered onto the dock. "Hey, Charlie," he said.

Charlie downed the last of a beer, looked up and asked if Schroeder wanted a Schlitz, knowing full well he wouldn't take it.

"How long you been at this, now?" Schroeder laughed, pointing to the faded teakwood.

"You want that in weeks or years?"

Schroeder asked if he'd seen a man matching Barker's description the day before.

"Oh, you know how it is down here. People meander in and out of here all the time. Just pull up to the store there and walk around, lookin' at us like we're in a zoo."

Schroeder chuckled. "Yeah, they do," he said. "Yeah, they do. So, you didn't notice him?"

"Can't say I did. Casper's in the shop if you want to talk to him."

Schroeder ambled away stopping at his slip, checking the lines and bumpers. Cleats held tight. He stepped aboard and removed a couple twigs that had collected in the bow. He heard a boat motor cut off and saw Casper make his way to the gas pump on the end of the dock. Someone had just pulled in off the river to fill up. Schroeder wandered into the shop, a makeshift parts store, grocery, bait & tackle and gas station, one pump on the water for marine fuel, one out front for cars. A woman stepped in, and paying no attention to the fact he wore a police uniform, asked Schroeder to pump her gas. He told her to go half a mile up into town. She looked annoyed.

"Hey," he said taking a seat on a stool behind the counter. "I don't work here. Go up into town. Go on. Go." He shooed her out like a disobedient child. She left mumbling about never stopping there again as two men came in carrying a bucket.

"Minnows," one said.

"How any," Schroeder asked.

"Two ought to do it."

"You got it." Schroeder took their bucket to the back and half filled it with water from the minnow tank and scooped out a couple dozen minnows. The men left seven bucks on the counter, walked through the store, picked up a pint of whiskey and collected their bucket making some joke about the chief having to take a second job. Schroeder laughed and told them to tell Casper he was waiting.

"We're doing a caldron this weekend," one of them said.

"Chili," the other said.

Schroeder told them if it was George's chili his stomach couldn't take it.

"That's what the beer is for," the men said in unison.

Schroeder took up residence on the stool again. Casper ambled through the back door, the screen smack announcing his arrival. He was a pudgy fellow, somewhere between sixty and eighty. All Schroeder knew was he'd been there for as long as he could recall.

"You sent that lady away?" he asked.

"Yeah."

"Too important are ya, to pump her gas?"

"Yes," Schroeder chuckled. "I suppose I am."

Schroeder asked his questions and all Casper could tell him was that yes, he'd seen Barker the day before and yes, he'd been in the store and like the two men who'd just been through, he bought a pint. "He held up the flask to show me as he walked off and just like always, the money was on the counter. Fifty cents short, but I'll get it next time."

"So, you didn't get a look at him," Schroeder said.

"What do ya mean, a look? I was across the marina when he went in. It was Barker, but that's all I can say. Shows up here every few days. Hiding, I think."

"From what?"

"Life."

Schroeder knocked on the counter and Casper walked him out.

"Been a good week for bass if you've got the time," Casper said. "About a mile out. Finney came in yesterday morning with a couple of five pounders."

"Never been much for night fishing like him."

"To each his own."

Schroeder went to the hospital emergency room, loitering at the nurses' station until a doctor arrived with word on Geneva. She'd suffered a mild heart attack. They'd know more in a few days.

~

Harold stood outside the doorway of the morgue. A young girl, a teenager in a red and white striped dress, asked if she could help him. Her youth and innocence seemed misplaced in this part of the hospital but there she was, juggling an armload of magazines and two vases of flowers.

"Would you like me to find someone to help you?" she asked with an easy smile, one that at this point in her life still came naturally. She had no sense yet what a person standing in that hallway, by that particular doorway, was coping with and this made him smile at her.

"I'm fine, dear," he said. "I'll find my way." She moved on down the hall, her gathered skirt bouncing with her steps, her white Keds squeaking on the linoleum.

A man behind the door heard the exchange and opened it. He was in his forties and had that look about him of a man on task but not particularly engaged. "You looking for the coroner, because he's not here."

Harold asked to see August Maxwell. "He just came in this morning. Drowning. Young man. Large fellow. Early twenties."

"He's here. But I can't let you in without authorization."

"Don't you need someone to identify the body?"

"Yes, but I need the police on hand for that."

"But I need to see the boy. His mother was just brought into emergency. I need to be able to tell her if it's really her boy or not. She needs to know. You understand. You have a mother, don't you?"

"You still have to wait."

The man closed the door. Harold knocked quietly, begging. The door opened.

"Come on in. Just don't touch anything."

Harold only had to see the hulking mass under the white sheet to know it was Augie. He stepped over to the stainless steel table, thinking it was probably too cold and hard for Augie, then thinking what did it matter? Augie wasn't in a position to notice discomfort any more. "Let me see him."

The man pulled the sheet from Augie's head. A bit of dry mud flaked to the table. The cut on his cheek was swollen and the bruise spread from his eye to his jawline. "He's naked!" Harold shouted. "He was naked in the river?"

The man said he'd just stripped the body.

"It's not a body," Harold said. "It's August Maxwell."

The man sighed and stepped back, giving Harold a moment to collect himself.

Harold thought he'd be OK, that he'd be unmoved. But the sight of Augie's lifeless face, the face that always smiled, now swollen and cut; eyes that squeezed into little slits when he was happy, now closed; hands always busy, fidgeting, now motionless under the smooth white shroud. All this shook him beyond measure. Before the man could stop him, Harold lifted the sheet to see the lightning bolt tattoo but saw a massive bruise and then lifted it off farther, revealing his entire torso covered in deep blue bruises. Something welled in Harold, hard and violent. When the man took the sheet from him, Harold almost slugged him, not for anything he'd done, but just because he felt like slugging someone.

Harold left the morgue walking the long hall the candy striper had disappeared down. He found his way to the emergency room and Geneva.

She was awake, sweaty, her hair pasted to her head, her mouth gasping for air. A bottle of clear liquid hung from a stand with a tube connected to a needle in her arm.

"Did you see him? Did you see my boy, Harold?"

"Yes."

"Did he look peaceful?"

Harold had never lied to Geneva. It was something neither of them could tolerate, so for her to ask such a ridiculous thing made him question his answer.

"There's nothing peaceful about death," he finally said, skirting the issue.

"It was him, though, was it? No mistake?"

Though he saw the desperation just beneath her expression, he knew she harbored no delusions of it being a mistake. He pulled a chair from the corner and sat down. The truth would come out sooner than later and he knew he had to tell her the fact of Augie's condition before she heard it somewhere else.

"He was beaten, dear girl. He was roughed up pretty bad."

Geneva made no outward gasp or sound of any kind. "I know it." She looked into Harold's eyes. "I saw the picture. Didn't even look like him anymore." She looked away, bracing herself. "How bad was it?"

Harold hung his head. "Bad."

She began a quiet yowling as the tears welled. A nurse came in and told Harold to leave.

By late afternoon, the search at the river came up empty. The local paper reported the activities were nothing more than routine procedure after finding the drowned man that morning.

CHAPTER FIFTEEN

Schroeder was happier that day to be pulling into his driveway than most any other day. It was only four, but he was exhausted. He wasn't used to dealing with dead bodies, accidental or otherwise, and today there'd been two. Over the years, he'd investigated a handful of deaths, but never one of questionable cause like Augie. And though Aunt Eunice's passing was a relief, she was the last of her generation, a realization that left him all too aware of his own mortality.

Tammy bounded out of the house, pointing to the Dodge Dart in front of his police car.

"Hi, Dad," she said in her typical chipper tone. "Can you pull out? I have to leave." She came up to his car window, asking where his Buick was.

"Servicing," he said.

"I'm sorry about Aunt Eunice," she said.

Schroeder just smiled and told her to have a good time. They jockeyed cars, and Tammy headed out to meet up with friends. As she drove away, they waved, and a bit of his heart went with her, envying her carefree youth.

Grace met Schroeder at the backdoor with a kiss. "Bought some ground round today," she said. "Feel like grilling burgers?" She kissed him. "I'll make some patties while you take your shower," she said, but he stood in the kitchen as if glued to the floor. "Go on," Grace urged. "You'll feel better after a shower."

He half smiled, pulled a beer from the fridge, and stepped outside. "Coals first," he said.

As Schroeder poured charcoal briquettes into his grill, Janey Donahue sat on a swing in her backyard next door, holding a book in her lap, too preoccupied with events at the river the day before to read it. "Hey there, Janey," he hollered over the fence.

His voice startled her, and she looked up to see the chief smiling at her. "Hi," she said back with an automatic smile. She watched him squirt a stream of lighter fluid into his grill.

Over at Finneys', Ben sat at the picnic table reading a book, drinking root beer. He heard Schroeder and looked next door to see him drop a lighted match and step back as the flames leaped up. Looking a little further into the next yard, he could see Janey. She waved at him, drawing Schroeder's attention to Ben. Schroeder nodded. Ben nodded back.

"Your mom take the kids to Jackie's again?" Schroeder asked.

"Yeah," Ben answered. "Aunt Jackie's pool."

Trish arrived and parked her bike in Finneys' driveway. Ben turned to her and saw the bruises on her legs. Harboring the delusion that the chief was ever-vigilant, always alert to his surroundings and events that may or may not be suspicious, Ben quickly threw a Frisbee at Trish, hitting her in the gut, stopping her from stepping into Schroeder's line of sight.

Trish hollered at him.

He told her Linda was waiting inside. She went in.

Preoccupied with the multitude of unsettling events of his day, Schroeder paid little attention to the kids and went inside to shower, hoping to wash the day down the drain.

Next door, up in Linda's bedroom, Linda and Trish sat on one of the beds. The cat sprawled across Linda's lap. Trish's legs dangled over the edge, feet squirming with nervous energy. Her red bruises were blooming deep blue in the centers. Ben came up and leaned against the doorframe, arms crossed, watching them.

Eric's voice came from the stairs. "Hey. It's us."

"In here," Ben said. Eric and Jason came in. Ben closed the door. "Did Schroeder see you?" he asked.

"No. We're not idiots," Jason said.

Ben went to the window, eying the squad car in the drive below. "I think the chief's on to us."

"That's bullshit," Jason argued.

"No. It isn't." Ben pointed to Trish's legs. "Your sister's running around with handprint bruises all over her legs. He saw her."

Trish pointed to Jason and said she was always bruised up. "He beats the crap out of me regularly."

"I do not."

"Yes, you do."

Eric intervened. "No, he doesn't, but she's always covered in bruises."

"She's a klutz," Jason said with a snide grin.

"Am not."

"Are too."

"Stop it!" Ben told them.

"Has anybody said anything about your legs?" Eric asked. "Did Mom?"

"Mom did. This morning. I told her it was Jason, pulling me off the couch because he wanted it all to himself."

"That was quick thinking," Ben said.

"Naw," Eric said. "He does it all the time." He told Linda to get Jane to come over.

Linda looked out the window and dropped to the floor, hiding. Eric and Ben rolled their eyes.

"For crying out loud. Just act natural," Ben said.

"Go on," Eric said. "Call Janey."

Linda knelt down at the window, pretended to smile, and in an almost fake girl voice, called out to Jane. "Hey there, Jane. Wanna come over?" Jane shook her head, and Linda ducked back down. "She isn't coming."

"Make her," Ben said.

Linda called out again, saying she had the new Teen Magazine. Janey didn't budge. "Herman's Hermits are on the cover!" Janey got off her swing.

Eric swore under his breath from the corner.

"What's going on?" Jason asked. "Why's everyone so freaked?"

"You didn't tell him," Ben said.

"Tell me what?"

Ben took a newspaper off a dresser and shoved it at Jason. "That guy you were beating on yesterday?" Eric said. "They pulled his body out of the river this morning."

Jason felt reality slam him upside the head. He let go with a nervous laugh but stopped cold when he saw Ben glaring at him.

"Read it!" Ben demanded. "Read the fucking story!"

Jason skimmed it. "Oh shit," he said.

Janey came into the room, startled to see the boys. Linda motioned her over to the bed, where she sat down between the two girls. She looked at the cat. Linda put it down and whispered something in her ear.

"He's dead?" Janey shouted.

"Be quiet!" Ben told her, closing the window.

Janey started crying, barely squeaking the words out, asking if Jason killed him.

Ben tried to calm the situation. "No. No, Janey. Nobody killed anybody. Jason only got a couple good kicks in. And he ran off. Right, Jason? You said he ran off."

Jason silently panicked, replaying in his head every punch and kick, the blood splatter when he hit him, the falling and getting up, the stumbling into the bush and into the river, the splashing. The stillness.

"Jason!" Eric whisper shouted.

Jason stuffed his hands in his pockets, eyes to the floor. "Yeah. Yeah. The guy ran off. Like I said."

"We didn't kill anybody, got that?" Eric reassured everyone. "We did what we had to do. What the hell were you doing down there anyway?"

Linda spoke up quickly. "Smoking."

"What the hell?" Eric shot back.

"Why down there?" Ben asked.

"You guys talk about the river all the time," Trish told them.

"Yeah," Linda said. "Like you're exploring the Amazon or something."

"Shut. Up. Everybody!" Ben said. "I have to think! We're forgetting something here. What if that other guy killed him?"

The room went silent, then burst with everyone talking at once.

"Why would he want to kill the guy?" Eric asked.

Ben shot back at him. "Oh, jeez, maybe because he saw him try to rape your sister!"

Trish asked Linda what rape meant, but Linda shrugged.

"No one was raping anybody," Eric said.

Ben threw up his hands. "Just what the hell do you think was happening down there?"

"Everybody shut up!" Eric said again.

"Anybody says anything, to anybody ..." Jason threatened. "Just don't even think about it."

"What if Chief Schroeder asks me about ..." Janey asked, sneezing.

"About what? He asks you anything, you lie!" Jason told her.

"I can't lie."

"You're a girl! You come by it naturally," Jason said.

"I do not!" Janey shouted.

"Do too!" Jason shouted back.

Trish told Jason to shut up. So did Linda.

"You shut up!" Jason shouted.

"Everybody shut up!" Eric whispered. "Listen! Everyone settle down. Just act normal. Jane, you don't have to lie, just smile and shrug. He's not going to have any idea about us. Why would he?"

Ben stood in the corner, his arms in a vice grip over his chest.

"Ben, you with us on this?" Eric asked. "We all keep quiet?"

Ben was quick to respond. "Yeah. Absolutely. Not a word, man."

"Girls?"

"Nothing," Linda said. "We say nothing."

Janey's mom called out for her, and Janey opened the window and hollered back she'd be right home.

Eric asked her if she was OK. It was obvious she'd been crying. Linda grabbed the cat and pushed it in Jane's face.

"Hey!" Jane said, pushing it away. "I'm allergic."

Linda just smiled. "Exactly. Your red eyes? From the cat."

"See?" Jason mused. "I told you you're all liars."

The enclave disbanded. Janey and the boys poured down the steps, through the kitchen and out the back door. Ben came back in to find his dad standing in the living room with a cold beer in hand. Phil Finney held his son's gaze for what seemed forever.

"You got a ride home," Ben said.

"Your mother has the car."

This was the extent of their conversation.

~

Next door, Grace followed Schroeder into the backyard with two bottles of beer in hand. He looked at them and laughed. It was Aunt Eunice's cheap stuff. He took one and clinked it against hers. They drank in silent tribute.

"I went over to Eunice's," Grace said. "After they took her out. Thought there might be something of the family to salvage."

"Let me guess. This beer was all you found," Schroeder chuckled, and she nodded.

Grace kissed his cheek and sat down in a lawn chair. He watched her stretch out her plump tan legs and wiggle her painted pink toes in the grass. In his mind, she hadn't changed much from the kid she used to be, and he was suddenly swarmed by memories of Al's bar and living in the Main Street house. The images were so vivid it was like he was present in each moment, leading him to conclude life was moving way too fast. Time was winning. He was losing. "I wouldn't be who I am if it weren't for her," he said. "My entire education can be summed up in what I learned from Al Hightower sitting on that stool behind his bar waiting for her."

Grace sat very still, something she'd always done for him. Even as a kid, when he'd come over to her house, he'd just sit in silence sometimes, working a thing through in his head. Given enough time, he'd often share his thoughts. There was a delicate line between letting him stew and encouraging him to talk.

"Earth to Andrew," Grace said softly after a few minutes passed. She was the only one left who called him by his given name. "How'd the rest of your day go? You know, after you had to contend with two dead bodies."

"And how do you know that?"

"I heard something about it from Sandy. He was leaving Eunice's as I was arriving."

"I wish my men wouldn't talk to you. They're supposed to keep police business to themselves."

"Don't be too hard on him. He was a little, uh, discombobulated, I'd say. I think Eunice and her place was a bit much for him."

Schroeder looked at her, trying to decide how much to share. "You know that theory of threes?" he asked. "The old wives' tale, that bad news always comes in threes?" He checked the coals, now settling to a quiet low flame, and sat back down. "This morning it was Aunt Eunice, who did us all a big favor by dying, and then the drowning at the river." He took a swig of beer, his mind darting between Eunice's vacant stare, the ash lingering on her cigarette, the men scouring the riverbank, Barker's beat-up face, Geneva's screams of grief, the doctor in the hospital, Augie's dead body -- it had been a busy day. He looked up to the sky, at nothing in particular, just an effort to clear the clutter.

"So, what was the third?" Grace finally asked.

"Huh?"

"The third thing."

When he didn't answer, she said she'd go get the patties. As she rose, Schroeder told her there might have been another victim. She sat back down.

"Something happened down there to that poor kid at the river. There was some kind of fight with more than a couple people involved. And, well," he was about to tell her there might have been a young girl involved, but he stopped short. "Nothing to worry about. Just a tough day rattling my brain."

~

Next door, Eric and Jason took off on their bikes together, but Jason cut away, saying he was going back to the river to look for the shoe again. Eric told him to forget it, and Jason skidded to an abrupt stop in the middle of the street.

"That moron is dead, Eric! The shoe! They find that, and they can put the girls there and then us. They'll say we killed him. We're dead. We're fuckin' dead!"

"Every girl in grade school has the same damn shoe. I swear to God, if you go down there, I'll kill you myself. Look. The paper didn't say anything about murder. And that shoe's at the bottom of the river."

"You don't know shit, Eric. I kicked him so hard. He spit blood."

"Couldn't have been that bad if he ran off. You've gotta cool it."

Jason looked at his brother trying to decide how much to say, if he should tell him the truth or just live with it. Before he'd decided, the words just came out. "He didn't run off."

"What? What the hell are you saying?"

"I'm saying I left him there. In the water. I'm saying I think he drowned. Goddamn it, Eric! I think I killed him!"

"Why the fuck didn't you say anything!"

"What difference would it make?"

"What difference would it make if you let that dumb shit drown? Really? You better hope to hell you're wrong! You don't say a word about it. Don't even think about it. And you stay the hell away from the river!" He looked to Jason for some kind of recognition. "Well?"

"Yeah. Not going to the fucking river. Got it." Jason rode off, pedaling hard toward home. Eric rode close behind. His stomach cramped. He skidded to the curb and threw up.

Trish didn't want to leave Linda's room and crawled onto one of the beds, clutching a large stuffed rabbit. Linda told her to go home, and the way she said it, so angry, left no room to argue.

CHAPTER SIXTEEN

"Eric! Hurry up if you want a ride to drivers ed," Rose hollered, purse on her arm, keys in hand. "Eric!" She glanced at Jason, finishing his breakfast at the table, and told him to stay with his sister while she ran errands. Rose was ready to pull out of the drive when Eric finally jumped in the car.

Jason went upstairs.

Trish watched the car turn the corner. Her heart pounded. She looked up at the ceiling, her anger with her brother stronger than her fear of him. It had only been two days since the river, one since they found out Augie died. She had no tools to process the intensity of her emotions. She launched up the stairs, shouting.

"You killed that man! Didn't you! I told you to stop kicking him! He tried to help me! But you kicked and kicked until you killed him!"

Jason charged at her, forcing her backward down the steps. At the bottom, he pushed her into the living room. Trish pushed back hard as she could. He held his ground. She kicked him, and he took it, looking out the window.

"I told you to stop kicking him!" she yelled, kicking him in the shin. "How does that feel? Huh?"

Jason clenched his jaw, breathing hard through his nose, afraid of what he might do to her.

"He wasn't fighting back," she yelled, "and you just kept kicking and kicking!"

When he'd taken all he could, he grabbed her by the shoulders and slammed her onto the couch. She recoiled to a corner.

"I didn't see you running to his rescue!" He almost spat the words at her. "Did you? Did you go see if your dumb, fat friend was OK? No! You killed him just the same as I did! If I'm going to jail, so are you! We all are! Is that what you want?"

"No," she mumbled.

"I didn't hear you! You want to go tell Mom and Dad? Chief Schroeder, maybe? Yeah. You go tell your little story about how you were naked at the river! And how we came along and had to save your ass! And how we killed that dumb shit! See how that flies!" He raised his hands as if he was coming after her but spun away, then turned back to her, fists clenched.

Trish stiffened, unable to take her eyes off his hands. His voice went quiet, giving his words more threat. He glared at her with utter contempt. "You don't get it, you stupid little shit. If you tell one person, just one ..." He hesitated and started to leave the room but stopped. He pointed at her, his hand shaking. "This. Is. All. Your. Fault."

He left the house, something Rose would call him on at dinner.

~

It was late afternoon when Schroeder looked for Geneva's hospital room. Lightning flashed, illuminating the window at the end of the long hall, sending shards of light along the polished linoleum. He found her propped up in bed, thanking a nurse for bringing her a glass of water. The sight of Schroeder brought a flood of tears. The nurse told him she needed her rest. "Five minutes. No more."

"You should have just let me die," Geneva said, pausing to catch her breath. "You find out what happened to my boy yet?"

"I'm sorry, Mrs. Maxwell, I don't know anything yet. We'll keep looking into it. Don't worry. You just rest and get your strength back."

Her tears abated and she adjusted her sheet. "They just brought me a menu for dinner. You believe that? A menu. And that bathroom," she said as her eyes closed. "It's huge."

"They'll take good care of you here." Schroeder said as he left her.

One floor up, he found Manny Horowitz sitting at his wife's bedside and knocked softly on the doorframe. Manny glanced up and waved him in.

"Sorry to see you here, Manny," Schroeder said. "How's she doing?"

"I'm doing just fine," Mrs. Horowitz said, opening her eyes. "Don't know what all the fuss was about."

"You had appendicitis. That's what all the fuss was about," Manny said, irritated with her. "Like I told you, came home yesterday," he said to Schroeder. "After fishin', I found her on the floor writhing in pain."

"I was not writhing. I was ..."

"You were a mess, that's what you were."

"Be nice to me," she said with a little grin. "I just had surgery."

"Yes, my bride, you did."

Schroeder chuckled at the exchange, watching the old man soften under his wife's smile. He walked over to the window to inspect the four-story view. Lightning struck nearby. Dark skies released a torrential downpour. "You called me?" Schroeder asked.

"You called the police, Manny? Why'd you call the police?"

Manny appeared to be at a loss.

"You called the station, Manny. Said you saw something? From this window here?"

"Oh! Yes!" Manny joined him at the window and pointed down to a large hedge.

"Wouldn't have thought much of it, but with the body washing up and all, well."

"Oh, my Lord," Mrs. Horowitz said. "A dead body at the river and my Manny finding it! Horrible business, just horrible."

"Yes, well, certainly unusual for us," Schroeder said. "So, what did you see that you wanted me to know about?"

"It was later in the afternoon. Day before the body landed on the Jetty. I saw a little girl. Down there. Late afternoon. I was alone in here waitin' for them to bring Agnes up from recovery. Was looking out when I saw a girl ride a bike out from behind that big hedge down there. There's a boy with her. A teenager. She rides off. Didn't see anything more because they brought Agnes up."

"I was lucky they got me in," Agnes said. "Had to call the surgeon in."

"Took his sweet time, too," Manny grumbled.

"They fix her up?" Schroeder asked. "The surgery?"

"Yes, yes. She'll be fine in no time. She's a tough old bird," Manny said.

"Who you callin' old?" Agnes sniped.

"About those kids," Schroeder asked. "Can you tell me anything about the girl? Or maybe her bicycle?" Lightning struck again, and thunder broke all around them.

"I don't know."

Agnes was quick to assist. "Well, did it look like Laurie's bike with streamers and a basket? Did it look like that? Laurie's one of our grandkids. Just got her a new bike last year. She's such a cutie."

"He didn't come here to hear about our kids, Agnes." Manny rubbed his head, thinking. "Didn't look like a kid's bike. No streamers."

"And the girl? How old do you think she was?"

Manny looked to Agnes. "Reminded me of Laurie a little bit. Longish hair. About eight or ten, maybe."

"Well, that certainly narrows it down," Agnes said, rolling her eyes.

"It's hard to tell with kids, dear."

"I see," Schroeder said. "Well, in any case, that's very helpful, Mr. Horowitz. I won't bother you anymore. If you think of anything else, just call the station. They'll let me know." Schroeder headed to the door but stopped to rest his hand on the hospital bed. "Thanks again," he said. "You take care, and I hope you get home soon."

"I hope they keep me a while," Agnes said. "I could get used to being waited on."

Schroeder turned in the doorway. "Uh, I'm so sorry, but what did the boy look like?"

"The boy?" Manny said.

"From the bluff."

"I don't know. Teenager. Jeans. Shirt."

"Tall? Short? Hair color?"

"I don't remember. Really. They were wheeling her back in from surgery and …"

"Don't worry about it," Schroeder said.

~

From the hospital, Schroeder went to track down the mayor. Nothing was going to be easy about the exchange. "You need to talk, Abbott?"

The mayor spoke with a disconcerting calm. "Did you know they've called an emergency meeting? It's going to be Sunset Beach or my ass on a skewer. I'm not even sure they care which it is."

Schroeder said nothing.

"You should've told me you broke up a fight with Negroes down there."

The chief shrugged.

"I don't want to hear this shit from the general public, Chief." Abbott yelled. "I need to hear that shit from you!"

"That fight has nothing to do with this." Schroder wasn't used to being second-guessed. He didn't like it and walked out.

That evening was no cooler than it had been at noon, hotter still in the town council meeting chamber. The air conditioning was on the fritz. It was standing room only, angry voices shouting over each other.

"One of those carnies is dead! Who's next? One of our kids?"

"Shut it down!"

"It's the damn Coloreds! They did this!"

"Close Sunset Beach for good! It's the only way to keep them out!"

"Burn that hellhole to the ground!"

"Shut it down before we have to call in the National Guard!"

The mayor banged his gavel so many times the mallet broke off, flying to the front row.

Schroeder sauntered over, picked it up, and handed it back. He turned to face the crowd, seeking out several of them. Silence moved like a wave from front to back.

"You all need to get a grip before somebody does something they regret," he said. "Right now, this fear, this panic? This is more dangerous than anything going on down on the boardwalk. Settle down and let me do my job. Just take a breath." As he walked out the door, shouting again filled the hall.

It was after eleven that night when Schroeder opened the bedroom window wide. A cool breeze lifted the curtains. He stood taking in his neighborhood, the roofs, the trees, dark windows, lit windows. Then he looked down to the Donahue driveway and noticed Jane's bike leaning on the side stoop. It was purple, with purple and white streamers and a big purple basket, everything the bike under the hedge at the bluff was not.

He sat down on the edge of the bed. Grace reached over and touched his back. "Smells like rain again," she said.

"I love that smell," he agreed, lying down next to her. He drew her to him and spoke quietly. "I've got an odd question for you."

She nestled in.

"If something awful," he began, "I mean really horrible, happened to Tammy, do you think we'd know. Even if she didn't say anything?"

"Like what?"

"Anything. You'd know, wouldn't you?"

"Yes. I think we'd both know something wasn't right with her. Why? Do you think something…"

"No, no. Nothing to worry about."

"I'm going to miss her next year."

"Where do you think she'll end up? Western or State?"

"She hasn't decided yet." Grace looked into her husband's eyes. "You're sure everything is OK?"

He smiled and squeezed her. "Yup."

She kissed him and grinned.

"I know that look," he said. "What's a hot number like you doing with a guy like me?"

"Just a sucker for a man in uniform, I guess."

As another storm rumbled in the distance, Andrew and Grace made love.

CHAPTER SEVENTEEN

The news of Augie's death hit Gar hard, hard enough to make him grateful to be retiring in a week's time. He missed the boy's smile, his eagerness, and maybe more than anything, his simple nature. Gar worked in a solitary job because he didn't think too highly of humanity. He thought most people were either outright liars or inadvertent ones. Augie didn't know how to lie. There was always an emptiness when Sunset Beach closed for the season, when Augie wasn't there to wave every morning, to walk with him, to ask him if he had a good night up in his little box. It was such a simple exchange, easily taken for granted, but it endeared the boy to Gar. He loved Augie.

Walking the tracks alone Saturday morning, standing on that broken square of sidewalk, it grated Gar's every nerve knowing Augie had been beaten, that he likely died alone. What little faith he had in mankind before Augie died was entirely lost after. He went home, changed his clothes, and headed down to Casper's. Even his wife knew the only cure for his mood was the river.

He arrived to find Charlie and Casper busy setting up the cauldron. Phil Finney and half a dozen other men were setting up tables. Others were prepping the chili ingredients, cutting hot peppers and onions, unwrapping pounds of Cajun sausage, and opening cans and cans of beans and tomatoes. A quart jar sat amid all this chaos, holding the secret spice mix no one was privy to but the two guys who concocted it.

Gar avoided them all until Casper called out to him. "Suppose we'll see a lot more of you out here soon, eh?"

"That's right," Charlie said. "Joining us retired lot, aren't ya."

"I am," Gar hollered. "Thursday. My last night is next Thursday."

It was only nine in the morning, but the men hoisted a beer to him.

Schroeder sauntered up, about to head out on the lake for a few hours. When he was hit with a barrage of questions about the investigation, men more interested in getting rid of Sunset Beach than the fate of a dead carnie, he walked away and decided to forgo the gathering later.

Gar uncovered his 15' Lyman outboard. She was the most pristine boat at the docks, her golden fir planking buffed to a sheen, her white hull gleaming. Schroeder offered a hand with the ropes and asked how Gar was doing.

"Sad business, Chief. Just too sad. Need to get on the river, clear my mind a bit." He hung his head.

"I hear that. I suppose I'm doing the same thing. Just need to get out to open water."

"Such a sweet kid. Who would do that to him?" Gar pulled the cord to start the motor. "You gonna find him? Whoever did this?"

"Doing my best." Schroeder tossed the bow line.

Gar backed out slowly, his motor puttering through the marina to the river, where he opened her up, the whine of her Evinrude carrying upriver.

~

The Tuesday before Labor Day, a week after Augie's body was discovered, Trish sat alone in her room, alienated from her only friends. Linda and Jane cut her off. She heard her mom take a phone call in the hall and could tell it was Gramps by the way she talked. Her voice was always softer with him, like a child. Suddenly, the door opened.

"You don't want to run out to the cabin, do you?"

An hour later, Trish was strapping on her puffy orange life jacket at the lake, pushing the canoe into the water. Bert drew a circle in the air, indicating she should stay close. She paddled out a bit and practiced turning and backing up, both moves easier than going straight for a solo paddler. Bert started to glaze a loose windowpane.

The sky, overcast all morning, held little threat until it changed hue, turning a dim shade of yellow. Bert didn't bother to turn on the radio. He knew what was coming and shouted to Trish to get back fast. It started to sprinkle.

"Patricia! Get a move on!"

She'd never seen the sky turn so dark so fast. She pushed hard to shore. A siren whined from another lake over. Bert hollered to hurry up. She hit the beach, jumped out, pulled the canoe up onto the grass, and tied it to a post. Bert told her to leave it and get to the cabin. A deep purple mass filled the eastern sky. A stiff wind kicked up as he grabbed her hand, rushing her into the cabin. "Time to head for cover," he shouted. They'd barely gotten to the door when a large branch cracked above them and fell against the screen porch.

Trish stopped to watch trees bending further than she'd ever seen, and her hand slid out of his. Another branch cracked overhead and crashed not far away. "Did you hear me?" Bert shouted, grabbing her arm hard. "Get inside! Stay away from windows!"

"But we always watch storms."

"Not this kind!" He pulled her inside and she stumbled over a box of paperback books, spilling them. She reached to pick them up when he yanked her into the bathroom. When the light switch didn't work, he reached around the corner to the nightstand for a flashlight and turned it on. Pulling the door shut, they hunkered down in the cast iron bathtub. Bert's arms wrapped his granddaughter.as wind pummeled the cabin. Creaking came from the other side of the wall, then loud cracks, and Bert folded himself over Trish, waiting for the worst. There was a crunching sound, scraping, and more cracking as if the cabin was being ripped apart. Glass shattered in the front room, and something pounded a wall, then a heavy thud hit just outside the door. Bert yanked the shower curtain down, draping it over them. The wind roared outside and whistled through the cabin. Things banged about. Something slid along the floor on the other side of the door.

"It's going to be all right," he said. "It's going to be all right."

Bert was the only person in Trish's life who ever hugged her or held her hand or told her things were going to be all right. This was the first time she didn't believe him.

When the silence suddenly hit, it was like going deaf. Bert climbed out and pushed the door open, telling Trish to stay put. He found shattered windows, the bed rain-soaked and littered with glass shards, twigs, and pinecones. In the kitchen, a branch rested in the kitchen sink. Glass littered the stove and floor. The tree had crushed the entire porch, blocking the door. He opened the other door by the fireplace by prying it with a poker. He called for Trish, and she gingerly stepped through debris. She looked to the mantle, and sitting on its perch was his pipe, the only thing undisturbed.

Standing out front, they saw trees down everywhere. Branches and furniture were half submerged in the lake. Somebody's aluminum dock was wrapped around a tree. Bert looked behind him to survey damage to the cottage. The roof appeared intact. The porch could be rebuilt. He considered himself lucky.

Trish looked out to the shore and ran in a panic. The skiff was still there, but not the canoe. She scanned the shoreline and out to the lake but couldn't see it among the other boats that had broken free of their tethers, some of them listing. An irrational panic spun within her. She did not yet recognize this feeling, though it would follow her for years, grabbing hold of her heart for lesser reasons than a lost boat, or a drowned man, or boys beating on a drunk.

When Bert came to her side, she couldn't even look at him. Nearly hysterical, she told him she'd pulled the canoe up high enough. She tied it tight enough. She was sure of it.

"It was a pretty good blow," he said.

"But it's my fault!" she sobbed.

"Nothing's your fault. It was a storm. Probably a tornado." He drew her to him, but her arms did not wrap around him as they usually did. They were folded to her chest, her hands clenched in fists. "It's just a boat, Princess. All that matters is that we're not hurt."

"But I secured it! I know it!" She pushed away.

"Nothing is ever as secure as we think it is," he said, taking her chin in his hand and lifting her sobbing face. "Hey. It's not as bad as all that. Bad things are always going to happen. It's what you do next that counts. You understand?" He held her tight until her erratic breathing stopped and her body relaxed.

Somewhere in his embrace, her panic dissipated as if his body soaked it all up. Her tears stopped. She stepped back and wiped her face.

"Will you help me look for it?" she asked.

He said it sounded like a good plan and then started to laugh. He pointed up. He'd found the canoe intact, lodged in the branches of two white pines.

~

As the storm approached Edgewater, Schroeder half hoped it might be a good enough blow to knock Aunt Eunice's house to the ground, but it had run out of steam by then, and the old bones of the house stood up to what wind there was. Schroeder proposed to the fire chief he burn it as a training exercise. "Beats the hell out of hauling all her crap to the dump," he said.

Two days later, fire crews from three county-wide departments prepared to run drills on Eunice's apartment house. Dozens of people lined the property watching. Trish saw Linda and Janey standing with other kids snug to the cordon rope. She walked toward them, but when Linda saw her, she got the other girls to work their way to another spot.

Schroeder leaned on his squad car behind the gawkers, feeling little more than relief. Out of the corner of his eye, he noticed one of the carnies from Sunset Beach approach Ben, standing alone at the edge of the ravine. A blasting air horn interrupted Schroeder's attention, but only momentarily.

Flames appeared in a back window. Crews ran in, successfully extinguishing it. This exercise was repeated three times. Some in the crowd cheered. Others booed. They wanted a raging inferno.

The fire chief shouted to the crowd, explaining the perils of smoking in bed. He lit a cigarette and instructed one of his men to place it on a mattress in a front bedroom. Nothing happened. Somebody in the crowd shouted to get on with it. Firefighters stood in packs inside and out as the mattress smoldered. The fire chief continued giving instruction on fire prevention and what to do in a fire. Inside the house, one of the firemen nudged things along with lighter fluid, and flames erupted. The whole room lit up. Two firemen bolted out the front door. The crowd cheered.

~

"I got my eye on you."

Ben turned with a start when he heard the gravelly voice behind him.

"Eyes on the fire, boy. Eyes on the fire."

Ben looked at the man's sneering face. The stench was almost overpowering. "What do you want?" Ben asked, more annoyed than scared

"Oh, I want a lot of things," Barker mumbled, cocking his head to the side. "Mostly, what I want right now is for you and your friends to keep your mouths shut." Ben started to walk away, but Barker stepped up and blocked him. "I was never gonna hurt that little girl, ya know."

"Like hell, you weren't."

Thick black smoke roiled out a window.

"Any of you tell anybody about that, and I'll tell them that friend of yours killed Augie, beat him to a pulp and drowned him."

A room in the back of the house filled with flames.

"We didn't kill anybody. Maybe you did. To keep him quiet."

Barker smiled. "Oh," he said, "we all know the truth, don't we? You don't get it. That boy and his mama and me, we go way back. Let's say I tell Miss Geneva you boys killed her only boy. She'll send somebody after you. Probably me. Ain't nowhere you'll be safe."

Commanding shouts rallied firefighters to swarm the house. Some ran inside. Others pulled more water hoses into position.

Ben tried to maintain calm, turning away from Barker. Barker jerked forward again. "Just so you understand me," he said quietly into Ben's ear. "I know where you all live. I know where those girls live, where they go, what they do. You tell a single soul what happened at that river, and …" His unfinished thought hung in the air. "You tell on me …" Barker said, walking away, his voice with a singsong lilt. "I tell on you."

Schroeder watched the entire exchange unfold, not knowing what to make of it. He was about to go to Ben when, like a bomb, the house exploded, blasting out windows. People screamed as debris flew and wood cracked and snapped. Flames roared like a Gemini launch.

Firemen bolted out the front door, flames chasing them and shooting and up the stairway, feeding off Eunice's stacks of newspapers, engulfing the second floor. The crowd ducked, then cheered.

Firefighters scrambled to hose down the surrounding trees before the sky-high flames set the ravine on fire. Schroeder looked around but couldn't see Ben anymore.

CHAPTER EIGHTEEN

Friday of Labor Day weekend, Rose and Trish sweltered in the back seat of the Chevy, waiting. Rose took her hanky, wiping her neck. Eric sat behind the wheel, wiping his sweaty hands on his jeans. Fred stood at the passenger side glaring at Jason, who stood on the back stoop, arms crossed.

"You're coming," Fred barked. "Get in the car."

"Am not," Jason countered and put his hands in his jeans pockets.

"Look, it's not like this is how I want to spend my Labor Day weekend, so just get in and shut up."

Rose smiled through the window, saying if he didn't want to be grounded till Christmas, he'd better get his backside in the car immediately. Jason looked at Fred, at Eric, then demanded to sit in front.

"Get in the back. Now," came Fred's abrupt demand.

Jason went to Rose's side to get in. "Not a chance," she said.

Trish got out so Jason could get in. To the middle.

"Get in," Jason told her.

"Not a chance," she sneered.

"Get in the damn car, both of you," Fred said. "Now."

"I get the window," Trish insisted.

"Trish, dear," Rose urged. "Get back in."

Trish refused.

"Jason, get in the goddamned car," Fred demanded. "You're skating on thin ice as it is."

Jason got in as close to the end as he could and wouldn't budge. Trish pressed her way in, shut the door, and they sat plastered against each other, rivers of sweat between them.

Hot air buffeted through open windows on the drive out. No one spoke except for Fred's continual commentary on Eric's driving. "Slow down. Speed up. Not so close. You don't have to turn your blinker on half a mile before you turn."

Labor Day weekend's schedule was crowded enough with a baseball tournament on Sunday and Monday without spending Saturday cleaning up storm damage at the lake. Fred didn't want to go any more than the boys, but Rose insisted. "My folks aren't getting any younger. The place will be ours someday, so just try to show some interest."

Storm damage along the way was evident in stacks of freshly cut wood sitting next to huge piles of branches on front lawns. Somebody's outbuilding sat mangled in the middle of an alfalfa field. A silo had fallen in on itself. A barn was collapsed to rubble.

They arrived at the cabin to find the broken window sashes had already been replaced and the fallen trees cut and stacked. The carpenter was due in a week to rebuild the porch. The debris in the house was cleaned up, and branches from up and down the shoreline were being piled at the beach, ready to burn. The power was still out, so no pump meant no water. Bert and Myrtle would have been content to be on their own, but the plan had been made, and with phone lines down, there was no way to call off the little invasion. Everyone would just have to pretend to tolerate each other.

"Buckets of water," Bert told them as they climbed out of the car. "You go to the bathroom, you need a bucket of lake water to flush."

"Welcome to paradise," Fred muttered under his breath. Rose gave him a look he knew meant "we're all miserable, so just keep quiet".

The evening passed around a lakefront bonfire fueled by storm debris. It was not a social event so much as a tiresome task prolonging the day's endeavors. Neighbors came and went, keeping watch, stirring the pile to make it burn faster.

~

Jason's hostility was evident to everyone throughout the next day. He was belligerent with Eric, resistant to Rose, and when Trish got too close to where he cleared branches, he shoved her. She fell on a stick, the resulting gouge bleeding through her shirt. Bert sent the boys down the shore to help a neighbor haul a fallen tree out of the water.

When chores were finished, Eric and Jason swam out to the raft. Trish paddled around in the canoe, retrieved from its pine perch undamaged beyond a few new dents. When Fred heard Eric's panicked shouting for Trish, he looked out to the lake and saw the canoe upside down with no sign of his daughter. He hollered to Bert and they both ran, Bert stopping for breath. Fred kicked off his shoes and dove into the water. Bert knelt down to untie the skiff. Myrtle watched and thought she saw him falter and sit down, but he got right back up and into the boat. Fred was halfway to the canoe when he saw Eric push Trish up out of the water. She was coughing and thrashing. Jason had flipped her from underneath, something the kids did to each other, but this time, she had no warning and hit the water on the wrong side of a breath. If not for Eric's quick response, they could have lost her.

Bert got the skiff to them and Fred helped Eric hoist Trish up and in. Eric held onto one side of the boat as his dad climbed in the other. Fred shouted to the raft, to Jason, who was by then standing on it. "Goddamn it, Jason! What the hell were you thinking? Get your ass in to shore! Right now!"

Eric righted the canoe. Bert threw him a line and towed it in. Eric swam to shore and made himself scarce.

Rose and Myrtle watched from halfway between the cabin and shore. Once Trish climbed to the dock and it appeared the crisis was over, Myrtle suggested Rose get a better handle on her children. Rose bolted into the cabin, Myrtle right behind her. "All I'm saying is they're teenagers now, and if you don't corral them soon, God knows what kind of trouble they'll get into. And that Jay Jay. You better put the brakes on that boy before . . ."

"Thank you, Mother, for that little tidbit. I hadn't thought of that before. I'll take it under advisement." She went upstairs to pull the kids' stuff together. "And stop calling him Jay Jay!"

"Don't go getting all snippy with me," Myrtle hollered from the bottom of the steps. "I'm just telling you what it looks like from here."

"Of course you are. You always are." Rose threw Eric's duffel down at her mother's feet.

"Always what?"

"Telling me what it looks like." Rose picked up socks, underwear and shirts from the floor, stuffing them into another duffel. "What everything looks like. If the lawn isn't green enough or the sidewalk isn't perfectly edged, it looks like indigents live there. If my shoes don't match my purse, I look like white trash." She threw another duffel downstairs, clipping her mother's knees. "Well, you know what?" she said, looking down at Myrtle. "I don't care!"

"All I'm saying is if you paid a little more attention to your children . . . "

"God damn it, Mother, just shut up! For once! Just keep your judgments to yourself!"

Bert appeared at the foot of the steps. "What seems to be the problem here?" It was a question that always went unanswered. Myrtle disappeared, and Bert handed the duffels back up to his daughter.

"Nobody's going anywhere," he said. "Jason refuses to come in off the raft. And I won't be responsible for him." He then suggested it was the smarter course of action to do nothing and let him settle down on his own. "He'll come in when he's ready. How about you go sit in the shade with Fred. Take him a beer. Your mother and I will start dinner."

Something about her father's voice, his certitude and calm command, had a way of defusing even her most volatile emotions. Rose came downstairs, skirted her mother in the kitchen, grabbed two beers from the cooler, and went outside.

As Myrtle pulled potato salad from another cooler and collected buns, condiments, and plates, Bert set out half-frozen burgers from the bottom of yet another cooler.

Jason sat on the raft facing away from shore. He didn't have a towel and was getting sunburned, but he didn't budge. He tried to tell himself he hadn't meant to hurt his sister. He'd just done what he always did. But this time, there was something different about it, an indifference. Ever since the fight at the river, he felt splayed open, like every dark thought he ever had was bleeding out into the world, changing him, and it was all her fault. Sitting on the raft after almost drowning his sister, he feared the darkness had taken over.

Fred started to go after Jason. Bert stopped him. "You go out there now, as mad as you are, it will only make things worse." Fred backed down.

Trish changed into dry clothes and undid her braids, pulling her wet hair back into a ponytail. As soon as Rose saw it, she called her to the picnic table, took out the rubber band and began finger combing it to braid it, snagging it, tugging.

"Stop it!"

"Hold still."

"That hurts!"

"It does not!"

When Rose finished, Trish walked back inside, pulled something off the counter, and went to the bathroom.

Rose yelled at her to come back out. Bert told her to let the girl be, and he took the skiff out to Jason.

Fred tossed his empty beer can and swore under his breath. Rose went back inside, choosing her mother's ire over her husband's.

When Bert pulled up to the raft, Jason wouldn't even look at his grandfather.

"You need to get a grip on whatever this is with you," Bert said. There was no anger in his voice. "What you did was reckless and dangerous. You're on a precarious perch right now. It's only a matter of time before you slip up and find yourself in real trouble."

Jason looked him in the eyes. "Maybe I already did." When asked to elaborate, he shrugged and looked away.

"Are you coming with me?"

"Nope."

Bert left him there.

Back on shore, walking past Fred, Bert told him to open his eyes before it was too late. "Something's eating at that boy."

"You think I don't know that?"

The two men had a momentary stare-down before Bert stepped away to put the burgers on the grill. When they were cooked, he rang the dinner bell.

Jason did not budge.

Trish slowly descended the steps, walked through the kitchen past her mother and grandmother, dropping her braids on the floor at their feet secured with rubber bands on both ends. She'd cut them off, leaving her hair cropped short and ragged. Both women stood speechless.

Eric appeared at the picnic table long enough to fill a paper plate before parking himself under a tree.

Trish ate without making eye contact with her parents or grandparents.

Myrtle took a breath to speak, only to have Bert's glare stop her cold.

Rose reached over to touch her daughter's cropped hair, but Trish ducked and slid to the end of the bench.

Fred opened another beer.

Bert left the table without finishing his burger. He grabbed his pipe from the mantel inside and headed out for a walk. Trish followed, the two of them walking in silence as they had countless times before.

Bert lit his pipe, its pungent aroma wafting around them. Smoke from two fires drifted from down the road, people burning branches.

They turned around halfway. By the time they got back to the cabin, dusk overtook the woods, darkness muting definition. Sharp-edged shadows melted. A welcoming glow filled two windows, one in the kitchen and one in the bedroom. Myrtle had lit lanterns and was already in bed reading one of the dog-eared paperbacks she'd rescued from the woods.

In the guest room, Rose climbed into bed, too irritated to sleep.

Fred sat drinking a beer at the picnic table in the dark, staring out at his son, now little more than a dark spot on the raft's dim surface.

Trish went up to her bed in the sleeping attic. Eric was already there, reading a book by flashlight. Before she had a chance to speak, he told her to shut up.

"But what if he comes back in?"

"He won't."

CHAPTER NINETEEN

"Jesus Christ. Who called it in?" Saturday morning, Schroeder stood next to the bed in his boxers, listening to dispatch tell him about a dead body. "Call in County. We may need them down there."

He took a sip of the coffee Grace had just handed him. "Dead body at Sunset Beach," he told her. She gasped a bit, then looked at him with a sad smile that spoke volumes. She pulled a clean uniform from the closet and laid it out for him.

Schroeder drove to Sunset Beach into a barrage of flashing lights. Local and county sheriff units were already clogging the entry to the boardwalk. He hit his horn, and a path cleared for him. The sheriff met him at his car door.

"It's all yours, Chief. We haven't touched a thing. Just here for support."

Schroeder nodded appreciation and slowly climbed out of his car. The sheriff pointed down the boardwalk. "Around back."

Schroeder ambled by Geneva's closed concession stand and slipped between Barker's ball toss booth and the Wicked Flyer ticket booth next to it. He approached Ted and Frank standing guard behind Barker's game booth.

"Not every day you see something like this," Frank said with a bit too much levity. "Damn near got his head cut clean off!" Schroeder's expression did not change, something Ted knew meant "keep your mouth shut".

Schroeder stood in the doorway, unprepared for what he saw. Barker lay on the floor in a congealed pool of blood, his neck cut wide open. A spray of blood spattered the floor all the way to the wall. A bloody handprint smeared the doorframe. One bloody footprint on the floor led out into the gravel. "Tell me none of you stepped in this blood."

"It's clean, Chief," Ted assured him. "No contamination."

Schroeder nodded his satisfaction. "Need to be sure on this stuff."

Though Barker's room was messy, nothing seemed out of place, broken, or knocked about. Even Barker's body appeared not to have disturbed anything when it fell. Schroeder stepped carefully around the blood. He studied Barker's battered face, then stepped out into the sunlight, rubbing the sweat off his brow.

Frank said he thought the taffy lady did it. "Retaliation for the drowning."

"Don't go making assumptions," Schroeder said.

Frank shot back. "You aren't the only one who notices stuff. This guy was the last one to see her son, wasn't he? Down at the river, by the fishing shack?

Manny told me. After you went down the path the day we found him. He said . . ."

Schroeder cut him off. "Keep your theories to yourself."

Frank stepped back, scuffing the gravel.

Schroeder rolled his eyes. "How 'bout you follow that blood trail through the gravel before you destroy it all together."

Frank threw his hands up and walked slowly toward the tracks looking for little bloody bits of stone, until he hit pavement, and the trail disappeared.

"Don't see how Geneva could do this anyway," Schroeder told Ted. "She's still recuperating."

"No, Chief," Ted said. "She's in her stand. But she couldn't pull this off after a heart attack, could she?"

Schroeder surveyed the area from the train depot across to the warehouse at the river. "Never know. No murder weapon yet?"

"Not yet."

"Well, let's enlist a little help and turn this place upside down."

"Maybe destroy it in the process?" Ted joked.

"Wouldn't break my heart." Schroeder pointed to the slick of blood on the floor and the footprint. "Anyway, unless the taffy lady wears Tracksters these days, I think we may have to look somewhere else." He saw Ted's glazed expression. "Running shoes."

Schroeder drew his attention to the smeared handprints. "See if you can pull a useable print and look for more." He called out to Frank. "When you're done over there, I want photographs of everything in here. Everything. Real film. Not those Polaroids." He looked back in at Barker's gaping throat. "Ted, before you do that, I'll get some county boys over here to stand guard. We need to talk to everyone out there. One of them saw something. I want to know what."

"Oh, we have the guy who called it in," Ted said.

Schroeder leered at him. "And you were going to mention this when?"

"Sorry, Chief. It was one of the carnies, Harold. The older guy. Seems pretty reliable."

"I'm going to need more coffee," Schroeder said.

"Want me to get that for you?"

Schroeder chuckled, saying fetching him coffee wasn't in his job description. He was about to make his way between buildings when Gar called out to him. "Just the man I need to see," Schroeder said with some relief. "You're my eyes and ears down here. What can you tell me?"

"Not a damn thing," Gar said. "Not a goddamn thing! Thursday night was my last shift. My replacement was on duty. I just came over to see what all the fuss was about, and I heard about Barker there."

"Of all the times for you to retire," Schroeder said. "This is the worst. You think you can get me in touch with the guy who was on watch?" Gar said he'd hand-deliver the man and re-educate him in the process.

A crowd began to gather at the edge of the boardwalk, gawkers who'd heard sirens all through town. As state troopers arrived, they were enlisted to block off entry. Schroeder looked around until he saw Harold, Sam, and Ivan standing together down the boardwalk. He pointed to Harold and waved him over. Harold made his way slump-shouldered and with a hitch in his step.

"Hell of a way to start a Sunday morning, eh?" Schroeder said to him. "I understand you found the body?"

"No, no. I called it in because the telephone is in my office at the arcade. Ivan found him and . . ."

Before he could finish, Schroeder called Ivan over.

Ivan rolled his eyes and shook his head. Sam shoved him, and he finally made his way to Schroeder. His threadbare dungarees, roomy enough to drape over his beer belly, were held up with only one shoulder strap, the other hanging off the back of his sweat-stained T-shirt. The stink arrived before the man. "I didn't do it," he said. "I didn't slice his head off."

Harold told Ivan to behave.

Schroeder rolled his eyes at Ivan. "OK, but you found him."

"Just answer the man's questions," Harold said.

"Yeah," Ivan said. "Told that guy over there all about it. Told that other guy over there, too."

"And now you're going to tell me."

"Look," Ivan said. "He knew we had work to do this mornin'. Shit to fix. I went to get him, and his door was open, and he was there on the floor dead."

"How'd you know he was dead?"

"Well, all the blood was my first clue," he said with a sneer. "And he was covered in flies. That was a pretty good indication."

Schroeder shrugged. "I suppose it was."

"Harold," Ivan said. "Tell him what you saw."

"Harold," Schroeder said, clearly exasperated. "You saw something?"

Harold was reluctant but finally answered. "I did. Saw a man. Running away."

"What time was that?"

"I don't know. Around five-thirty, maybe. That train come through normal time. Was a while after that. You should be able to tell from that train."

"And what were you doing walking about at that time of morning?"

"My old pal Arthur," he said.

"Arthur?"

"Arthritis. My back, knees, my hands." Harold held up his hands. All the knuckles were swollen and bent. "Gets so bad some nights, it's just easier not to try to sleep. I'm always shooing teenagers out of here."

"Can you describe the man you saw running?"

"Skinny. Not quite six-foot. Ball cap. Hair stuck out from under."

"What color was the hat?"

"Don't know. Those floodlights are yellow, changes the color of things, ya know? Couldn't say for sure. But he looked like that boy who runs the pier every day or so. Reminded me of him."

Schroeder looked hard at both men. He didn't want to hear any more. He wanted it all to go away. He wanted it simple, random. No kids, no locals, just random violence. "Anything you want to add or change?" he finally asked.

"Nope," Harold said, shaking his head. "That about does it."

"And you didn't see anything else, Ivan?"

"Nope. Nothin'."

"You're shuttin' us down, aren't ya," Ivan asked.

The air of disappointment in his voice surprised Schroeder. "Yes, Ivan. I'm shutting it down."

"Fuck all," Ivan shouted, stomping his foot, spinning around. "You hear that, Sam? They're fucking shutting us down!" He continued to shout obscenities all the way down the boardwalk.

"All of you!" Schroeder shouted. "I want all of you at the station this afternoon! Need to get you all fingerprinted and get your stories officially."

"I ain't tellin' you shit again," Ivan yelled.

Schroeder looked over to the concession stand where Geneva was heaving the taffy pulling equipment out of the booth, pulling, pushing, and forcing the cart over an obstruction. It finally broke free and plowed forward onto the boardwalk. Schroeder hollered to her. "Nice to see you've made such a full recovery."

She stopped and leaned on the booth, panting, sweat oozing from every pore, trying to catch her breath. Schroeder walked over.

"Closing up shop then?" he said.

"Well, I assume you're shutting us down, aren't you?" she snapped, gasping. "What's a few less days? It's our last week anyway."

"Did you see anything last night? Anything that could help us with the investigation?"

"No. I was in my trailer. Resting. Doctor said to take it easy. So I was."

Schroeder looked at the cart. "This is taking it easy?"

Geneva shot back. "So what are you saying? I got no one left to help me! First Augie and now Barker? I've got no one left! If it kills me, it kills me. What else am I gonna do?" She pointed to the other officers in the parking lot. "Ask one of them to help me?" She stood upright, wobbled a bit, pushed Schroeder out of her way, and shoved the card down the boardwalk, wheezing. "Get the hell out of my way!"

Schroeder stepped over and took hold of the cart for her. She pointed forward, and they walked. "Some people seem to think you might have something to do with Mr. Perry's death," Schroeder said.

Geneva laughed at such ludicrous formality. "Mister Perry? Don't know I ever heard it said that way. Why would I want him dead? We go back a long ways, Barker and me. Was my boy's best friend."

"Then why would you think he killed your son?"

"What? I never thought that. Barker was mean as hell, but he'd never lay a hand on my Augie. I know that sure as anything." She hesitated for a moment. "Oh, I was angry when you told me my boy was dead. What mother wouldn't be? And he was with Barker that day, but my boy was a wonderer. A trusting soul. Who knows what or who he ran into to end up in the river. All I know is that man dead over there was always good to Augie. Always. My boy loved him."

Schroeder did not appear to doubt or believe. He simply listened the way he used to as a kid in Hightower's bar. Listen without judgment, Al always said. The alcohol brings out all kinds of pain, and there's no telling how much is real or imagined. Eventually, Schroeder applied that logic to just about anything a person said. He believed in the reality of the moment, which isn't always the truth of the day.

"You want suspects?" Geneva asked. "Real suspects? What about that Colored kid he beat up so bad? I bet he came back here and cut him. They're good with knives. The Blacks."

"You let me do my job. And for your own sake, I suggest you keep your ideas to yourself. You keep talking like that, and you'll bring the Feds in on this. Next thing you know, we'll have the National Guard swarming about. I don't think you want that. Do you? Do you want that, Mrs. Maxwell?" His eyes demanded agreement.

"No, Chief," she yielded. "We wouldn't want that."

Schroeder told her to get Herald to take her to the station to make a formal statement. "Don't even think about leaving town."

Engaging the help of the sheriff's department, Schroeder initiated a search for the murder weapon, utilizing state police crowd control. As a few men moved slowly through the dune grass, others spread out, searching every ride, booth, and rollercoaster car. Suddenly, the sky busted loose, and rain came down in a deluge.

The crowd disbursed to their cars but did not leave. Officers continued searching. Schroeder directed the county cops to go two at a time to search the trailers. "You're looking for a drop of blood. In the sinks, drains, towels, clothes. You're looking for a knife. You're looking for anything that might be pertinent."

Geneva sat in the arcade out of the rain, watching what seemed like a swarm of locusts sweep through the park. A dozen men began going booth by booth, combing through decades of cast-off machine parts, moth-eaten stuffed toys, and boxes of debris left over from decades of neglect. They pulled floorboards and tore out walls. Schroeder went through Geneva's concession stand, emptying the freezer, opening every box of hot dogs. He emptied the fridge and every cupboard, finding nothing.

An officer sorting through her taffy cart removed everything to the boardwalk until all that remained was her knife drawer, something Ralph had made for her. Schroeder pulled it out and set it on top. Each knife had a spot carved just for it, and every spot had a knife in place. He motioned for the officer to take it.

Geneva yelled that she needed that back. She was ignored.

Ivan stood in the doorway of his trailer refusing them entry, demanding to see a search warrant. Harold told him to get out of their way. Ivan stepped down and watched two men go inside with wet feet and sopping wet clothes. He listened as his place was ransacked. "That's my home you're tearing apart in there!"

Schroeder went to the trailers, waiting for something to turn up, anything that would put an end to this thing before it had time to fester. A trooper stood in Herald's doorway holding up a leather strop and straight razor. "Don't see any sign of blood," he said.

"Take it."

"And just what the hell am I supposed to shave with," Herald griped.

"Grow a beard," Schroeder said, walking away.

The rain let up to a drizzle. A ruckus by the Wicked Flyer ticket booth drew his attention. Harold, Sam, and Ivan followed.

An angry crowd with hammers and pry bars charged onto the boardwalk, determined to tear the place down. Officers pushed and shoved, trying to hold them back, but they advanced, one man swinging a sledgehammer to the ticket booth, another using a pry bar to dismantle the picket fence around Kiddie Korner. Harold, Sam, and Ivan watched, seeing no point in intervening. There was no coming back from this. There would be no last gasping breath for Sunset Beach. It was dead, little more than a corpse with bones to pick. A state trooper hit his siren, and a dozen officers overpowered the crowd.

Schroeder walked over and stood in front of them, silent, looking at them like a father admonishing misbehaving children. He did not speak until they quieted. "You know this is private property," he said.

Disparate voices called out.

"This place should be condemned!"

"We don't want a Watts riot in our town."

"This has nothing to do with Watts."

"The hell it doesn't!"

A man waving a pry bar over his head hollered out. "I declare this hell hole condemned! Now, let's tear it down!"

Schroeder called out. "Really, Mark? That you back there with that rusty old pry bar? You want me to take you and everyone else down to the station? Because that's what I'm tempted to do. This is a crime scene."

Several cars pulled up and the mayor pushed his way through to the chief, taking a stance next to him. "This will be taken care of," he said. "You have my word on it." The shouting erupted again. Somebody yelled Bull shit!

"This sort of thing takes time," the mayor said.

"What's it going to take, Abbot," somebody yelled. "Two of them murdered already? Who's next? One of us? You?"

Schroeder snapped back hard. "Somebody's gonna get hurt in this rat hole if you keep this up, and then what? Let this mess sort itself out. Go home. Stay away from here." Schroeder looked over to the empty concession stand, then down to the other end of the boardwalk. Geneva sat at the picnic table, watching him. "Look," he said, "it's closed down now. Go home."

"Yeah, but just for the season!" someone hollered.

"There's nothing more you can accomplish," Schroeder insisted. "Go home. Now!"

The group began to spread out and filter off the boardwalk. There were grumbles but no further objections spoken aloud.

"Demorrow!" Schroeder called out. "Come over here."

Merv Demorrow stepped out of a cluster of men and approached the Chief.

"Get control of these people," Schroeder told him, "or I'll haul you in on inciting to riot."

"You can't do that."

"The hell I can't."

Schroeder held his ground until every last one of them pulled out of the parking lot.

CHAPTER TWENTY

A few hours later, Schroeder stood in the morgue alongside Scotty, the coroner, a man who appeared too young for the job. In front of them, on a tall metal table draped in a white plastic sheet, lay Barker's remains. Schroeder uncovered the body to the shoulders.

"Nasty, eh?" said Scotty. "Cut clean through the trachea to the vertebrae. Not easy to do." He flipped on the overhead lights.

"You really ought to keep this place locked up, Scotty."

"It's not like this is a dedicated forensics morgue. Hospital needs access. You do know this is a holiday, don't you? I had to leave a perfectly good game of hoops. Got my ass whipped last week. Was getting even today."

Schroeder offered an insincere smile. "Well, I appreciate you coming in, seeing as how this is a murder investigation and all."

"Yeah, yeah. No mystery here. Cause of death is basic decapitation."

"That's your technical evaluation, is it? I thought you went to med school for this."

"I did," Scotty grinned.

"Your mother thinks you became a coroner instead of a doctor to piss off your father."

"Everything pisses off my father. And I am a doctor."

Schroeder picked up a bag of clothes from a shelf below. "This his stuff?" he asked. "It's evidence. What's it doing here?"

"Ask your guys. Not my responsibility."

Schroeder pulled out Barker's pointed boots. "So these would do some pretty specific damage if you got kicked with them."

"Sure."

"They'd leave a particular imprint."

"Most everything does."

"Do the boots match the bruising you found on August Maxwell?"

"Our floater? No. I don't think so. You can check for yourself." Scotty pulled out a file folder and spread out a bunch of 8 X 10 photographs of Augie's body, placing the close-ups of his torso contusions on top. "Look here. You see that? Those boots didn't cause these bruises. Was something blunt. That one there and this one have stripes."

"Stripes?"

"Yeah."

"What would do that?"

"Don't know. I can look into it if you want."

Schroeder accidentally knocked the file folder to the floor and bent down to retrieve it. He noticed Scotty's shoes – high tops with vertical rubber ridges on the toe.

"Naw," he said. "Don't bother. If it didn't kill him, I'm not interested."

"Fair enough. But there are a couple other things you need to see." Scotty showed him a photo of the gash on Augie's right cheek. "A cut there would have been very bloody. And I'm pretty sure this gash was caused by that guy's ring." He lifted Barker's onyx ring from a stainless steel bowl. "See that? There's a gouge in the gold there. See that sharp edge? There's blood. Lots of blood."

"You put that together yourself?"

"Two carnies dead. Yeah. I took a look."

Schroeder smiled.

"What."

"You've got a knack for this stuff, kid. Forensics."

Schroeder thought for a moment, then took a couple slow mid-air swings, trying to work out what would have resulted in the injury. "Left or right? The ring?"

"Right hand, middle finger."

Schroeder made a fist and swung in slow motion at Scotty, who corrected him. "No. The gouge and blood were on the back side, away from the fingertip. Try backhanding me."

Schroeder took a slow, wide, back-handed swing, stopping just short of Scotty's cheek.

"Yeah. That would do it," Scotty said.

"You're positive he was hit with this ring?" Schroeder asked.

"I'll test it, but I'm betting the blood on the ring is a match."

Schroeder smiled again. "Anything else?"

Scotty lifted the sheet off Barker's torso, revealing a myriad of bruises in a variety of colors. "This guy looks like a punching bag," Scotty said.

"Yeah, well, he pretty much was."

"This massive discoloration here is blood settling in the corpse. These others are indicative of injury. This one here was from the night he died." Scotty pointed to the most prominent bruise on his rib cage, a puffy mound of deep blue the size of a fist. "It's shifted a little, but you get the idea."

"Shifted?"

"Yeah. Dead bodies do that. These green and yellow contusions are probably a week or so old, hard to tell. Sort of depends on his basic overall health, which was pretty horrible. Liver, probably shot. Kidneys, I'm guessing I'll find out they were ready to fail. Heart. Lungs. I'll know more when I cut him open. X-rays show several broken bones and fractures that healed badly. Probably never had them set. Hell, if that blow to his chest had been two inches higher, it would have killed him." He flipped on a light behind an X-ray of Barker's ribs. "See that knob there? A broken rib that never healed properly. A punch just right would have shattered it, perforated his heart and lungs. Game over." He drew Schroeder's attention back to the body.

"Headless here? These old contusions? I'd say he got them the same time as our floater, roughly ten days ago."

"I wish you'd stop calling them names." He watched Scotty pull the sheet back over Barker's head. "You're saying they were in the same fight."

"Sorry. Mr. Maxwell and Mr. Perry. Yeah, I'd say they were in the same fight. Timing would be right."

"And the new injuries to Perry's face? And his rib bruises. Recent."

"Within a few hours before he died. Around one in the morning. Died around five."

"How much strength would it take to cut clean through his neck like that? A lot of force?"

"All depends on the blade. Even with a good swing with a sharp blade, it takes some effort. Whoever did this? They knew what they were doing."

"Why do you say that?"

"It's very neat. Very clean. No blood smear like you'd get if you hesitated or didn't anticipate arterial spray. It's messy business. And cutting through the trachea? Not easy. You can get hung up on it. His carotid, jugular, and trach are almost surgically cut."

"You saying a pro did this?"

"No, I'm not saying that. But it was either a really lucky slash or, well, I don't know what I'm saying, Chief. Not supposed to jump to conclusions. Just supposed to give it to you straight and let you do the jumping." Scotty shrugged. "Oh, one more thing," he said with a hint of embarrassment. "Our floater didn't drown."

Schroeder's eyes narrowed.

"Hey, that's why they call it a preliminary finding," Scotty told him. "He was as good as dead when he hit the water."

"And why am I just now hearing this?"

"It's in the report. Didn't you read it?"

"When did you send it?"

"When did you ask for it?"

Schroeder sighed in exasperation.

"Hey, I'm not being a smart ass. There's protocol. I hang onto this stuff until your office asks for it. I called when I was ready. Talk to your office."

"This report," Schroeder said. "On this guy. I'm asking you now. Get it to me as soon as you have it. The Maxwell report, too. On my desk. ASAP."

"Yes, sir."

Schroeder put Barker's stuff back in the bag and took it with him, stepping back in. "Hey, Scotty. Good work here."

"Be sure to tell my dad. That'll really piss him off."

~

By nine o'clock Sunday morning, the Hudsons had returned home from the lake. Fred was in his easy chair sorting through the Sunday paper with the smell of bacon wafting from the kitchen. Rose walked in, wiping her hands on a towel, saying she'd just heard the news on the radio. "Some guy got his throat slit at Sunset Beach last night."

"What? A local?"

"They said it was somebody named Chesterfield Pearson, Perry, or something like that. Ran one of the game booths." She called for the boys to get into their ball gear. Breakfast would be ready soon.

"First the drowning and now this. It's time they just level the place."

"Lowlife degenerates."

Out on the front stoop, Jason listened through the screen door. "Holy shit."

~

At the same time, Schroeder leaned against his patrol car in River Park on a woodsy stretch of land upriver a few miles from town. From under a dense canopy of Sweetgum trees, he watched a few cars pull up to one of the pavilions and unload balloons, boxes, and coolers. Pouring coffee from a thermos, he hadn't yet taken a sip when Ben appeared, running out of the woods, followed shortly after by a dozen other runners, none of them wearing baseball caps. He waved Ben over, but Ben kept running. "Oh, come on," Schroeder urged. "Let them go. You'll catch up to them."

Ben jogged over to the chief, barely breathing hard. "How many miles?"

"Ten."

"Them too?"

"No. I met up after my first five. What do you want, Chief?"

Schroeder looked down to the imprints in the dirt at Ben's feet. They didn't match the print at Barker's doorway.

"New shoes?"

"I have a few pairs."

"Well, I suppose you go through them, don't you? Ten miles a day."

Ben shrugged. "Not every day." He shook out his arms and said he really wanted to keep running.

Schroeder ignored him. "Haven't seen you running the pier at Sunset Beach recently."

"I run the beach a couple times a week. I like wet sand." He looks down the dirt road at his pack disappearing around a bend. "Don't remember when I ran there last."

"Really? I'd think with your commitment to training, you'd know exactly . . ."

Ben rolled his shoulders and said he should catch up to the others.

"Where's your cap? Don't think I've ever seen you run without it. Why is that, anyway? Why wear a hat when you run in the dark most mornings?"

"Hair."

"Hair?"

"Keeps it out of my eyes. Got a haircut. Don't need it."

"Ah. You did. Looks good." Schroeder glanced off to the river to two men in a skiff, fishing lines in the water.

"Look, man," Ben said. "I gotta run. See you around."

"Yes, go. Sorry to interrupt your rhythm."

Ben took off jogging, lifting a hand when Schroeder hollered out thanks, then upped his pace, but not too much, afraid the chief would get the wrong idea, like he was running away. He had to keep a measured pace, look unfazed, normal, but he could feel the adrenaline pumping through his system, and he wanted to sprint as fast as he could until he made it past the day, the winter, the year, and was at State or U of M, far away from Edgewater. He took a path into the woods. Glancing back to see the chief get in his car, Ben lost his footing and stumbled the same way he'd stumbled in Barker's booth the morning before, slipping in the blood, landing in the thick dark pool of it, the reflex to catch himself, his hand landing in it, sliding, Barker's lifeless stare and the panic that rose so fast he couldn't breathe, and he bolted outside leaving his sticky palm print on the doorjamb as he scrambled away. Now in the brush at River Park, he crawled to his hands and knees and threw up.

Schroeder cruised by the two baseball diamonds being prepped for the Babe Ruth Baseball Tournament. The first game started at 8:30. Families were spilling in from around the county. Eight teams. Two ball diamonds. Winner takes all.

~

By noon, the two-day Baseball Tournament was in full swing. Seventy-four degrees, clear skies, a perfect day except for mutterings everywhere about the murder the night before.

Teenage boys in white-striped uniforms gathered in groups, teams identifiable only by the color of their caps and socks. The small bleachers adjacent to the dugouts were packed with women and children. Men and boys clustered nearby and along the baselines behind families sitting on blankets with picnic baskets and coolers.

The Tigers beat the Yankees in the first morning game and were in the third inning against the Eagles. Jason and Eric's Pirates barely scraped by with a win over the Wildcats. By mid-afternoon in the bottom of the fifth, Pirates were down by three runs against the Cardinals.

Women sitting with Rose were growing frustrated. The Pirates had had a winning season but were doing horribly in the tournament. They wanted Jason pulled out. His pitching alone was about to lose the game.

The announcer's booth doubled as a concession stand where Trish stood in line for a hotdog. The groans from the Pirate bleachers gave her a little smile. If they lost, the day was over. She could go home. If they won, she'd be stuck there till seven or eight and have to return the next day.

Fred stood with other men alongside the dugout. Schroeder wandered up, out of uniform.

"Off duty there, Chief?" one of the men chided. "With two murders to solve?"

Schroeder shrugged.

Fred didn't take his eyes off the game.

Jason threw a wild ball and was about to walk a second batter. Eric was giving him signals from behind the plate, but Jason kept shaking him off.

Schroeder told Fred he'd heard the storm hit pretty hard out at Bert's place.

Jason pitched another ball, almost taking out the batter's knees.

"Yeah," Fred said.

Jason threw another wild ball, and Eric scrambled to catch it, prompting Fred to shout out. "Get your head in the game!" The batter jogged to first base. The runner on first jogged to second, sending the runner on second to third. Eric and the coach went to the mound, talking too quietly to be heard.

"I don't know what Jason's problem is," Fred grumbled. "They should just pull him out. He's not snapping out of this."

With the bases loaded, Eric gave Jason a signal, but Jason shook him off again.

"I don't get it," Fred said, watching Jason pitch another wild ball. "He started the summer out so good."

Jason threw again before Eric was even in position, and the ball went rogue. The batter shot to first. The runner on second made a dash for third. The runner on third made it home. With the bases loaded again, Jason shook off another signal. Eric charged out to the mound, yelling for a time-out.

"What the hell?" Eric yelled at Jason.

Parents started shouting. Kids cheered.

Jason charged off the mound, ramming into his brother. "It's your stupid ass calls!" They both hit the ground hard, wrestling in the dirt, their words illegible. Eric grabbed Jason by the shirt. Both the coach and Fred ran out.

Schroeder remained on the sideline, watching both men try to pull the boys apart. Phil Finney watched from the opposite sideline. Schroeder ventured over to him, feeling what he was about to do could well be the most difficult thing he'd ever done as a cop.

Schroeder knew Phil the way neighbors know each other. Which is to say, they hardly knew each other at all. There was the occasional beer in the backyard, small talk at sporting events, but Phil was a quiet guy, older than Schroeder by four, maybe five years. Grace hadn't gleaned much from Margaret except that Phil was from somewhere in upstate New York, and they met in a little town on Lake Erie. She was fresh out of college, teaching home economics after the war. He taught history. They married, but when Ben came along, they realized his pay alone at that school wouldn't be enough to support a family. Margaret had a sister in Edgewater, so they moved, and Phil started teaching at the high school. When more kids came along, he picked up shifts at the box factory in the summer. Between the two jobs, he supported his wife and six kids. Beyond that, the Finneys were an enigma.

Schroeder stepped up beside Phil as Jason and Eric were escorted off the field. "First year Ben isn't playing, eh?"

Phil grunted and nodded almost imperceptibly.

"I need you to do something for me, Phil."

Phil looked at Schroeder with a vague air of consternation. They were not men accustomed to asking favors of each other.

"I need you to bring Ben into the station this afternoon. Do you know where he is? Think you could make it in an hour?"

Without a shift in expression, Phil asked why, but Schroeder said it was just a formality. A new pitcher took the mound, warming up. The pitch went wide.

"I'll see what I can do," Phil said, walking away.

By this time, Trish was in the back seat of her dad's car, hugging her knees, rocking back and forth. Seeing Jason and Eric rip into each other ignited memories of the river, and she couldn't breathe. All the fear and panic she'd held inside was beginning to escape, bit by bit, at inopportune moments.

CHAPTER TWENTY-ONE

Ben and his father waited in Chief Schroeder's office.

Phil lit a match, lit a cigarette, pinched the match, and put it in his pocket. "Whatever this is," he said, "the truth is all you need."

"You don't know that."

Phil looked hard at his son, seeing something he couldn't work out.

Ben's silence belied the chaos in his head. He rubbed his hands hard on his pants. He could feel the chief standing in the hallway watching him. When Schroeder finally stepped in, closing the door behind him, Ben couldn't look him in the eye.

"Sorry about this, Phil."

Phil looked Schroeder in the eye, then looked at his son, whose eyes were glued to the floor. "Get on with it," he said.

"We're just here to talk, Ben. I just need to …"

Ben shifted in his seat. Schroeder's voice faded away. He tried to shove Barker's empty stare out of his head.

"Ben, you still with me?" Schroeder asked, his tone cautious.

"Yeah."

"I have a witness who puts someone like you at Chesterfield Perry's game booth yesterday morning."

Phil looked hard at the chief, then at his son.

"Could have been anybody," Ben said, trying desperately to be casual. "What makes you think it was me?"

"It's nothing, Ben," Schroeder said it in a manner meant to calm tender nerves. "I know you run down there. That may be all they saw. You on your normal run. But I'm going to ask you to bring in your running shoes."

"Which ones?"

"The ones from yesterday."

Schroeder pulled an inkpad from his desk and laid a fingerprint card in front of Ben.

"We're not doing that," Phil said.

"It's just a formality. I have to do this." He reached for Ben's hand.

Ben looked to his dad.

Phil nodded.

Schroeder took Ben's fingers, one at a time, rolling them on the pad, then to the card. It was as difficult for Schroeder as it was for Ben. When he finished, he waved to an officer in the hall who came and took the card.

"Just talk to me, Ben," Schroeder said, giving him a towel for his hands.

Ben's lungs felt tight, the way they did when he ran in winter. No matter how he rubbed, like Barker's blood, the ink would not come off.

"Did you run down at Sunset Beach yesterday morning?"

"I don't remember if it was Friday or Saturday."

Phil turned his face to Ben. "Look at me," he said. Ben didn't. "Ben, look at me."

Ben finally lifted his eyes to his father and, seeing his calm, took a breath and felt his shoulders release some tightness.

"It was early," Ben said. "Yesterday. Maybe 5:00. 5:30. I don't know."

"That's a little early for you, isn't it? I usually see you coming home when I leave. Around seven."

" I go early sometimes. It's been so hot."

"OK. Why did you go to Mr. Perry's living quarters that morning? Did you have a reason?"

"No more," Phil said.

"What?" Schroeder asked.

"I said no," Phil repeated.

"Dad, it's OK. I was just running. I saw him lying on the floor in the open door."

"You what?" Phil raised his voice.

Ben calculated carefully what to say. The only moment that counted, the only moment that Schroeder was asking about, was Saturday morning, his run, and seeing the body. It was the truth. There didn't need to be any lie except of omission. Cut the story to the bone, he thought, like writing an essay: premise and support. He settled his mind, putting aside everything from the half-naked girls at the river, the fight, Jason killing Augie, Barker's threats at the apartment fire, and all that blood on the floor around the body. None of it was relevant. "I didn't go looking for him. When I run the pier, I take the boardwalk and cut through between the ball toss and the building next to the roller coaster. That's when I saw the door was open. I stopped and looked in and saw his head. I stepped in to get a closer look and saw the blood. Lots of blood, and I stepped in it and slipped, went down, slipped getting up, and ran away."

Phil flicked the hot ash from his cigarette into Schroeder's empty ashtray. He folded the remaining butt and put it in his pocket.

Schroeder asked why Ben hadn't reported it.

"Seriously? He was dead!" Ben allowed the emotion to show. It would help his story. "You may see that sort of thing every day, but I don't!"

An officer appeared in the doorway, catching Schroeder's attention with a simple nod.

"What did you do after you left Sunset Beach?"

Ben didn't answer.

Schroeder waited.

The silence was overwhelming.

"I ran," Ben finally said. "I went home and showered all the blood off. I ran to the dump and burned my shoes in an oil drum. I didn't say anything because of this."

"Because of what?" Phil asked.

"Because of this! I was scared! You. Me. Here! It's my bloody footprint! My bloody prints on the door jam. I didn't want to be a suspect! I could lose any chance of a scholarship."

Leaning forward on his desk, Schroeder asked the one question he did not want to ask. "Ben," he said quietly, "did you have anything to do with Chesterfield Perry's death?"

Ben looked up, his eyes wide. "No! Chief. No. No, I didn't kill anybody!"

"OK," Schroeder said. "Thanks for coming in. I know it wasn't easy. You did good, Ben." He stood up and said Phil and Ben were good to go.

"You're grounded," Phil said on the way out the door.

"No shit," Ben said.

The district attorney waited for Schroeder in the hall, arms tight across his chest. "Well, may not be a confession, but . . ."

Schroeder shut him down. "I cut him loose. We got nothin'."

"It was his print on the doorframe."

"Yeah, and he explained why it was there."

"I don't know," the D. A. argued.

"Did you see his hands? He wasn't in a fight. Somebody beat Perry before they killed him."

"Or somebody else beat him. Then the kid killed him."

"Why on earth would he do that? We're cutting him loose," Schroeder insisted.

The D.A. hesitated. "OK. We'll play this your way for now. I just hope to hell you know what you're doing." He was about to walk away when Officer Sandy walked up, pointing to the other side of the room where two men sat in chairs.

"They say they were in a fight with Barker last night behind a bar."

Schroeder looked at them, closed his eyes, and shook his head. "There, ya want me to arrest them, too?" he asked the D.A..

Ben and Phil walked out of the police station in a daze. "You run. You come home. That's your life now," Phil said. "We're not telling your mother any of this. Now go walk it off. Don't come home till you've got it out of your system." He told his son it was just death and life was full of it.

Ben walked back alleys to the beach. Climbing up dunes into the saw grass, his legs felt like dead weights. He watched families below, playing, laughing. Teenage girls in bathing suits sauntered in ankle-deep water, drawing attention from boys tossing a football.

They don't know shit, he thought. He repeatedly rubbed his hands on his jeans, mindlessly trying to wipe off the rest of the ink. His heart raced, trying to push aside his rage and fear, trying to push out of his mind Barker's gashed neck, blood still oozing out, trying to forget the man's eye that, for an instant, seemed locked with his.

Life as he knew it changed at the river, an incident that by itself might have been processed and absorbed without much effect. But someone died. They should have told someone. Schroeder maybe. He was a good guy, he'd have – would have what? Hauled Jason in on manslaughter charges? Hauled all of them in on charges?

None of them helped the poor dumb bastard in the water. Ben left the river that day, thinking how lucky they'd been. But he was beginning to realize the whole mess had a momentum of its own, like a slow landside capable of destroying everything in its path.

CHAPTER TWENTY-TWO

Tuesday morning found Chief Schroeder sitting on a bench under a large oak along the Grand River on Michigan State's campus. His eyes scanned for a particular face, one he hoped to remember. She saw his wave and slowly approached the tree.

"Helen. I need you to do something for me," he told her.

"How'd you find me?"

"I'm a cop."

She laughed.

An hour later, Helen reappeared with Charles and Deon.

Charles was subdued but distrustful. "You being here isn't a good thing, is it?"

"Can't be too serious," Helen said. "He's not in uniform."

"It's just routine. I have to ask you a few questions," Schroeder said. "Did any one of you happen to tell anyone about your visit to Sunset Beach?"

Deon was quick to jump. "What do you mean? You mean that we were there or that we almost got the shit kicked out of us?"

Charles elbowed him to shut up.

"I wish the hell you'd stop doing that!" Deon sniped.

"Then don't say shit that makes me do it," Charles retaliated. "Anyways, it was me, not you, who got it."

"Well?" Schroeder asked.

Helen said she hadn't told anyone and assured him that Shirley hadn't either. "She still lives at home, and she'd never be allowed out of the house again if they knew."

Schroeder looked at the guys.

"We're not stupid," Charles said.

"Good," Schroeder said. "I also need to know where the four of you were on Labor Day weekend."

"Why?" Deon objected. "What are you going to accuse us of?"

Charles elbowed him again to shut up.

Helen said she was on campus all weekend. "Classes started today. And Shirley was visiting relatives over the weekend. In Chicago."

Charles said they had practice all weekend to get ready for the season opener.

"Specifically, I need to know where you were Saturday morning around four."

"What? Sleeping. In my dorm room," Helen said. Deon and Charles nodded.

"And your roommates would swear to that?"

"Swear? What the hell is this?" Deon balked.

Schroeder suggested he just answer the question.

"Yes," Charles said. "They'd swear to it. I busted my ass in practice and was zoned out on muscle relaxers."

"My roommate wasn't here," Helen said. "She went home for the weekend. Didn't come back until yesterday. But my suite mates saw me, they ..."

Schroeder interrupted her. "What about you, Deon?"

"I was drunk on my ass," Deon said. "Started drinking after practice and spent most of the night throwing up before I passed out on the bathroom floor. I'm sure they'd all be happy to tell you all about it."

"Good," Schroeder said. "Thanks."

"What's this about?" Charles asked.

"Just covering my bases. Don't worry about it. I'm not even on duty now. Just scoping out the school for my daughter."

Helen looked him dead in the eye. "Must have been something real serious for you to have to lie about talking to us."

"Yeah. It is. But you don't need to worry about it."

"But?"

"Believe me, the less you know about it, the better," Schroeder said. "You ready to take UCLA?"

"No sweat," Deon boasted. "Those California boys won't know what hit 'em."

Charles grinned. "They'll be cryin' all the way home."

Schroeder laughed. "Go on," he said. "Back to class. Don't need you flunking out. Need you out there on the field."

CHAPTER TWENTY-THREE

Wednesday morning after Labor Day, Fred sat at the kitchen table, drinking coffee and finishing a plate of scrambled eggs. Rose buttered toast at the counter, hollering to the ceiling for Eric and Jason to hurry up. Trish walked in wearing a new dress, carrying bright new gym shoes and a new binder. Her newly shorn hair had been professionally trimmed into a pixie cut. She ate a few bites of cereal, half a piece of toast, and was out the door, leaving Rose griping about leaving food and dishes on the table.

"Frist day," Fred said. "Cut her some slack, why don't you."

"What does that mean?" Rose shot back.

"Would it kill you to smile at them once in a while? At any of us?" He grabbed his suit jacket from the chair and left Rose standing alone in the middle of the kitchen with her mouth hanging open.

Trish walked to school looking forward to having someplace to be, something to do, a routine again. When she saw Linda in the hall, she ran up to her, but Linda turned away. When Trish grabbed her blouse, Linda yanked free.

"Just leave me alone," Linda barked. Trish watched her walk into Mrs. Jackson's classroom. Janey was already in the room, in the front row.

Mrs. Paulson called from down the hall. "Trish, are you coming?" Mrs. Jackson smiled at Trish as she pulled the door closed.

Trish walked into Mrs. Paulson's room confused, certain there had been an error. When she was assigned a seat in the back, it felt like a punishment. She'd always been mid-room by the window. Mrs. Paulson spent the morning laying out goals of the semester. Having a different teacher in a different room left Trish feeling empty in ways she didn't understand. She didn't want to talk to anyone. During reading period, words on the page were jumbled. Her mind couldn't to focus. Her name was called to go to the front board with three other kids to solve an arithmetic problem, but she didn't hear anything. Three times, her name was called before a girl next to her nudged her. Standing at the board, Trish stared at the numbers stacked one on another, but they seemed like strange symbols. She stood there, her back to the class, her eyes welling, chest pounding, feeling like something terrible was about to happen. Three little words slipped out quietly. "I don't care." When asked to repeat herself, she shouted them. "I don't care!"

Mrs. Paulson was a seasoned teacher. She knew kids get moody. In dealing with outbursts, there's a fine line between escalation and calm. She went to Trish, touched her shoulder, and softly asked her to return to her seat. "We'll try again tomorrow." Trish went to her chair and quietly let the tears fall.

After lunch, three short bursts of the bell announced the first duck and cover drill of the year. Mrs. Paulson stood in front of the class, clapping her hands. "You know the drill. Quietly, please."

When Trish crawled under her desk, Todd grabbed her ankle, and she kicked back fast and hard. It was a reflex, her mind snapping back to Barker's grip when he yanked and flipped her. Her foot split Todd's lip, and they were both sent to the principal's office.

~

In the backyard, under a threatening sky, Rose pulled clothespins from a sheet on the clothesline, burying her face in the freshness of it. She loved that smell, not like anything that came out of the dryer. There was something about sunshine. She snapped the crisp fabric tight and began to fold it repeatedly until it fit into the basket. The phone rang, and she ran to catch it.

"There's been an incident," Mrs. Burns said. "One of the boys grabbed Trish's foot during a duck and cover drill, and she kicked him. In the face. I've sent them both home."

Though it sounded like a simple act of defense, Rose did not challenge the principal's decision to punish Trish. This silence, instead of speaking up for her daughter, grated on her almost as much as the injustice itself. She went back out, grabbing sheets and towels off the line just before the rain hit. At the back door, she saw Todd running into his house down the street. "Of course, it was Todd," she muttered. "The little juvenile delinquent."

Inside, Rose laid out a daisy-patterned pillowcase on the ironing board and shook the BubbleUp bottle repeatedly. She wet her finger on her tongue and tapped it to the iron with a sharp snap. She was pressing out a resistant wrinkle when a rain-soaked Trish walked through the back door. Kicking her shoes off and to the landing, she walked through the kitchen without making eye contact.

"I know," she grumbled. "I'm grounded." She retreated to her bedroom, closing the door quietly.

Rose had no idea what to say, so said nothing. Mothers were supposed to find the right words. They were supposed to know how to berate or comfort their offspring, depending on the circumstance. But she was not in a position to contend with her child's discord. She was a woman going through the motions while some irrational resentment simmered below her placid surface.

Rose turned on the radio, catching the top-of-the-hour report.

"In Edgewater today, the police still have no suspect in custody for the murder of Chesterfield Perry. His body was found over Labor Day weekend at Sunset Beach Amusement Park. The investigation is ongoing. Local officials are seeking legal avenues to demolish the park. Father Merchant..." Rose turned it off, splattered more water, and pressed on.

~

The second week of September saw the little caravan of trailers pull away from Sunset Beach for the last time. The investigation stalled, and Schroeder had no basis to hold Geneva, Harold, Sam, or Ivan.

~

It was the end of September when Schroeder stepped into the mayor's office. "Got the paperwork in order, Abbott?"

"Yeah. Done deal." Abbott Carver was anxious to have the whole mess done and over with. "We pay to demolish the place, and with any luck, we'll own the property by spring. Hell, it took our attorney forever just to figure out where to send the notice. Apparently, taxes get paid by an accountant in Texas, but the owner is somewhere in California."

"Everyone thinks you're stalling," Schroeder said.

"Oh, it's worse than that. They blame me for the murder."

"They don't care about that murder."

"Yes, they do," Abbott insisted.

"No, they don't. It was pretty damn convenient, don't you think? Gave them a good reason to close it down. A nice, irrefutable, palatable reason. Something to take the focus off closing it down just to keep the Coloreds out."

Abbott looked at him, surprised. "I wasn't entirely sure where you landed in all this."

Schroeder cracked his neck. "You're a pretty big State fan, aren't you?"

"Damn right. Tied with U of M last weekend. Should have won."

"You know that kid, the halfback who ran the ball for the tie? Charles Morgan?"

"Hell of a play."

"He's the kid from the fight last summer."

"What the hell?"

"He was down on the boardwalk with friends, nice kids. Somebody picked a fight with him."

"Who'd be stupid enough to pick a fight with him? He's huge."

When Schroeder stayed quiet, Mayor Carver put it together. "Shit. It was Chesterfield Perry, wasn't it?"

"I don't remember who it was."

"Bull shit. Yes, you do. It was Perry. And that makes Morgan the mystery suspect I've been hearing about from every goddamned merchant in town." The mayor shook his head and started to pace. "Shit! This gets out, and this whole town is going up! We'll have every paper in the fucking country poking around here!"

"No," Schroeder said. "He's just a scared kid trying to hang on to a football scholarship. There was no incident report. No paper trail. No reason for him to do anything but steer clear of here. And my officers don't know who the hell they were, so there's nothing to tell. You need to calm down, Abbott. Take a breath. If it was going to blow up, it would have by now. People want it to disappear. Not erupt. No one's going to come forward."

The mayor sat down hard in his chair. He looked to Schroeder, about to say something, but held back.

"Those black kids?" Schroeder said. "They thought they had the right to enjoy themselves like any of the rest of us."

"I'm not so sure I like this town anymore," Abbott said. "Grew up here. Just like you. Things need to change."

"Nobody likes change."

"I do. I like change," Abbott said. "I like progress. Hell, I campaigned on progress."

"Too much progress makes people uneasy," Schroeder said. "They get scared. We're tribal creatures, pack animals. We get threatened by outsiders."

"I had no idea you were so philosophical, Chief."

A moment of calm seemed to arrive, but the mayor couldn't quite let it last. "If they knew about that kid, the fight, they'd pin it on him in a heartbeat."

"Naw. Bad for business. Look, the kid is clean. He and his friends all have good tight alibies."

"You're certain?" Abbott asked.

"Certain."

"Something else is pretty much certain," Abbott said. "I'm losing the election."

"Yeah. I'm afraid you are," Schroeder said on his way out the door.

Drizzle ran into rivers on the squad car's windshield as Schroeder took a long draw from his coffee cup. He turned his collar up, got out, opened the trunk, and pulled out a large placard, a handful of nails, and a hammer. He walked up to the entrance pillar to Sunset Beach and nailed the sign to the post.

"This property condemned. Trespassers will be prosecuted."

~

On Friday, the first of October, a crowd of over two hundred gathered to watch a bulldozer take out Geneva's concession stand and work its way down the boardwalk. The photograph of the dozer plowing through the old dance hall made the front page.

~

At dinner, Jason pulled the chair out from the kitchen table with a start. Fred watched, thinking everything the boy did lately was too abrupt. His words were un-tempered. His eyes were dull one minute and lightning sharp the next. Jason sat down hard, and dragged the metal chair legs hard across the linoleum.

"Jason!" Rose scolded. He did not look at her.

A plate of cold white toast hovered in front of him. "Jason," Fred said. "Take some."

Jason took the plate from his father. Across the table, Trish's chair was empty.

Eric ladled white sauce onto his plate, stirring around in the bowl for any sign of chipped beef. He found some and dropped it to his toast. White toast. White sauce. Tough, salty meat that tasted like blood.

Jason said he wasn't hungry. Rose put a piece of toast on his plate and piled it with the pasty-looking glop. "I'm not hungry," he repeated. Rose pounded the ketchup bottle and poured a river of thick red ketchup onto her plate, red oozing into white until her fork intervened, creating swirls of pink and red around wrinkled shreds of meat.

"I'm not hungry!" Jason shouted and bolted away from the table, charging out the back door.

Rose did not take her eyes from her plate. Eric watched Fred. Fred had run out of words. He'd yelled and counseled and reprimanded and attempted to sympathize, but all these efforts failed to impact Jason's behavior, except possibly to make things worse, yet even that would have implied influence where none existed.

"He'll work through it," Eric said quietly to his father. His words startled Fred. They made him feel small, his son offering him counsel, and seeing the slight tilt of Rose's head, he knew she thought so too.

"Well, he'd better work through whatever it is fast," Rose said. "Because I've had about all I can take."

"May I be excused?" Eric asked. Fred nodded, and Eric left the room. Eric had become the quiet voice of reason, the calmer of nerves, the ever-obedient son attempting to maintain some minuscule semblance of peace. Rose scraped the boys' plates into the trash.

Across town, Trish cut into a roasted carrot at her grandparents' table and dipped it into rich brown gravy. Myrtle made a pot roast, knowing it was her granddaughter's favorite. The weekend before, Myrtle made a blueberry pie, another favorite. The week before that, it was biscuits with honey, all served on the pheasant plates, the dishes she used from September through November, before the Thanksgiving plates came out, and then the Christmas plates.

At Rose's request, Trish spent every Friday and Saturday with her grandparents that fall. There was no explanation offered, and none was required.

Bert and Myrtle's home was elegant with its polished antiques, woven rag carpet, and tapestry upholstery. Exotic knickknacks carefully arranged on custom shelving never had a speck of dust. The beds were always made, corners tucked tight. A cleaning lady came in twice a week, a middle-aged woman from across town who changed and washed the linens, vacuumed, dusted, washed windows and waxed the kitchen floor. Myrtle did her own laundry except what was picked up and delivered weekly by the dry cleaner.

Trish slept in a four-poster bed that was so tall she needed a stool to get up on. She had a private bathroom with little pink seashell soaps. The house sat on the bluff, and her bedroom faced the lake, making it a dark room at night, no streetlight in her face like at home, just the night sky. The tracks ran just below the house, and whenever a train went by, the house vibrated. It wasn't so noticeable in the daytime, but when it woke her in the middle of the night, shaking her bed, her mind went to Sunset Beach, Geneva's cigarette stuck to her lip, her yellow teeth and sour odor, and Augie's silly smile. Then she remembered his cries for help. And the river. And Barker's piercing eye just inches over her face. And everything that came next replayed in varying degrees of detail, some of it distorted as happens sometimes in the twilight between waking and sleeping when reality mingles with imagination. It always took a long, lonely time to slip back into sleep.

~

The Hudson household was better off when Trish was nowhere near Jason. Though he'd always pestered her, something changed over the summer. His jabs were meaner. She seemed fearful. Things got broken. A dinner plate shattered when he threw it in the sink rather than hand it to his sister. The lamp cracked when he threw a pillow at her so hard it knocked the lamp off the table. The glass in a frame of Great Grandfather Hudson broke when Jason slammed a door so hard it fell off the wall.

School nights were manageable to the extent Trish and Jason occupied the same space for so brief a time, ten minutes at the most over dinner. He avoided her in the morning by leaving before she came out. If she walked into the living room, he went upstairs. When she went to bed, he came back down.

It wasn't obvious initially to anyone but Eric because it had been his idea to keep them apart. "If seeing her sets you off, just avoid her." It was a simple solution. Doable. But what was wrong with Jason had no simple solution. Just knowing Trish was in the house, on the planet, breathing, reminded him of the river, of the three or four minutes that turned him into a murderer. That singular memory continually flooded him with fear. It was not fear of being found out or sent to jail so much as fear of his temper, the persistent anger clawing its way to the surface every minute of every day. He was afraid he hated her so much and had to try so hard to hide it that he might be capable of seriously hurting her. Even killing her. The canoe incident was proof. Such thoughts only served to compound his fear, for how does a kid actually consider killing his sister without one day doing it?

Eric had no idea what went on in Jason's head. He couldn't comprehend an interior life so tortuous. Eric's world was visual, tactile. He lived on the surface of things, tidying up loose ends until everything looked as it should. Attempting to tie up Jason's loose ends was getting more and more difficult.

CHAPTER TWENTY-FOUR

One week into November, Abbot Carver was voted out of office.

Two weeks into November, the downtown Christmas decorations went up.

Three weeks into November, the first snow arrived, just a dusting, but enough to get people talking about winter.

Trish got home from school to see her mother crying on the phone. She'd never seen her mother cry. Until that moment, it hadn't crossed her mind that her mother ever cried, but there she was, with mascara stripes on her cheeks.

Rose looked to the girl and snapped. "Go to your room." She glared at her daughter. "Now, Trish! Go!"

Trish went to her doorframe and listened.

"Yes," Rose said to the phone. "I'll be right there. I'll meet you in the emergency room." Trish asked what was wrong, and Rose snapped again. "I said go to your room, and I meant it!"

Trish slammed her door.

It opened hours later when Fred came in to find her still in her school clothes, sitting on her bed, the dull yellow glow of a bedside lamp illuminating her face. Fred stood in silent dismay.

"Is mom still crying?" Trish asked.

"No, honey," he said. "Mom left. She's . . ."

"Can I come out now?" she interrupted. The question shocked him.

"Have you been in here since you got home?" he asked, hoping to hell Rose hadn't left her alone. She nodded.

"Your mother is at the hospital with Grandma. Gramps had another heart attack, sweetie."

Trish looked up at him with a stubborn look of betrayal. "Is it bad?"

"We'll see," he said. "He should be home in a few days."

Trish began to cry, tears spilling forth until she buried her face in her pillow. Fred rested his hand on her shoulder.

"Come out for dinner when you feel up to it. Grilled cheese and tomato soup." He left her there, alone, with the door open, checking on her from time to time, hoping that letting her alone to cry it out was helpful, but afraid maybe he was failing her somehow.

She lay in bed wishing Gramps was holding her the way he did at the lake after the tornado. If he was there now, she'd tell him about the river, about Augie's death, and Jason, that she was afraid Ben killed the other man. She'd spill it all just to stop feeling so twisted up. By the time Fred brought a tray into her, she was over the worst of it.

~

Rose took her mother from the hospital. Bert was stable and sleeping. Myrtle appeared stoic, resigned, but distant. She did not confide her grief to her daughter. She seemed, above all else, indifferent. It was a ruse that Rose could not see through.

Cobbing, Rose yelled at her mother to show some emotion as if tears alone proved love. Myrtle obediently took the sleeping tablet from her daughter, put it on the settee, and told her to go home. There was no hug, no consoling between the women. Rose slammed the front door on her way out.

Fred waited in the kitchen under the glare of the overhead light. The kids were sleeping. He'd spoken with the doctor. He knew Bert had had another heart attack and was resting comfortably. He hadn't heard from Rose since mid-afternoon when she called to tell him there was an emergency. She hadn't called with an update or to say when she'd be home. He'd fed the kids. Watched TV with them. Got them to bed. And he waited, working his way through his second glass of bourbon. He wasn't a big drinker, usually only at parties. But tonight was special. Tonight required fortitude.

Car lights pulled in the drive. He heard the door close and the screen screech open. Rose pushed the back door open, surprised to see Fred sitting at the table, his back to her. He did not rise to meet her. He said nothing.

"Oh dear god," she said, stepping up from the landing. "Dad's had another heart attack!" A fresh wave of tears spilled from swollen eyes.

Fred looked at her without compassion.

"Did you hear me?" she said. "Dad could have died! Where were you? I told you I was going to the hospital!"

"Eight hours, Rose."

"What does that mean?"

"You walked out on your daughter eight hours ago. You left her alone in her room in an empty house. She didn't know where you were or what was happening."

"You know where I was. At the hospital. Then I took Mother home."

"She didn't know, Rose! You just left her. For eight hours, you didn't bother to let me know what was going on."

"I thought you'd come to …"

"You're not a child anymore, Rose. You're a grown woman with responsibilities. You have children who count on you. You can't just go running off as if they don't exist, without a word, and expect me to run to your side and take care of you. I was here taking care of our kids."

"He's my father! What was I supposed to do? Pretend I'm not scared to death of losing him?"

"No. Be scared. But don't forget you have a family who feel the same way about him. And you. You disappeared, and they were scared."

"I can't do anything about that!"

"The hell you can't! Just for once, you could put their feelings ahead of your own. You're not the only one hurting. How can you be so thoughtless?"

Rose stood stunned, eyes wide, quaking.

Fred told her to stop acting like a selfish child. "You're their mother! Start paying attention, or I swear . . ." He stopped himself.

"What if I don't want to be?" It blurted out without benefit of filter. Her face looked as if everything she'd ever wanted to say had finally been said, and she was released from some impossible torment. "What if I don't want to?"

"Oh, that's rich," he said. "Wake your ass up, Rose. Before it's too late."

"You can't talk to me that way."

"It's about time someone did."

Fred went to bed. Rose drove back to her mother's house. Myrtle told her to go home and closed the door on her daughter. Rose went home, undressed, and crawled in bed next to Fred. He rolled his back to her as she did to him.

~

Bert survived another event during the night. He went home a few days later, diminished and weak. Trish wanted to spend the night with them over the weekend like she always did, but Myrtle said no visitors.

A light snow flurry began as Trish left the house Saturday morning. She didn't say where she was going, and Rose didn't ask. She knew. By the time Trish made it the ten blocks to Myrtle and Bert's, her shoes were caked with snow, her hair soaked, and her hands freezing. Myrtle met her at the door.

"Your mother is on the way."

"I want to see him."

"He's sleeping."

Trish slipped out of her coat, dropped it to the floor, and pushed past her grandmother into the hall. "I want to see him."

"By the fireplace," Myrtle said, resigned.

Trish turned down the hall to the front room, to the stone fireplace where a gentle fire flickered behind a black mesh screen. Gramps sat in a wingback chair facing it, wedged into the chair, wrapped in a blanket, sleeping, his head leaning against a wing. He was so pale, so still. So small. He'd always been large in Trish's mind, tall and sturdy. Now, he looked frail, like the chair alone supported his body. She knelt down on the floor, soaking in the warmth of the fire. She touched his knee, and his eyes opened. He took a quick breath as if startled, then smiled when he saw her.

Myrtle watched from across the room. Rose stepped in quietly behind her, still in her car coat.

"It's snowing," Trish told him. "It's beautiful."

Bert's words were breathy. "Yes. It is."

Rose walked over, kissed her father's head, stirred the fire, and put another piece of wood on. "Come on, Patricia," she said. "Time to go home."

Rose never called her Patricia.

Bert reached for Trish's hand and gave it a squeeze.

Trish went home with her mother. "You can't just . . ."

"I know," Trish said, without needing to hear the rest of the reprimand.

Myrtle kept with tradition and hosted Thanksgiving. Bert showed little improvement and did not come to the table. Trish ate on a tray table next to his bed.

~

Rose's Christmas tree crowded the small living room, its colored bulbs doubled by reflection in the front window. She gathered up empty TV dinner trays as Andy Williams began singing, "It's the hap-happiest season of all …" Trish sprawled on the couch, Eric on the floor. Fred folded up tray tables and put them in the closet. He asked Eric if it was a home game next week. "You think the coach will start you?"

"No game. Christmas break."

"Ah, well, that makes sense," Fred said. "It's sneaking up on me a bit too fast this year." He looked out at snow sifting through the corner streetlight. The day's accumulation turned lights strung over bushes into soft glowing clouds. Mrs. Finch's blue spruce, entwined with double the strings of previous years, stood as the focal point of the block. Brilliant lights shone against glass wax stencils of reindeer and holly in every front window except for the Cantors. It felt like a scene out of every daydream he had when he was stationed overseas: healthy kids sprawled around a living room, a nice neighborhood, a job good enough to put food on the table and buy new shoes every year. It was everything he thought he ever wanted. But it was harder to maintain than he ever imagined.

He watched a city plow stop out front. Conner Pitcher came out of the house across the street and climbed in. They turned the corner, heading away toward downtown.

"Must be bad if they're taking Conner back to work," Fred hollered to the kitchen. "The new mayor's making it look like he's on top of things. You watch. He'll have Pitcher call in every plow driver on the payroll."

"Well," Rose called back, "if that's what it takes."

Fred grumbled. "You don't know what you're talking about."

The phone rang. Trish watched her dad answer. It was a quick call, and something about the way he quietly hung up seemed wrong. Rose approached from the kitchen and met him in the hall.

"We have to go to the hospital," he said. "It's your dad."

Fred grabbed their coats from the closet while Rose collected her purse. "What's going on?" Trish asked. Eric looked to his dad for clarification, and Fred shook his head. Fred and Rose rushed out the back door without boots or gloves. "You kids be good," Fred hollered.

Jason came downstairs when he heard the back door close. "What's going on?"

"Something happened to Gramps," Eric said.

"What do you mean?" Trish asked.

Jason taunted her. "He's probably dead!"

Eric told Jason to shut up. Headlights pulled out and away.

"Dead! Dead! Dead!" Jason shouted at Trish, and she flew off the couch and started punching him as hard as she could.

"Shut up! Shut up! Shut up!" she yelled, landing one punch after another. Jason didn't hit back but kept trying to push her off. Eric tried to grab her, and she kicked back, arms and legs flailing wildly. Eric got a good hold on her from behind and pulled her up off her feet, holding her, his arms wrapped around her, squeezing. She kept fighting to get free, but he held fast. The harder she fought, the tighter he squeezed.

"It's OK," he told her almost in a whisper. "It's OK," but her body stiffened. Eric held tight and started to cry. His knees gave out, and they both collapsed to the floor. Trish broke free of him and went to her room.

Jason kicked a Christmas package across the room, opened the front door, and tore out into the snow, running down the middle of the street barefoot in six inches of snow.

Later that night, the wall clock chimed twice as Trish stood in her pajamas in the dark hallway. She peered into the living room at her mom sitting alone on the couch. Rose's wet cheeks shimmered. Trish didn't move, waiting for Rose to say something. There was a moment of doubt, of wondering if her mother would turn her away. Rose reached out a hand and drew her daughter to her.

"He's gone," Rose said quietly.

"I know," Trish said.

Rose put her arm around the girl's shoulders, but it was not enough to reduce the distance between them.

Bert's visitation three days later was well attended by community leaders, friends, and total strangers. James Franklin came up to Myrtle with a story of how Bert gave him a job when no one else would when he got out of jail. Many people told Rose and Fred how grateful they'd been when Bert didn't put them in the street when they came up short on rent.

He kept my boy out of jail.

He got me to sober up twenty years ago.

He loaned me money to start my business when the bank wouldn't.

He convinced me to leave my husband when everyone else pretended not to see the bruises.

These stories from strangers, like gifts, were bestowed with humility and gratefulness. Myrtle saw herself in each of them and wondered how she could have thought she was the only one to have benefited from his generosity of spirit. Still, she did not share her own story. The only one who knew her history was lying in a box at the front of the room.

~

Chief Schroeder and Grace drove through town on their way to a Christmas party. It was only 6:00, but dark as midnight. A high-pressure system had moved in, bringing a blast of cold arctic air. The sky was clear, full of stars. All through town, Christmas lights glowed through a veil of fresh snow. He drove slowly along the bluff, taking in the city's light display, when the flashing lights of a squad car down at Sunset Beach caught his attention. He pulled to the curb on the bluff and watched as a spotlight scanned the snow-covered rubble of what was once the amusement park.

"You want to go down there, don't you?" Grace asked.

He didn't say anything.

"Come on," she urged. "I'll be fine. One of your men is already down there. Let's go see what the fuss is about."

~

A bottle shattered against a bulldozer, and Jason stepped into the spotlight of the squad car. His winter jacket hung open. He wasn't wearing boots. Behind him, what remained of the roller coaster scaffolding stood like a skeleton against the night sky. Officer Ted got out of his car to confront him when the chief's headlights approached from behind.

"Leave me the hell alone," Jason yelled.

"Can't do that," Ted said. "You need to come with me."

Schroeder pulled up in his Buick, more headlights on the boy. He heaved a heavy sigh.

"Isn't that Jason Hudson?" Grace asked.

"Yeah. Yeah, Hun. It is."

He rolled down the window, and Ted leaned in, saw Grace, and smiled. She smiled back and turned up her collar against the chill.

Schroeder told Ted to go back to his rounds.

"You sure, Chief?" Ted asked.

"I got it," Schroeder reiterated. "Keep it off your log, too. Understood?"

"Got it," Ted said. "Off the log."

Ted got back in his squad car and pulled slowly away.

Schroeder rolled the window closed, turned up the heater, and looked at his wife. Grace half smiled. "Nobody ever said this job was easy," she told him.

"I won't be long."

Jason stood his ground in Schroeder's headlights, wobbling a bit, hollering. "Well, Chief Schroeder in the flesh. I'm all yours. Take me in."

"You want to tell me what's going on here, Jason?"

"I know you know I killed him!"

Schroeder felt like his world just slammed to a stop. He looked back to Grace in the car, then to Ted's disappearing taillights, wondering if maybe he'd made a mistake letting him leave. "Who, Jason. Who'd you kill?" He almost choked, just asking the question. "Not Chesterfield Perry?"

Jason leaned forward and threw his hands up. "Who? The ball toss guy? Hell no! It was that half-wit. I beat him to fuckin' death. I saw him fall in the river. I heard him splashing around, and I didn't do anything! I let him fucking drown! I'm a murderer!"

Schroeder couldn't believe it was right in front of him all the time. He heaved a sigh of palpable relief. "So, it was the three of you? Ben and Eric with you in this fight?"

"At the river," Jason said. "We got into a fight. But we had to."

Schroeder hung his head, shook it, and looked back to Jason. "Jesus Christ almighty, Jason. Tell me everything. Start at the beginning." He started to walk toward Jason, stopping when he saw his clenched fists. "Jason," he said as convincingly as possible. "Nobody killed Augie."

"Bullshit!"

Schroeder stepped closer.

Jason took a step back.

Grace watched from the car.

"Not bullshit," Schroeder said. "God's honest truth."

"You don't know shit!"

Schroeder stepped to within a few feet of him and stopped.

"You weren't there!" Jason yelled, his voice cracking.

"Jason. The fight didn't kill him. You didn't kill him."

Jason worked this around a bit, sorting out whether to believe or not. "I don't get it."

"You didn't kill him, Jason. Nobody did. It was an accident." Still seeing no response from Jason, he insisted. "You – didn't – kill – him. He didn't drown. He choked to death, Jason. Sometime that night. Long after the fight. He choked. On a wad of taffy."

"I didn't kill him?" Jason asked. "I didn't kill him." He unclenched his fists. He fell to his knees in the snow. He began to cry, his body quaking, openly bawling, screaming out as if some beast had burst out through his chest and flown off. He keeled backward into the snow.

Schroeder watched, waiting for the emotion to subside before offering a hand up. "Stand up." Jason didn't move. "C'mon, stand up."

Jason rose to his feet, unsteady.

"What started it?" Schroeder asked. "The fight."

"That Barker guy," Jason said. He wanted to stop talking, to just leave the rest out, but it spewed out of him. "He . . . he had my sister pinned down in the bushes."

Nothing the kid could have said would have hit Schroeder harder. He grabbed Jason by the shoulders and squeezed. "What the hell are you saying? All of it! You tell me right now!"

"The girls. They were half naked and . . ."

"Jesus Christ!" Schroeder let go of Jason before he accidentally hurt him. He took a step back. "And you didn't think to tell anyone? Report it? Was she hurt? Did he do anything to her? God damn it, Jason, what were you thinking?"

"We saw Janey going down to the river alone, and Eric and Ben wanted to follow cuz they thought it was sort of weird . . ."

"And?"

"We followed her down the track bed. Linda was screaming up the hill, and Barker was on top of Trish, and she wasn't wearing any clothes, and ..." Jason stopped when the look on Schroeder's face scared him. He'd never seen a man so angry.

"What do you mean they weren't wearing any clothes?"

A sudden gust of wind stirred some snow into a whirlwind.

Schroeder looked back to Grace. He needed equilibrium even she couldn't provide.

"Hell, I don't know. They said they fell in the river or something. Janey went home and washed their clothes?" Jason closed his eyes and weaved, turned, and threw up.

Schroeder told him to eat some snow.

Jason spit the last of it, put a handful of snow in his mouth, and then spit that out.

"Good. Now, keep going, Jason. Tell me what happened."

"Ben knocked the guy off Trish."

"Who?"

"The tall one. Barker. He had her pinned down, and we started kicking him and hitting him. And that other guy, the fat one, his face was all bloody before we got there, and he was shouting, and I hit him, and he ran, and he fell, and I kicked him over and over and over." Tears streamed down his face, overwhelmed by the catharsis of confessing. "He ran into the bushes and into the river, and he splashed a lot and cried out, and then he went all quiet, and the water stopped splashing, and I didn't do anything. I didn't help him. I just let him drown, but you said he didn't drown, so I guess everything's all fine and dandy then, isn't it?" Jason glared at the chief.

The wind came on in earnest, and Grace watched through a wash of whipped-up snow.

Schroeder grabbed Jason by the arm tighter than he should have and dragged him toward the car.

Before stuffing him into the back seat, Schroeder told Jason to be quiet. "You get me? Not one fucking word!"

With Jason ensconced in the back seat, Schroeder got in the front and drove. Grace knew better than to speak. She saw something in her husband's face she'd never seen before. It was something akin to fear. When he drove to the station instead of home, he handed her the keys. "I may be late," he told her. He transferred Jason to a squad car as she pulled away.

~

Across town, Eric lay in his room wondering where Jason had gone off to, what he might do. It felt like the whole world was about to implode. The furnace cut off. The ductwork snapped as it cooled. The silence seemed interminable as he waited. He just didn't know what he had waited for. It wasn't Jason. It was something intangible. Consequence, maybe. He was waiting for the consequences of what they'd done. The screen rattled as a gust of wind hit it.

Eric went downstairs and found his dad at the kitchen table in the dark, the only light filtering in from the back porch light. He turned on the kitchen light.

"Your mother's staying at Grandma's tonight."

"Good. I mean, OK."

"Where's your brother?"

"I don't know. We need to talk, Dad."

Fred watched Eric's hands shake as he got a glass of water. He couldn't figure out why he hadn't asked his kids months ago what was bothering them. He'd told himself it was just puberty issues, problems that would blow over eventually. Now, it felt like he'd missed something serious. He told Eric to sit down. "Just begin. Whatever it is, just get it out."

The furnace kicked on with a click, and Eric listened to the fan groaning through the floor until the fan kicked on, sending cold air billowing up his pant leg. His skin tightened, the hairs on his legs stood on end. He looked at his father, suddenly angry with the man, so pathetic in his ignorance. For months, Eric had been the one keeping Jason in check. How could a father be so blind? He fidgeted with a hangnail on his thumb. "You know about that man who drowned in the river?"

"Last August? Yeah."

"We were there. Jason, Ben, and me..."

"What do you mean, you were there?"

Eric looked at his father with cold eyes. "Janey and Linda, too. And Trish."

Fred sat up straighter. "The girls? What were they doing there?"

Eric slapped his hand on the table against the interruption.

"OK, son. Go on."

Eric's words fell like tacks from his mouth, every point sharper than the next. "We found the girls hiding in their underwear down at the river and..."

"You what?"

Eric could see the veins along his dad's forehead bulge. "They'd been in the river and..."

Fred felt every fiber of his body tense.

"... that Barker guy was on top of Trish..."

"What the hell?" Fred shouted. Not since the war had he felt such primal rage.

Eric kept talking, word after word, because it had to all come out. It had to. "We got him off her, we beat him up, we kicked him and kicked him, and that fat guy, Jason chased him and . . ." Even the rage in his father's eyes could not stop him, and the rest of the tale was told. Every detail. Every move the rest of the summer. But when it came to why Jason almost drowned Trish at the lake, why he was so angry all the time, the words refused.

"What aren't you telling me?" Eric was silent. "You left something out. Eric?" When Eric refused to speak, Fred shouted. "God damn it, Eric!"

Eric almost whispered. "Jason thinks he killed the taffy lady's son. The fat guy. He thinks he killed the fat guy."

Fred could barely catch enough breath to tell Eric to go to his room. When Eric hesitated, Fred shouted "Get the hell up to your room!" Eric ran upstairs afraid of his father for the first time in his life.

Fred stepped outside, sucking cold air into his lungs, hoping to quell the fire, wondering how in the hell his life had gotten so out of control. Thoughts of finding a lawyer for Jason fell away to finding out the thing he most needed to know above all others: Had Patricia been raped. He would have to mask his own vulnerability and fear. He would have to be strong in ways he never imagined. He had to go to the source. When his breathing settled and his hands no longer shook, he went back inside.

He stood in the hall outside his daughter's bedroom. There was light under the door. He opened it. It was only seven, but it had been an exhausting day. Trish was already in pajamas, curled up tight in her blankets, holding a snow globe.

"Gramps gave this to me last year, remember?"

"It's been a rough day, hasn't it?" Fred stepped inside and closed the door. The questions he had were impossible to ask. He sat at the foot of her bed. "I need you to talk to me," he said quietly. Her eyes looked up to him, so sweet, so innocent, so willing.

"What's wrong, Daddy?"

"Eric just told me about the river."

Her eyes widened. She pulled the snow globe tight to her chest.

"It's alright," he said, knowing full well it wasn't ever going to be alright. "I just need to know something. And it's very important. I need you to be completely honest with me. I need you to tell me the truth. Do you understand? The truth."

She nodded.

"Did that man touch you where he shouldn't have?" The words came easier than he thought they would, but waiting on the answer was like a knife in his ribs.

"What do you mean?"

"Just tell me what happened."

"Well, Linda and I were hiding behind a bush . . ." Embarrassment made her hesitate.

"Go on."

"... we were down at the river ..." She talked slowly. "Linda tooted, and the men saw us, and one of them chased us up the hill, and Linda got higher than me, and the man grabbed my feet, and I kicked him really, really hard, and he pulled my legs, but then he let go real fast when he saw my face like he was surprised I was just a kid. I think he said that, that I was just a kid, and that's when Ben hit him, and the fight started."

"That's all that happened to you. He didn't do anything else to you?"

"What do you mean? Like I said, he let go of me right before the boys showed up."

There was a moment when time seemed to stop, when Fred saw the truth in his daughter's eyes and was certain she hadn't been sexually assaulted, and some mechanism clicked within his heart, and time reset.

"So, you weren't hurt," he said.

"I'm OK," she said almost too quietly to hear. "I'm OK," she said again and repeated it over and over until the tears came and she sobbed, "I'm OK. I'm OK," and Fred pulled her into his arms and held her tight, both of them crying. "I'm OK, Daddy. I'm OK," she cried, feeling for the first time since it happened that she was indeed alright. He sat there holding her until they both calmed.

"Is mom coming home?"

"Not tonight."

"Good."

Her response startled him at first, until he realized he felt the same way.

Tucking Trish back in, Fred turned off her light and went upstairs to Eric. "You did good, son. I'm glad you finally told me. It explains a lot about, well, things will be different now." He watched Eric's eyes well up. "That's a lot to carry, isn't it? You can let it go now. I've got it." He watched Eric quickly wipe his face. "What about Jason? What if he killed that man?"

"That's mine to deal with now. You need to let it go."

CHAPTER TWENTY-FIVE

As Fred left the boys' bedroom, lights pulled into the driveway.

"I thought Mom was staying at Grandma's," Eric said.

"She is." Fred looked out and saw the squad car. He headed downstairs and told Eric to stay put.

The wind caught the back door screen as Jason opened it. Icy snow blew in.

"The door, damn it!" Fred shouted and then saw Schroeder behind him, carefully closing the screen and the inner door, checking to see they were secure. Jason took the steps from the landing, leaning on the wall for support.

"I'll talk to you later," Fred told his son. "Leave your coat here and take off those wet shoes." Watching Jason struggle with his coat, Fred finally grabbed it and pulled it off. "Get upstairs!"

Jason tried to kick off his shoes and slipped, falling to his knee before scrambling upstairs, wet shoes and all.

Fred shook the coat and dropped it on a chair before stepping aside for the chief.

The two men stood silently in the kitchen, both somewhat shell-shocked. They'd known each other since junior high. They'd never been friends. Fred ran with a tight circle not known for their generosity. Schroeder had been a loner. No matter how old they got, there was always a trace of who they'd been when they were kids. Old animosities were ancient history, but the outdated resentments and jealousies still ran just below the surface.

"He's drunk?" Fred asked.

"He's drunk."

Neither of them wanted to go further, unsure what the other one knew, but Fred saw something in Schroeder's eyes. In light of what he had just heard from Eric, he had a hunch the chief had just heard something similar from Jason. "How bad is it?" he finally asked.

"I could ask you the same thing."

"How long have you known, Andrew?"

"About half an hour. You?"

"Just now. Eric told me what I hope is all of it."

They sat down at the kitchen table.

"You go first," Fred said.

After hearing Schroeder's version, Fred said the stories aligned. When he heard the boys had nothing to do with Augie's death, he fought back tears.

Schroeder stalled for a moment before asking the hardest question. "I need to know for certain that nothing happened to Patricia, that she wasn't . . . abused. Assaulted. That she wasn't . . ." Schroeder stumbled over the words.

"She fought him off," Fred said. "She's tough. Then the boys got to him. But as near as I can tell, he didn't touch her."

"Thank God for that."

Fred shook his head. "Why the hell am I just now hearing about this from my son instead of you?"

"I knew there were kids involved. There was a girl's gym shoe found at the scene and . . ."

Fred bolted from his chair, and it slammed into the cupboard. "And you didn't investigate further? You didn't figure it out? It was Patricia's shoe. I remember the day she lost it. Her mother griped about it for a whole week!"

Schroeder nodded for Fred to sit back down. He didn't. Schroeder reminded him there were way more kids in town than adults. "How in the hell was I supposed to know who was involved or what even occurred? I kept it out of the papers on purpose. If it came out that two carnies may have come after a little girl? Come on, Fred. You know this town. They'd have burned the place down."

"And I'd have poured on the gasoline!"

"More people might have been hurt or killed. Those kids would have been all over the papers. I was trying to protect them. You. Hell, everyone."

"She's my daughter! If they'd beat that carnie to death right then and there, I'd have had no problem with that."

"Stop talking, Fred."

"What do you mean?"

"Fred, I beg you. Just stop talking."

To that point, Fred had not thought beyond the fight. "What are you trying to say, Andrew? There's more? What the hell is this all about?"

"Where were you all over Labor Day weekend?"

"At the lake. Cleaning up after the storm. Came home Sunday morning. But what. . ."

"Chesterfield Perry."

"What? Who?" It suddenly came to Fred what was happening. "You think my boys had anything to do with the death of that asshole? For Christ's sake, his throat was slit! Who would do that? Kids? Are you out of your fucking mind?"

"No, Fred. I'm not. But my gut says there's more to this. And it's going to be difficult for everyone. Things are going to happen. Things have to happen. We'll all get through it, but I'm just warning you, it won't be easy." Schroeder got up to leave.

"One way or another, I'll have your badge for this."

"No, Fred. You won't."

Schroeder hesitated at the door. "When did you leave for the lake? When you went to clean up."

Fred looked Schroeder hard in the eyes. "I seem to remember you told me to stop talking."

~

Fred walked upstairs slowly, attempting to process all the events he now knew to have torn his family apart, wondering how to comfort a boy who, for weeks, had seen himself capable of murder. But first, he had to swallow his anger.

He walked the length of the hall, focused on what he might say to Jason, but came up empty. The half-man, half-boy lay sprawled on his bed, hiding his face, pretending to sleep.

"I know what happened," Fred said. "Are you OK?"

Jason rolled over. The light was not dim enough to hide the puffy eyes. "Hell of a thing you've been living with. You know the truth now. It's time to move forward. Put it behind you."

Jason tried to be stoic, but another round of tears hit him head-on.

"You'll be fine," Fred said. "We'll all be fine." He looked over to Eric. "Let's just keep this between us for now. Your mother has enough on her plate. You with me on that?" Jason nodded. "As far as your sister . . ."

Jason said he hated her.

"No, you don't. It feels like you do right now. I don't know what to tell you except to give it time. Just give it time."

Fred was halfway down the steps when he heard Jason ask the impossible question.

"Why didn't I help him?"

Fred turned back around with the only words he could find. "That's something you're going to have to figure out on your own."

Jason needed to talk, but Eric told him to shut up. "But it's all better now," Jason insisted. "We're in the clear."

Eric understood there would be consequences beyond the day. Jason just hadn't gotten that far yet.

Fred stood at the living room window, staring out at horizontal snow. He would not sleep the rest of the night. He would keep watch over his family with a ferocity he'd never felt before.

CHAPTER TWENTY-SIX

CHAPTER TWENTY-SIX

It was nearly eight o'clock when Schroeder pulled into the Finneys' driveway in the squad car. He did not engage the lights, but the message was delivered just the same. He was surprised to see Phil come to the door with his coat on. Ben stood behind his father, zipping his jacket. Margaret stood around the corner in the hallway. Linda and the kids were in their rooms.

"Fred called?" Schroeder asked.

"Eric," Ben said.

Phil told Schroeder he'd drive Ben.

Schroeder hung his head. "Can't do that. He's officially a suspect in the death of Chesterfield Lee Perry." These words, spoken quietly, were intended only for Phil, but Margaret heard, and she'd read every word the paper reported about Barker's murder, including a gruesome description of his near decapitation. When she heard Schroeder say Ben and suspect in the same breath, her mind snapped to a vision of her son cutting that man's throat. It was a millisecond of terror she could not disguise. And Ben could not pretend he hadn't seen it.

Phil followed the squad car through what had turned into a full-blown blizzard. There were no other cars on the road. Wind howled as he parked and watched two officers meet the squad car and escort Ben into the police station. He turned off the motor but couldn't make his body get out of the vehicle. There was a knock on his window. It was Chief Schroeder. Phil followed him in where a handful of officers stood around, their expressions a mix of surprise and assumption of guilt. He wanted to punch each and every one of them. As Ben was led down a hall, Schroeder corralled Phil into his office.

"Do you know why we're here?" Schroeder asked. Phil did not answer. "If he'd told the whole story when he was in here last summer, if he'd just . . ." Schroeder clenched his jaw to keep from losing what little composure he'd mustered. "It doesn't look good, Phil."

"Let's just get to this."

"You can call a lawyer if you want to."

"He doesn't need a lawyer."

Ben was led to what seemed a spare office with a wall of file cabinets. He sat in one of two chairs in front of an empty desk. The only thing on the desk was a large ashtray full of butts. When the chief and his father finally stepped in, closing the door behind them, Ben couldn't look either of them in the eye.

Schroeder took his coat off and hung it on a rack in the corner. He motioned for Ben's coat, then Phil's, but they did not comply. They just unzipped and took their gloves off.

Schroeder took a seat behind the desk. Phil remained standing, opened a book of matches, and lit a cigarette. He snuffed the match between his fingers and put it in his pocket.

"Tell me what happened at the river last August," Schroeder said.

Ben looked up to his dad.

"He asked a question," Phil said. "You answer it."

Ben shifted in his seat. "What do you want to know?"

"I want your version of what happened."

Ben spoke slowly without inflection or emotion. When Eric called, he said it was all out in the open, so all he had to do was corroborate. "There was a fight. Eric, Jason, and I got into it with two men from Sunset Beach."

"Sure you wouldn't rather take your jacket off?"

"I'm fine."

"What were you and Patricia doing coming up from the river later that day?"

"What?"

"You were seen. Both of you."

Phil, leaning on a file cabinet, took a long drag. Ben looked over to him. "Just tell the truth, son," he said.

Ben sat silent, averting his eyes.

"Look, Ben," Schroeder said, his patience strained. "I've heard it all. Right now, I need your version of it. Just get it out." He heaved forward over the desk, glaring at him. "Stop dickin' around here, Ben!"

Ben looked Schroeder dead in the eye, stunned.

"What happened down there, Ben? What did you see?" Schroeder's voice got louder, meaner.

Ben finally blurted it out. "We were looking for a gym shoe. It was Trish Hudson's. She lost it when that animal was on top of her, and she couldn't get free. But I stopped him. I got him good!" Ben's hands started shaking, and he pressed them to his jeans, rubbing them slowly back and forth, his torso moving with each stroke, eyes focused on the floor.

Schroeder watched Phil close his eyes and drop his head. In all the years they'd been neighbors, he'd never seen the man express the slightest emotion or heard him string more than a dozen words together. This reaction was new.

"Ben, why were you at Chesterfield Perry's living quarters at 5:00 in the morning on Saturday last Labor Day weekend?"

"I told you already. I was on a run, and I saw the door was open and . . ."

"Ben?" Schroeder was pleading with this terrified kid for the truth. "What were you and Chesterfield Perry arguing about when the fire department burned the apartment house?"

"Nothing. Look! I haven't done anything!" Ben's anger could not be quelled. His words were chosen and delivered with care and defiance. "He told me he was watching all of us. If he even thought we were going to tell the police about what he did to Trisha, he'd tell the police we killed Augie. He started showing up everywhere. He followed me. I saw him watching Linda and Janey at the play park around the corner. I went to see him that morning to tell him to leave us alone. But he was dead. I did not go there to kill him. Hell, I wouldn't even know how to. And if you think I could do that, then just put me away right now because nothing matters anymore!" There were no tears. There was only resignation.

Silent to this point, Phil shouted. "Holy fucking shit, Schroeder. Get all your men together and search my house, the basement, the garage. Anywhere you like. We've got a boat in storage. Search that. Don't even need a warrant. You won't find anything because my son did not kill that reprobate. My son stopped a young girl from being raped. My son is a hero. And nothing you do will change that!" He flicked the embers off his cigarette into the ashtray and put the butt in his pocket.

The room fell silent.

When Schroeder finally said August Maxwell choked to death on a wad of taffy, Ben glared at the chief. "He what?"

"Nobody killed Augie," Schroeder said again.

"Would have been nice to know that!" Ben snapped.

Phil said that was enough. "What happens now?"

"Nothing," Schroeder said, his gaze falling to Ben. "I don't believe you had anything to do with it, but this gives you motive. The D.A. may want to run with it." His glance slid to Phil. Nothing about Phil's placid expression revealed his thoughts. "There are plenty of people in this town with motive,"

Schroeder said in an effort to reassure him. "Ben's just the only one we can place at the scene. Look. That carnie was bad business. But Ben, you should have told me everything the first time I had you in here. Withholding makes you look guilty. I understand you were protecting those girls and yourself. And Jeff from murder charges. You've done a lot of protecting at your own risk. And I honestly don't know how I feel about all that."

Phil lit a cigarette. "I'm taking my boy home."

"Tomorrow morning, you get yourself an attorney. You bring Ben back down here to write his statement. The D.A. will review it and make a determination as to whether there will be a search warrant issued. He'll raise some hell that I didn't get some judge to issue one tonight, but I just don't see the point. I'll deal with him. Come in as early as you can. He's got court in the morning. You don't want to run into him."

Schroeder put on his coat and walked Phil and Ben out to the parking lot. The front had moved through, leaving a peculiar stillness as snow fell in fat lethargic clumps. Ben took off walking, his jacket swinging open. Phil stood by his car, taking a long drag on his cigarette. Both men were silent in a moment rife with conflicting feelings.

Schroeder asked what Phil did in the war, an odd question under the circumstances but not unusual. It was what men said sometimes when nothing else seemed appropriate. "Don't think we've ever talked about it."

Phil's gaze followed Ben out of the parking lot to the street. "Motor pool," he said, dropping his cigarette to the snow and stepping on it. He opened the car door far enough that Schroeder had to step aside. Phil used the wipers to clear the windshield and drove off.

Schroeder looked down at the cigarette butt, then watched Phil pick Ben up half a block away. There would be no search warrant issued. He would see to it. No sixteen-year-old kid could have slit a man's throat as cleanly as it happened.

He walked to the squad car with one more stop to make. Pulling into his driveway, he walked next door to speak with Henry and Alice Donahue.

"Sorry it's so late," he told Henry at their front door. "We need to talk, and I don't want you to hear any of this from others." Henry let him in and told Alice to turn off the TV. Janey curled up into a ball, hugging a pillow. Henry took Schroeder's coat and draped it over a chair, anxious to hear the news without expectation it could possibly directly affect his family.

"You might want to sit for this," Schroeder said, at which point Henry and Alice took up positions on either side of Janey on the couch. Schroeder sat on the edge of an easy chair across from them. "Henry, Alice, were you aware your daughter was down at the river last summer?" To their blank expressions, he explained how the girls had come across two men from Sunset Beach. He left out specifics and kept it sparse.

"Not those men who were murdered, I hope," Alice blurted.

"They weren't both murdered. And I assure you," the chief added quickly, "neither of those deaths had anything to do with the kids." Schroeder watched Alice's eyes widen. "As near as I can piece it together, one of the men was bothering the girls when Ben Finney and the Hudson boys came by."

Henry interrupted. "What do you mean by bothering?"

"He grabbed Trish," Jane mumbled.

"What?" Alice blurted. "He what!"

Schroeder was quick to get on with it. "The boys came by. There was a scuffle." He paused. The words slipped out so easily, even he almost believed them. "That's all there is to it."

Janey shot a fast look at Chief Schroeder.

Henry glared at his daughter. "What do you think you were doing at the river, young lady?"

"Nothing, Daddy."

Henry stood up. "That's it," he said. "You're quitting your job, Alice. My mother obviously isn't up to watching Janey all day." Alice shot back that Henry was overreacting. Schroeder left the house as their argument ramped up.

Janey stopped him at the door, whispering. "What did you mean they weren't both murdered?"

The chief explained how Augie choked on taffy. "None of you were responsible for it." He watched her eyes well. "One day, you'll find a way to remember this in a way that doesn't hurt so much. Let this be is a good start."

He stepped outside. As the door closed behind him, he looked to his house. The Christmas lights were off. It was dark except for a light in the kitchen and Tammy's room.

Standing alone in his darkened living room, Andrew Schroeder had the sense that nothing would be the same in the neighborhood going forward. He would never again feel the peace of it and would think himself naive for every having thought it possible.

CHAPTER TWENTY-SEVEN

The day of the fight at the river, Augie was more scared than he'd ever been in his life. Everything went wrong so fast, all upside down and backwards, and he didn't understand. He didn't know why Barker went after June, or why Barker turned and hit him so hard that he fell down and saw stars, tasted blood, and felt the horrible pain in his face. Then those boys came and started hitting and kicking, and all he could do was curl up and take it. His face hurt. It hurt where they kicked him. He heard screaming and crying and shouting. He tried to get up and run, but he was shoved back down and kicked again, and there was more shouting. When he got to his feet, he ran as fast as he could but he stumbled and was kicked again and scrambled into the bushes, grabbing anything he could. Twigs scratched his face and arms as he crawled deeper into the underbrush until he fell into the river, water washing up over his whole body, sucking him in. He grabbed hard to a branch and hung on, reached for another and hung on, pulling himself up until only his shoulders and head were out of the water, chest heaving, gripping the bush so hard his hands hurt.

He pressed his head against the wet, silty earth, held perfectly still, eyes closed, playing possum. He heard the boys down the path cussing and kicking, and June yelling, but he couldn't look. He thought if he opened his eyes, they'd see him, so he stayed very quiet for a very long time, hanging on, his body in the river. When the noise finally stopped, and he couldn't hear the kids anymore, he stayed put. He heard Barker shuffle past and looked, but seeing the boys were still there, he couldn't call out. Barker did not stop. He kept walking, dragging his feet, holding his ribs. Augie watched the kids walk away, his grip still tight on the willow, his face still lying in river muck.

Long after silence returned, Augie made his way out of the river, his feet slipping in the mud and muck. His face stung where it was cut and swollen. He touched it, causing it to bleed again.

He wiped his bloody hand on his shirt, pulled some wet taffy from his pocket and crammed two pieces into his mouth, dropping the wrappers. The chewy syrupiness reminded him of home, of his mama, and safety.

His ribs ached where he'd been kicked. He rubbed them, but it made it hurt more. He sat down in the dirt and cried. He thought about trying to find his way back but thought maybe those boys were down the track, waiting for him, so he stayed, sure Barker would come back for him. He talked out loud to himself, working out whether he should leave or wait.

The afternoon seemed to go on forever. It was hot. Mosquitoes buzzed Augie's face. He slapped them away. When he finally got up the courage to walk out, he saw one of the boys walking toward him, looking for something in the bushes. Afraid of another beating, Augie climbed back into the bushes to the backside of a large willow trunk. The boy went away but Augie hid there all the rest of the day.

Barker never came back.

If Ben hadn't stopped Trish from looking for her shoe, if she'd gone just a little farther down the path, Augie would have seen her and gone to her. He would have gone home instead of hiding at the river deep into the night.

When wind sifted through willow branches above him, he cringed, imagining them reaching for him. The constant swishing of the leaves sounded like voices. Then, just as he was feeling his most hopeless, the wind blew the clouds away, and the full moon broke through, shining down on him. Geneva had always told him the moon was his friend, and this gave him courage. He climbed out to the track bed. "I'm going home," he said. "I will be brave."

He looked back and forth, deciding to go back toward the bridge, when something fell through the branches above him. He ducked. The wind had knocked something out of the tree onto a branch in a bush just a few feet from shore. It was June's gym shoe, dangling by laces just above the water. Augie knew it was hers. He'd watched it fly off her foot.

"She's gonna want that back," he said. "How's she gonna tell her mama she lost that shoe?"

He paced, looking out at the shoe, needing to get it, to give it back to June, to tell her he was sorry Barker hurt her. He unwrapped a piece of taffy and crammed it into his mouth, then another, and then the last of it, as if it would make him stronger, braver. His mouth was full of the sticky cud as he reached for a branch and stepped into the river, but he slipped with the first step, and the branch he held on to broke, and he gasped, and the thick stew of taffy and saliva slid drawn down his windpipe with searing pain. He tried to find solid ground but only slipped in deeper, falling onto his back, his head going under for an instant. Reaching wildly, he found only thin green willow branches to grab onto, but his weight was too much, and his grasp stripped them clean, sending long, narrow leaves falling like feathers around him. He thrashed about, slipped under, and erupted back to the surface, his last desperate gasp for air so strong it drew the wad of taffy into his trachea, where it would be lodged until the coroner pulled it out.

Augie's last gaze in life fell to the moon as he lay afloat in the river, his body rocking in the residual turbulence of his struggle. Soon, the stillness of the water returned, and the moon disappeared behind a cloud as if to grieve the young man whose buoyant body lay snagged in the lonely embrace of a thicket, his lightning bolt tattoo occasionally bobbing in and out of the water. In the morning, the wind stepped in, broke him free, and the river delivered him gently to the jetty to be discovered.

CHAPTER TWENTY-EIGHT

Though it was snowing at a rate of an inch an hour, Bert's funeral was well attended. After the internment, Rose drove her mother home, and Fred took the kids there. Myrtle and Rose were hosting a light lunch for close friends. The boys went around to the back door, to the basement rec room. Walking in the front with her dad, Trish couldn't make sense of things. All the Christmas decorations were still up. Myrtle went all out at the holidays with elegant garlands draping doorways, little birds with real feathers wired onto boughs of fir greens, brilliant red glass bobbles dangling, twists of holly berries, and glittered pine cones. Every surface held some gorgeous display. Trish had helped arrange the hand-painted crèche figures, brought home by her grandparents from a trip to Spain. She expected it would all be packed away, shoved into a room out of sight. It was too festive for death.

Her dad's attention was drawn down the hall, leaving Trish vulnerable to Myrtle's friends, women who wore too much perfume, who assumed a young girl would want to be buried in their bosom in the grip of fat arms, listening to platitudes.

"Poor, poor girl. He loved you so much."

"You were so lucky to have him as long as you did. I never knew my own grandfather."

"Your grandmother is going to need you to visit her every day for a while."

"We're all counting on you to help your grandmother through this."

She broke free from Mrs. Sexton, making her way to the living room, passing a table of angels resting on clouds of spun glass under a large upside down brandy snifter. She dodged Mrs. Wilcox, making her way to the dining room where the table and sideboard were end-to-end food, silver platters, silver and crystal candle sticks with long red tapers, and in the middle, a small artificial tree chock full of tiny lights and miniature fake fruits looking like they'd been rolled in sugar. From behind her, Trish heard a familiar rattling of a heavily laden charm bracelet. She slipped between people, narrowly escaping the grip of Mrs. Gast, a well-meaning woman, but she and all the rest all wanted something from her, some sign they'd given comfort when they only caused irritation. From the kitchen, Trish heard the boys playing ping pong in the basement, its clacking and smacking rising up the stairwell.

Myrtle busied herself, pulling little puff pastries from the oven. "Watch out, Dear," she said as if it were just one of her cocktail parties. "This is hot." Staying busy was her way of avoiding the gauntlet.

Trish wove back through the crowd to the lake room with the vaulted ceiling overlooking Lake Michigan where the Christmas tree stood, a twelve-footer this year, all lit up, packed with hundreds of ornaments, all beautiful, elegant, and tasteful. In the corner on a small table by the plant stand, an ornate wooden box held greens laced with tiny white lights, drenched in jewels, earrings, broaches, strings of pearls and glass beads. Nothing should be so beautiful when she felt so sad.

She heard a familiar voice from behind the tree, a man's deep, raspy voice. "Doesn't make much sense, does it, girl? Like nothing's changed." It was Mr. Carley, Gramps' fishing buddy. She took one look at him and burst into tears. Turning to run, she was scooped up by her father, who carried her to the car. The boys were already in it.

Rose stayed as long as she could to help, but she didn't want to be in that house where her father should have been, where she could still smell his pipe tobacco above the pine and cinnamon-scented candles. His boots still sat on the mat by the back door; his coat and scarf hung from the hook; his sweater, the green one with the leather buttons she'd given him for a birthday two, or was it three years ago, was still draped across the chair in the kitchen. Myrtle hadn't been able to move it.

Exhausted, Rose finally left around five, driving her father's Lincoln home, making her way down streets lined with waist-high snow piles. Christmas lights flickered in windows. A row of wooden reindeer stood half buried on somebody's front lawn, the sleigh leaning over under a shroud of snow. She pulled into her drive, wanting nothing more than silence.

Fred met her at the door and took her coat. She went into the bedroom to change without noticing the boys leave. Fred unplugged the Christmas lights, closed the front curtains, turned on a lamp, and waited for Rose to emerge. When she did, he knocked on Trish's door and asked her to come to the living room. He wanted her to know everything her mother would now know.

"I'm sorry to have to do this now," he told them. "There really won't be a good time for it, so it's better to get it out of the way." As he explained the summer's events to his wife, it took everything he had not to lash out at Trish. Like Jason, he held her accountable. Yet, she was only eleven and could not have known the ramifications of her actions or how much more horrific things could have been.

Rose listened. She should have been shocked, but his words – naked, assault, fight, murder – rescue – fell against her with dull thuds. She heard them but could not absorb them. She'd just buried her father, the one person who would have been able to explain it all to her, put it into perspective, tell her how to think about it. It was this sensation of isolation and abandonment that seemed to outweigh the greater implications for her family. When Fred finished, she sat in silence for a long time.

Trish sat isolated at the far end of the couch, tears streaming down her cheeks, looking at the swirls in the sculptured carpet.

Fred waited.

Rose finally looked at her daughter. "Did that man lay a hand on you? Did he touch you where he shouldn't have? Did he do anything bad to you?"

Trish's answer, delivered as if the question was absurd, was all either of her parents needed to hear. "Of course not."

Fred told her to go to her room. "This isn't the end of this," he said. "Just so you know. You're not off the hook."

Rose had but one more thing to say before her daughter disappeared into her bedroom and closed the door. "You're lucky you have such good brothers."

~

When Trish's door latch closed, Rose told Fred it was all too much. "I can't do this."

"You don't have a choice." His words were cold. "That girl in there needs a mother." He looked into his wife's vacant eyes.

"I'm lost."

"No. You're not. But it's time to wake up and grow up." He saw her eyes narrow. "None of this is about you." He wanted to shout but kept his voice quiet. "It's not about your grief. It's about our children. We could have lost her. We could have lost all of them." When her expression didn't crack, he could see none of it had registered yet. "Rose, your father lived a long, happy life. You were loved. But your own kids? Do you love them?

Do you even care what happens to them? Your baby girl was almost raped. Jason almost killed a man. Eric could have gone to jail as an accessory. We could have lost them all." When Rose still didn't respond, he stood up, torn between taking her into his arms to comfort her and slapping her as hard as he could. "You have a choice, you know. You don't have to be here. You can leave us all behind tomorrow, but right now? You need to pretend you're a mother and go comfort your daughter."

"I'm not leaving," Rose muttered as her husband left the room.

"Good," he said without turning to her.

There was only so much she could feel all at once, so she'd shut down. It was a habit to bury her emotions. She'd been well trained. "Never let them see who you are," her mother told her. Never let them see you cry. Never show weakness. Never let down your guard. Stand up straight. Fix your hair. Don't smile too much. Stop frowning. Stop talking. The directives from Myrtle were a never-ending stream of belittlement, countered only by Bert's affirmations of her worth. With his voice silenced, all she heard were a lifetime of reprimands. The first step in overcoming such indoctrination was awareness, but she had no idea what the next steps looked like.

"Do you love me?" she whispered.

"Yes," came a soft voice from the kitchen. "Yes, Rose. I love you."

Rose went to Trish. She looked about the room. Her eyes fell to a stuffed giraffe on the floor of the closet. She retrieved it, brushed its fur, and straightened a bent leg. "Dad, I mean Gramps, gave this to me when I was a little girl," she said. Her voice was soft, wistful, and unfamiliar to her daughter. "He'd been away on a trip and said when he saw this giraffe, he knew how it must have felt. He said he missed my hugs, and since giraffes don't have arms, they must miss hugs, too. He told me to be sure to hug it every day so it would know it was loved."

"He was a really good hugger," Trish whispered, almost too quietly to be heard. Had they been more practiced at such intimacies, they might have reached out, but something held them both back.

A knock on the door was followed by Eric opening it. "I'm sorry I didn't tell you sooner, Mom."

"I know," she said. "But you did fine." She hesitated. "I just want to put this all behind us."

Eric walked away, went upstairs, and did not come back down the rest of the night.

Trish whispered something too quietly to be heard, then said it again with more conviction. "It's what you do next that matters. Gramps always said it's what you do next.'"

Rose's eyes welled. "Yes," she said. "That's what he always said."

Without Bert, Rose and Trish each felt a vacancy and would, in time, turn toward each other.

~

Moving forward, evenings in the Hudson household were spent placated by television. Myrtle came for dinner on Sundays. Trish spent Saturday nights with her. Rose did her best to be fatherless, but at some point in every day found herself weeping. When the snow fell so softly it piled up inches high on the fence post, Rose cried for wanting to tell her dad. When Trish was five minutes late from school, Rose cried for worrying about her. When Rose burned the vegetables, made the bed, dusted the hutch, she cried, until one day the tears stopped, and life began to find its new normal.

CHAPTER TWENTY-NINE

For Myrtle, losing Bert was the amputation of happiness. With him gone, she was trapped in the pretense, left to live out the rest of her life in heels and earrings. The cabin had to go. She couldn't bear it without him. In the spring, Myrtle said nothing to the family about selling it and everything in it, along with the skiff, canoe, and Bert's fishing gear, until the papers were signed. Without inclination to soften the blow, she told Rose to hand over their cabin key.

Rose couldn't believe her mother was capable of abandoning something so much a part of her dad. She imagined he would always be out there in spirit, puttering, fishing, believing in years to come she would feel his presence there, a comfort. "How on earth could you do that?" she shouted at her mother. "How could you take that from me?"

"Stop being so dramatic," Myrtle sniped. "You can't afford to buy it. Fred doesn't make that kind of money, and I'm not going to give the place to him."

"To him? What about me? You could have given to me!"

Myrtle's silence meant there was nothing left to say, though there were volumes of explanations if only she didn't have so much to hide. Rose charged out of her mother's house, slamming the door behind her.

When Trish heard the cabin was sold, she realized she would not go fishing again. There would be no more evening walks down the wooded road. She would never again paddle the canoe or listen to the heartbeat of her woods. They were not her woods anymore, and she dreamed one night about the tornado, only this time it blew the cabin apart, and she ran through the debris calling out for Gramps, but he didn't answer. She woke crying so loudly she woke Fred across the hall. He stayed with her until she fell back to sleep.

The next day, Fred drove them all to the lake, unlocked the door with a spare key, and told them each to take something they wanted. Eric took the tackle box and a fishing pole. Jason took one of the canoe paddles just to piss off the new owners. Rose grabbed a peanut dispenser and the crescent moon from the bathroom door. Trish collected the pipe from the mantle and Myrtle's ratty canvas shoes. When they'd all taken what they wanted, Fred took his leave.

Trish believed giving the shoes back to her grandmother was a good thing, something to make Myrtle happy, like finding something she thought she'd lost. She rode over on her bike with the shoes in her basket.

Myrtle stepped outside with her hair in glossy, tight curls. Her beaded earrings matched her necklace draped in a perfect arc over the bodice of a linen dress.

Her lipstick was fresh. She was alone. There were no bridge ladies leaving or on their way. She had no plans for the day at all. She was simply prepared as she had always been before Bert died, before he stopped bringing home spontaneous dinner guests, before her life became one empty day after the next.

"What are you doing with those filthy old things?" she asked when Trish held out the shoes. Trish searched for a crack in the disguise, some hint that the grandmother she knew from the lake was still there.

"You left them behind," Trish said.

"Just throw them away. I don't want them."

Trish dropped them to the driveway and rode away so angry at so many things, tears drenched her face.

Myrtle reluctantly picked them up, dropped them in the trash bin, and let it slam closed. She was so angry at so many things that tears drenched her face.

The next time Trish visited, the ratty canvas shoes were on the step by the back door, and they remained there until Myrtle's passing many years later.

CHAPTER THIRTY

By the spring of 1968, there was still no arrest for Barker's murder.

With Vietnam in full swing, Ben enlisted in the Marines. Jason was drafted into the army.

Trish wrote letters to Ben, who wrote back, giving her the names of other soldiers to write to. She had little to say, especially to the boys she didn't know. She recorded the boring stuff of high school: Dances, classes, exam week, football games, marching band, what she got for Christmas. She often took paper to the beach and sat in the dune grass, no matter the weather, searching for words to explain how the air smelled before a storm or just after, what the waves sounded like thumping as they broke to shore, or how they swished on calm days; what the trees looked like in heavy foliage and naked against a steel gray winter sky. Her words always fell empty to the page. Still, she wrote them anyway, having no idea how important they were to those boys desperately needing contact with a world they feared they'd never see again. When one of the boys stopped writing, she wrote to Ben asking what happened to him but never got an answer. After a few months, she was only corresponding with

Ben. The other boys stopped writing. And she stopped asking about them.

In the beginning, much like Trish, Ben wrote a chronicle of daily life, observations on the weather, living conditions, the men around him. He never mentioned the river or Sunset Beach. There was so little of anything personal in his writing that the letters could have been meant for anyone. Though he could have refused to write to her, he couldn't extricate himself from the moment at the river, from his compulsion to intervene when he thought she was being raped. He and Trish were bound by that moment, the pivot point on which life as they knew it ended and the next began.

Six months in-country, his words began to break her heart. His onionskin pages were heavy with a horror she couldn't comprehend. In his new duty, he was surrounded by death. The mangled bodies of dead boys were delivered to him to bathe and prepare for transport back to the States. She read his philosophy of death, about the peacefulness in his task, saying the dead were beyond fear when they came to him, beyond wanting and longing and grief. They were safe again, out of the fight. In making death sound like an aspiration, she feared that even when he returned home, the person he used to be would be gone.

~

The first time Trish heard an honor guard fire a salute was at her grandfather's burial. A pale flurry of snow drifted over the cemetery as she sat on a cold folding chair with her parents, her brothers, Grandma Myrtle, and a few bundled mourners. The first shots blasted the air from three rifles. She jumped, and Fred reached over and took her hands in his. They fired again. And again.

"He was a veteran," he said, as if that explained the gunfire.

Two old men in full military uniform took positions at the casket, lifting the flag draped over it, snapping it tight. With sullen faces and white-gloved hands, they slowly folded it with sharp, practiced motions. The shell casings from the rifles were tucked into the tight triangular parcel and handed to Myrtle. Taps played in the near distance, a sound that Trish would, from that point forward, associate with sorrow.

Trish was sixteen the next time she heard an honor guard fire a salute. It was a beautiful summer afternoon. A robin warbled from a nearby tree against a deep blue, cloudless sky. The first blast felt like it shot straight through her heart, as did the second and the third. As the young Marines in their crisp uniforms stepped up to the casket, Trish's throat tightened. Beyond the crowd, she saw a boy she knew from school standing alone in uniform, slowly lifting a bugle to his lips. The sound of Taps drifted to the gravesite and hung there, raining down grief. One of the marines approached the line of chairs, stopped in front of Margaret Finney, and handed her the American flag they just retrieved from Ben's casket.

Somewhere in a jungle in Vietnam, Ben became one of those soldiers beyond fear, beyond wanting and longing and grief.

In Trish's heart, Ben would always be young, strong, the one who gave her his shirt, who fought for her, and who may have killed for her. His life was too short to dispel her delusions. In death, he became the fantasy none of the men in her life would ever live up to.

Jason returned home with medals, chevrons, bars, and insignia for bravery and valor. All would be put in a box inside another box and packed away. The only truth he knew with certainty was that something of him died alongside August Maxwell at the river. What was left may have made him a good soldier, but he would always doubt his worth as a man.

CHAPTER THIRTY-ONE

In 1967, on a blustery day in August, Phil took Ben out in the boat. News of Augie's death had hit the paper the day before. A storm looked to be hitting Chicago to the southwest. No telling how long it would take to hit the eastern shore. There was so much chop in the channel the motor came out of the water more than once. Clearing the piers, they slid from one swell to another, the wind whipping white caps. Phil headed straight out to deep water. He cut the motor. He lit a cigarette, bits of flaming tobacco flying away. He looked north to clear sky, then south to the darkening horizon. He hadn't said a word yet. Either had Ben. That's the way it was with them. Phil was a quiet man but somehow his children knew what he expected. The boat rocked with the occasional jarring slide off a big roller. Phil took a long drag and turned his attention to his son, silently demanding eye contact.

Ben raised his shoulders against the chill and said he didn't want to be out there when the storm hit.

"Then you better tell me what's been going on."

Ben's throat tightened. Fear and relief fought for dominance. He wanted to tell his dad everything but none of what happened was easily put into words because the words, once spoken, would change all their lives forever.

Phil never took his eyes off his son except to flick the last cigarette embers over the side, sending burning bits flying on the wind. He compressed the butt, folded it, and slipped it into his pocket.

When words finally found their way out, Ben spoke all of them, words like rape and blood and threat. He began with a simple declaration: Jason might have killed August Maxwell.

~

Friday morning, after his last shift as bridge tender, Gar walked the length of track behind the boardwalk. There was no retirement party. No gold watch. He stopped momentarily on the broken sidewalk, wondering what Augie would have thought. Much like Augie, Gar was a man of routine. He didn't like change, yet this year, more than most, change was constant. It made him uncomfortable. He went home to a hot cup of coffee, bacon, eggs, and fresh hot biscuits. His wife made no mention of it being his last night of work. She, too, was used to routine. After breakfast, he spent a few hours on the river trying to come to terms with having nothing constructive to do. By noon, he was home again, sleeping.

They went out to dinner that night, something they rarely did, but it seemed appropriate to commemorate the day. They did not, however, celebrate or make plans. Gar was a man of the night who would begrudgingly have to adjust to daylight hours. Whatever their lives might look like moving forward would come to them eventually. They were both patient people.

Four in the morning found Gar walking his neighborhood as he often did on his nights off. Standing under a streetlight, the air so still, he felt like a die-cast character in a model train layout. He was a man without purpose. He walked to the edge of the boardwalk before turning back. It was not his bridge anymore, and whatever the new tender was doing was of no concern. No point rubbing salt in the wound, he told himself. He sauntered back home through the alley lined with errant little garages, tidy trash cans, and small backyards cluttered with toys and picnic tables. Three bicycles leaned on a picket fence next door to his house.

His screen door hinges squealed as he opened it, and the stubborn back door needed a slight shove. Tasks, he thought, wondering what else in the house needed his attention. Upstairs in the spare room, he rummaged through a box of wood chunks. He chose a piece of basswood the size of a pack of cigarettes but eyed a much larger block of walnut salvaged from a downed tree the summer before. He retrieved it and set it on a table where it would stay until he discovered what it held. Once it revealed itself, he would chip away at it, taking as much time as it needed, time he now had in abundance.

With the small basswood and pocket knife in hand, he settled into his easy chair, the one at the west-facing window, its view of the lake carved from between two rooftops, the view that would have to suffice for the rest of his life. A sudden fog rolled in, cold and dense. He closed the window.

~

On the last night of his life, Chesterfield Lee Perry said the wrong thing to the wrong woman in a bar. Upon leaving, he was blindsided by the woman's husband and another man whose body weight was twice Barker's. They clipped him from behind, pushed him into an alley, and beat him senseless. He passed out between two trashcans.

Phil Finney rose at four that morning. Margaret woke when he stubbed his toe in the dark and let out a quick fuck it. He apologized for waking her and said he was going fishing. She asked him to turn the window fan off and told him to enjoy himself, then rolled over and fell back to sleep.

Phil pulled his tackle box from a shelf in the garage, loaded it in his car, and drove down to Casper's marina. He liked night fishing. Didn't matter what he caught. Always used the same spinner, a makeshift rig with a spoon lure he found entwined on a branch along the river a few years earlier. Its action in the water never failed him.

He wore a black windbreaker, not that he needed it, but sometimes night air rising off water could give a person a chill. It was different, night air. It smelled different than day air, like the sun stripped it bare. The night knew things a day never imagined. The night knew his truth, knew things he would have been better off to forget. There was no hiding from his past at night, and he found comfort in a space where he didn't have to try. The crescent moon overhead slipped behind a cloud, and things grew darker.

As Phil pulled out into the river, Barker awoke in the alley, still drunk, his face smarting from the beating. He scuffed his way onto the empty main street of downtown and glanced up the three blocks of darkened storefronts. He made his way to the bluff, along the lovely tree-lined park overlooking the lake. He sat for a moment on the edge of an ornate marble fountain, an acquired remnant of the Chicago World's Fair. Water trickled from multiple spouts over the marble heads of three bare-breasted women, one of whom seemed to look at him, pondering his presence at that hour. Off to his right stood the band shell where the municipal band would perform two concerts on Labor Day.

As the bridge siren wailed from the river, he stumbled down the steps of the bluff, longing for his cot and sleep. His ribs stung with every breath. His bad eye ached, swollen shut. He could taste the blood from his split lip. Down at the rail station, he heard the morning freight moaning in the distance. He looked for the approaching light. Still faint. Still down at the bend. No need to hurry.

Like so many other nights, Harold Caruthers couldn't sleep. It was too hot in his trailer. His back hurt. His knees hurt. His calves were cramping. He got up. Sometimes walking helped. He heard a shuffling on the boardwalk and caught sight of Geneva, her swaying gate recognizable even in the dark. "Can't sleep either?" he asked. She stopped cold, startled. "Yes, Ma'am," he said. "It's a hot one. Arthur's acting up. Just came out to walk it off."

"Go back to bed, old man."

Harold caught up to Geneva midway between the taffy booth and the arcade. "What you carrying there?" Something about her expression, an ease he hadn't seen in weeks, made him curious.

"It has to be done," she said, showing him her big taffy knife.

"No," he said, glancing to the ball toss booth and back at her. "Not with that."

"Has to be this knife. This knife has history," she said and took a step forward, but Harold blocked her way.

"It's not as easy as you think," he said. "Killing. It ain't easy in a lot of ways."

"Has to be done," she said. "I can't live in a world where Chesterfield Lee Parry walks free after abandoning my boy."

Harold took Augie's T-shirt from her.

"It's for the knife. For after," she said.

Harold could almost feel the boy's presence, imagining his gentle smile. "This won't end anything, dear lady. It will never be over."

"It's already over," she said.

Harold gave her back the shirt. "He wouldn't want this. Not in a million years."

Upriver, Phil cruised under the trestle bridge at the hospital, and the Hwy 63 draw bridge. On approach to the channel, he pulled over and tied up where boats tie up when marina transient docking is full. He climbed up the ladder to the gravel lot behind the warehouse. He lit a cigarette, tossed the match in the river, and checked his watch. Looking down the track, he saw the train approaching on schedule. Standing in the dark, he watched a man stumble across open ground behind the boardwalk. He took one last drag and field-stripped the cigarette, putting the folded butt in his pocket.

Bathed in the dim amber glow of a single floodlight, Barker wiped blood from a cut over his eye and pushed on the back door, expecting it to stick, but it flew open, smacking on a counter and bouncing back to him. He stepped inside and reached about in the dark for the pull chain to a light bulb suspended above him. Finally finding it, he yanked. The bulb danced on its wire, its beam darting away to the corner and back again, finally settling overhead with a sway.

The ground rumbled as the freight train blasted her horn, crawling slowly behind Barker, so loud, so close, her headlight so bright anyone else would have lurched forward to get out of her way. Barker was not phased.

Out on the boardwalk, with steel wheels screaming against rails, Harold grabbed hold of Geneva's knife and put it back in her booth, locking it tight. "Let's go sleep on it," he said. "One more night won't make any difference."

As they began their slow walk back down the boardwalk, Harold, much relieved to have intervened, a thick fog enveloped the piers, and with it came a sudden chill.

Phil crossed the field, now shrouded in mist. When the last boxcar slowly rolled by, he stepped across the tracks and through Barker's door. He yanked the light off. In one swift move, he pulled the man's head back by his hair and slit his carotid, jugular and windpipe. It was quick. It was clean. It was done. Phil was out the door and to the warehouse before the last car was even on the bridge.

Eyes wide in shock, with no breath to gasp, Barker collapsed to his knees, and like a felled tree, keeled over, his head propping the door open. If his life had flashed before him, if such myths weren't myth, it would have been cruel to again endure his abhorrent childhood and the bludgeoning later in life that remade him into the specter he became, reliving the years of muddling through anger and pain in a body always on the verge of failing him, his mind too vague to be of value. Yet, between those dark times were a handful of good years, and maybe in remembering them, he might have been restored to the brilliant young man whose wit charmed, whose pale blue eyes dazzled. If, even for a moment, he could have felt that command over his life again, perhaps dying was a gift.

The fog horn blasted, loud and foreboding, as Harold got Geneva settled in her trailer. With fog so thick he could barely see his own place next to hers, he went to find a coat and a blanket.

The fog had not yet reached up into town when Ben pulled on his running shoes. It was earlier than he usually went out, but he didn't want to be seen. He needed to catch Barker off guard. He was going to wake him up, threaten him, and tell him to leave them all the hell alone. He didn't have it all figured out yet, but with the element of surprise, he thought he'd get the upper hand.

The train wailed at a nearby crossing as Phil pushed off from his tether and motored under the swing bridge, shrouded in fog. Above him, the new bridge tender, window closed to the cold, had been deep into an engrossing novel when the freight came through. He had not noticed a skiff tie up, nor did he see a dark figure climb out of it. Now that the train was clear of the bridge, he opened it as duty demanded, then opened his book again, turning to a dog-eared page, paying no attention to a boat heading into the channel. With two long chapters left, he took a draw of coffee. He had not seen Harold and Geneva on their walkabout, or notice Harold, like a sentry, settle into a chair at her door, wrapped in a blanket.

Sifting through mist, Phil motored to open waters. His filleting knife hit the water with barely a splash, its curved blade catching the fading river current, sliding and rolling, hovering momentarily, almost weightless, then falling, carried away as much as down, through silty waters, sediment rising as if to collect it, to bury it deep in the soft stir of shifting sands until it came to rest, blade deep, in the bed of Lake Michigan.

The fog dissipated as quickly as it formed, the air warming around him. He found no judgment in a horizon so straight, so empty. Its vastness held an indifference he couldn't find in the Adirondacks where he was from. Their deep gorges, narrow roads, and tight hairpin turns smothered him when he tried going home after the war. Childhood memories felt contaminated by the things he'd done. Before the war, he had enjoyed his first years teaching history at the junior high. Returning to the classroom after the war, he wasn't the same man. He'd betrayed who he'd once been.

His brothers, ten and fifteen years older, sat out the war at home, working for the war effort but risking nothing. They didn't understand why he wouldn't go hunting with them, having no idea the hunting, gutting, and skinning skills they'd taught him gave him a reputation as a fine knifeman. He took no pride in the acts he committed in the name of God and country. Twenty years on, he was still learning to live with the memories. But he had not done those things only to come home and allow any man to put his family at risk. He felt neither pride nor remorse in taking Barker's life. It was like putting down a rabid dog.

He cast two lines in the water and began trolling.

~

The bridge tender read through to the end of his book, closing it with a snap in time to watch the sun come up, only then noticing the fog had cleared. He hit the siren and closed the bridge for an approaching train, paying little attention to a clutch of fishing boats traversing the channel, one of them Phil Finney, who pulled back into Casper's Cove around 7:00 with two bass and a six-pound steelie.

The End

Made in the USA
Monee, IL
07 April 2025